SPRING MAGIC

THE THORNE WITCHES BOOK 4

T.M. CROMER

To Sarah Hegger:
Thank you for making me a better writer!

The Thorne Witches

The Thorne Family Tree

Preston Thorne

Trina Gillespie — **Preston Thorne** ⚭ **Aurora Pennell** — **Ryker Gillespie** ⚭ **Gigi Thorne**

- Alastair Thorne — *Book 6*
- Holly Thorne — *Book 5*
- Summer Thorne — *Book 1*
- Autumn Thorne — *Book 2*
- Winter Thorne — *Book 3*
- Spring Thorne — *Book 4*
- Nash Thorne — *Book 7*

THE THORNE WITCHES

THE CARLYLE FAMILY TREE

CARLYLE

TRISTAN CARLYLE — M — GLORY ASHBROOKE

PHILLIP CARLYLE — M — KIERA PALMER

ROBERT KNOX — MARIANNE CARLYLE

ZANE CARLYLE
BOOK 3

KEATON CARLYLE — M — DIANE MARSHALL
BOOK 2

COOPER CARLYLE
BOOK 4

KNOX CARLYLE
BOOK 1

CHLOE CARLYLE

A banging on the door disturbed Knox Carlyle in the middle of his scrying. He shoved aside the small kernel of irritation. "One second!"

He closed his eyes, inhaled to the count of four, and released. Privacy at the Carlyle estate was a joke. He really should consider moving into his own place—*soon.*

Again, the banging started, more urgent this time.

Knox cast one last long glance at the woman reflected back at him then swiped a hand over the mirror. All was well for the moment. He could relax his guard.

"Knox? What gives, man? Open the damned door."

As he swung open the door, his cousin was poised with his fist in the air, ready to pound on the wood again. Impatience was alive and well in the Carlyle clan.

"Seriously, man? My 'one second' wasn't good enough?" Knox demanded.

Keaton's lips quirked in a sheepish grin. "Yeah, sorry. I need to know if you can watch Chloe. C.C. is in North Carolina, and Zane had an emergency pop up. Autumn and I had planned on a private dinner."

Keaton didn't need to stress how important his dinner with his new wife was to him. They'd only recently taken up where they left off years before due to a colossal misunderstanding. Finding their way back to one another had been a long, arduous journey.

"Sure. Go have fun. Chloe and I can either conjure something or grab a bite at Monica's." Knox referred to a local downtown diner that featured desserts to die for. His young cousin was always up for the triple chocolate layer cake.

"You're a lifesaver, man."

"I'm tallying up all the favors. One day I may need a kidney or something."

Keaton flashed an amused grin. "Thanks, Knox. Have I told you how much I like having you here?"

A snort escaped. "Because what's better than your own built-in babysitter?"

An outraged cry had both men ducking their heads into the hall.

Chloe's face screwed up in indignation. "I'm not a baby!"

Knox and Keaton shared a panicked look.

"I know you're not." Knox stepped up to the plate to soothe his eight-year-old cousin. "I didn't mean it that way, Chloe. It's a standard term for watching someone's kid." He scooped her up in his arms and blew a raspberry against her cheek. "Forgive me?"

She giggled and nodded as she wrapped her arms around his neck. He ignored the accidental pull of his hair.

"I forgive you, Knox."

"Good, because I have a special project I need your help with."

"You do?" Her honey-hued eyes flew wide.

"Indeed, I do, peanut." He tilted his head and made a face to indicate her dad. "But it has to wait until he's gone. This is Top Secret, I-could-tell-you-but-then-I'd-have-to-kill-you type stuff."

"Gotcha!"

"Now I want to stay and find out," Keaton complained.

"Nope. Only Chloe is allowed to know. I need her keen intellect and eye for detail," Knox swung her around for a piggyback ride. When the time came for Chloe's million questions—and it wouldn't be far off—Knox hoped like hell he could come up with something fun and creative to keep her occupied. Sometimes dealing with a highly intelligent kid was torturous.

"Fine. But don't think she won't spill her guts for a twenty and a bag of candy," Keaton informed him.

"I'm not a rat, Daddy!"

Autumn's arrival cut off the current line of discussion.

"There's my beautiful wife." Keaton's smile practically lit up the hallway. The man was head over heels.

"Well, don't keep her waiting. Chloe and I have things to do." After Keaton and Autumn kissed Chloe and left, Knox glanced over his shoulder at his young cousin. "Dinner at Monica's first?"

"Can I get a hot fudge sundae?"

"Is the sky blue?"

Chloe's scrawny arms tightened around his neck. "You're the best, Knox."

"I know. But for saying it, you get dessert first." He started humming the Mission Impossible theme as he crept down the halls of the sprawling two-story home. "Do we drive or teleport?"

Her excited squeak made him smile. Chloe was taking to magic like a duck to water, but there were still things her father refused to allow her to do without adult supervision, and teleporting was one.

"Will Dad get mad?"

"Not at you, and that's all that matters," he assured her. "So we doing this?"

By "this" he meant teleporting to the alley behind the diner. Knox knew the alley was usually abandoned except for the occasional stray animal, but he sent out a magical feeler first to be sure they had the all clear. It wouldn't do for their abilities to come to light in Smalltown, USA.

"Yeah!"

"Hang on tight, kid."

They arrived in the blink of an eye—much to Chloe's delight.

Hand-in-hand, they crept around the corner of the building and made a run for the front door of Monica's Diner, laughing the entire way.

The sight that greeted him stopped Knox short.

Spring Thorne.

She leaned her elbows back against the long counter, which had the effect of pushing out her perfect, pert breasts, as she flirted with Tommy Tomlinson.

But looks could be deceiving. They certainly were on the part of Spring. One had only to look at her to see a sultry siren with tawny hair and dancing jade-green eyes. But Knox knew she was far from the sexy goddess she appeared. Spring's bright-white aura was untouched, a clear indication of her virgin status.

Yet, based on the invitation in her eyes, she was clearly trying to rectify that little problem with Tommy.

Fury unlike any he'd ever known swamped him. It also confused him. He didn't want the complication that came with a relationship, and he absolutely didn't want the complication of Spring's innocence to contend with. But the sight of her making the moves on Tommy woke the beast in Knox.

When she threw back her head and laughed, her long, lean throat was exposed. That creamy expanse of skin was temptation itself. It begged a man to taste the silky sweetness there, to suck on her throat and to mark her as taken as a warning to all other men.

"Knox?" Chloe's uncertain voice penetrated the angry haze clouding his brain.

With great difficulty, he tore his gaze from Spring's beautiful body and glanced down. "Table, booth, or bar?" he asked.

"Booth in the back. Can we ask Miss Spring to have dinner with us?"

He suppressed a grimace. Chloe was a fan of all things Spring related: the flower shop, the Thorne gardens, the infuriating woman herself.

"It looks like she's busy."

"No, she's coming this way."

Knox's head whipped up. Sure enough, Spring sashayed in their direction with a wide, welcoming smile directed toward his little cousin. *Was it possible to be jealous of a kid?*

"Chloe!" she cried as if the sight of the child was the most delightful thing she'd ever experienced. And that was the crux of Knox's obsession with her. If she found the simple everyday that joy-filled, what would the serious aspects of life draw from her? He could only imagine what her enjoyment of sex would bring.

Chloe released his hand to run forward for a warm hug. "Did you already eat, Miss Spring? Do you want to join us?"

Wary eyes rose to connect with his gaze across the short distance. "I don't want to interrupt your dinner," she said in her soft, hesitant voice.

Knox should've demurred and told her that she wasn't interrupting, but he couldn't bring himself to offer up the social niceties.

"Knox doesn't mind. Do you, Knox?" Chloe turned wide, pleading eyes on him.

He forced a smile. "Of course not."

Spring squatted and, with the tip of her finger, tapped Chloe's nose. "Then I'll gladly accept."

As she rose, Tommy stepped forward and rested a hand on her waist. "I'll see you tomorrow?"

"Yes. I'll be there," Spring agreed.

Tommy's hand lingered as he tried to delay his departure.

The desire to sever that hand from Tommy's body just about caused Knox's head to explode. "Come on, Chloe. Let's leave these two alone for a minute."

"We'll be back there, Miss Spring," Chloe called over her shoulder as Knox practically shoved her toward the back booth.

With any luck, Spring would change her mind and head off with Tommy. While the image of the two of them together tore at his sanity, Knox silently hoped Spring would find another man to attach herself to. For the last six years, she'd taken every opportunity to throw herself at Knox. Each and every time, his answer was the same, "Not going to happen." She was like a pit bull with a bone and refused to accept no.

Remembering the sight of her on his doorstep in her tiny emerald bikini caused his saliva glands to dry up and his brain to malfunction. The gentle slope of her breast had scarcely been covered by the triangular scrap of material, and his hands had itched with the need to touch. The open longing in her bright green gaze had nearly been his downfall.

But he'd stuck to his guns. When she stalked away, he caved to his inner male-chauvinist pig and watched her ass twitch its angry rhythm until she was out of sight. He might have a strict policy of not getting romantically involved, but he wasn't dead. Any man with a pulse wouldn't have been able to tear his gaze from those firm ass cheeks.

He swallowed hard at the memory and pretended interest in the menu before him.

"I guess Miss Spring doesn't want to date you anymore, Knox," Chloe said as she openly watched her idol from across the room.

He stared in open-mouthed wonder at Chloe. *The kid was right!* Spring hadn't given him the time of day since the incident in her driveway about three months ago when he'd dumped a vase of water over her head. Maybe even before that, if he cared to examine the timeline.

Knox whipped his head around to where Spring stood with her hand over Tommy's heart. *Sonofabitch! She'd moved on!* Even knowing it was for the best, the fact made him irritable and out of sorts. She could do better than nerdy Tommy Tomlinson for her first lover.

"Are you mad?"

Hell, yes, Knox was mad. He was fit to be tied. But Chloe's quivering voice shot straight to his heart. Taking care to smooth his frown, he stretched his lips in what he hoped was a reassuring smile.

"Of course not, midget. Why would I be mad?"

"You look mad."

Mentally, he added practicing his poker face to his to-do list. His young cousin was sensitive to the most subtle changes in expression, and the people in her life needed to remain on guard so as not to

6

bring back the trauma she'd experienced at her horrible mother's hands. The two of them had that in common.

"Nope. I'm just hungry and hope that if Miss Spring plans to join us, she does it soon."

As if on cue, Spring arrived at their table. "I'm sorry to keep you waiting. Have you decided on what you're getting?"

Spring tried to slide in beside Chloe, but she had settled close to the edge of the seat and refused to budge. The mischievous spark in her wide, honey eyes caused the hairs on Knox's arms to stand on end. *The little troublemaker was trying to set him and Spring up!*

He rose and gestured to the bench beside him.

Although Spring's expression was watchful and overly cautious, she scooted across the old, cracked vinyl seat anyway.

Chloe beamed in delight.

Before he could stop the words, he said, "So, you and Tommy, huh?"

In the process of unwrapping her silverware, Spring paused. "I suppose you could say that." She continued to lay out her fork, knife, and spoon in a perfect line.

"How long have you been dating?"

She sighed and shifted on the vinyl seat to face him. "Go ahead, get the jokes out of the way."

"I'm not—"

"Oh, come on, Knox. Everything I do or say is a joke to you." She cast Chloe an apologetic glance. "Sorry, kid. I think joining you was a bad idea." To Knox, she said, "If you'll excuse me, I'll be on my way."

"No."

Her dark brows shot to her hairline. "Excuse me?"

"No. I…" What the hell could he say? Why didn't he move so she could be out of his hair? "Look, for what it's worth, I think Tommy is a nice guy." There, that should work. Then, his mouth opened again. "Maybe not the one for *you*, but…" He shrugged and studied the battered menu in his hand.

"You don't know how to *not* insult me, do you?"

7

"I didn't insult you," he argued. "I was paying you a compliment."

"Could've fooled me," she muttered. In a slightly louder voice, she asked, "Can you please scooch?"

"Why? I thought you were hungry."

"There you go thinking again," she said from between gritted teeth. The saccharine sweetness of her voice fooled no one.

If she didn't irritate the living hell out of him, Knox might've found her amusing.

"You deserve better than Tommy for your first—"

"Child present," she snapped.

"...for your first boyfriend," he clarified.

"I've had boyfriends."

His own brows shot up in disbelief.

SPRING'S MOOD PLUNGED TO DOWNRIGHT PISSY. WHO DID THIS puffed-up, self-important peacock think he was anyway?

Sure, she'd never had boyfriends in the truest sense of the word, but she'd had boys who were friends. And while she hadn't slept with a single one of them, they'd done other things like kiss or fondle private parts. She hadn't gone so far as to do the final deed with anyone. None of which was Knox's business.

"I've just remembered I have a few things I need to attend to tonight," she said.

"You're lying." He jutted his chin toward her menu on the table. "Figure out what you want for dinner."

His refusal to let her out of the booth until he was good and ready added to her ire. There they sat, glaring at one another, and all she could think was that she wanted to feel his lips on hers. To have those large work-roughened hands touch her in ways she'd only dreamed about. Her gaze fell to his wide, generous mouth before she shook her head and faced away from him.

Chloe watched them with wide-eyed wonder. "You fight like Mom and Dad used to," she said.

An icky feeling settled in Spring's stomach. She didn't like the look in Chloe's eyes. The girl was up to something, and Spring imagined it was a match between her and Knox. "Your dad and Autumn love each other, Chloe. They had to work through their issues."

"Does that mean you love Knox? That you need to work through *your* issues?"

Yep, without a doubt, the kid wanted to match them up.

"No, sweetie. Knox and I are far, far away from anything resembling love."

She could feel his intense stare on her, and she worked to keep her blush at bay.

"But I want you to marry him. Then you could come live with us."

A quick check of the general vicinity showed their table had become the center of attention due to Chloe's loud proclamation.

She cast Chloe a sickly smile and lowered her voice. "Not going to happen, kiddo."

The restaurant goers all heaved a collective sigh of disappointment. What the hell had they expected was going to happen? Did no one understand that she and Knox were as dissimilar as oil and water?

At one time she'd wanted him to notice her. Hell, she'd thrown herself at his feet on occasions too numerous to count. But all that was in the past, and she was determined to find someone who would make her feel wanted. Who didn't look at her as if she were the dirt beneath his feet. But who also didn't put her on a pedestal and believe because of her beauty that she was worthy of the best things in life. She needed someone to see her true self and love her anyway. Knox was not that guy.

As the youngest of the Thorne sisters, she'd scarcely gotten to know her mother's love before her mom had disappeared and been declared dead. Her father, in an effort to erase his painful memories, had traveled the world and ignored his daughters' very existence. There was never a doubt that Preston Thorne loved his girls, but staying at home was torturous for him without their mother. In addition, her father contracted for the Witches' Council and was always running off on one mission or another. The result was Spring's parentless upbringing.

It was the reason she'd sought out Knox at every opportunity. As kids, he used to take her mind off her loneliness. He'd acted as if having a child tagging around after him was no big deal. Whenever she would show up on the Carlyle estate, he had a horse saddled and waiting for her. It was as if he knew the exact moment she would arrive.

He'd been kind to her, and she'd fallen head over heels for him. It helped that he looked like a hero from a romance novel: windswept, sun-bleached blond hair on the long side, sapphire-blue eyes shielded by thick brown lashes, and a generous smile that melted her from the inside out every time it flashed in her direction. Yes, Knox was the whole perfect package.

Then one day, it all changed. All the kindness and caring he'd shown a lonely little girl evaporated into nothingness. If she were being truthful with herself, she knew the reason why. Somewhere around her fifteenth year, she'd decided to confess her love. Nineteen-year-old Knox had stared at her, aghast, and when she flung herself at his chest, he shoved her into a pile of horse manure.

But Spring hadn't given up. She bided her time and waited four years to try again. From that day on, she hadn't stopped trying to make him see her for the grown-up woman she'd become. Each rejection stung worse than the last. But each one made her that much more determined to win his affections.

However, nothing she did had worked. It was as if, once she turned fifteen, she'd ceased to exist for him. The only feeling he held for her was contempt. For six full years, she fought to make him see her. This past summer, Spring had finally gotten the message.

She'd shown up in a bikini to retrieve her sister's elephant from the Carlyle's olympic-sized, backyard pool. Spring had preened and displayed her wares, certain Knox would wake up and see her for the desirable woman she was. Instead he'd shoved her into the water—right next to Eddie the Elephant.

"Where's your pride, Spring?" he'd asked scathingly. "You keep up with this little slut routine of yours, and some man is going to take you up on your offer. When he's gotten what he wants and leaves you cold, you'll have nothing but self-disgust as your companion."

"But I love you," she'd whispered tearfully.

He'd sneered and shook his head. "Grow up."

That confrontation had been roughly nine months ago.

Since then, she'd avoided him whenever possible. She told herself he didn't deserve the love she had to offer. And while it was said the Thornes only ever loved once, she was determined to disabuse her family of that notion. Determined to find another love who was worthy. But until that day came, the Tommy Tomlinsons of the world would have to do.

She bit her lip and blinked back the tears of self-pity forming. Spring wanted nothing more than to teleport home, but to do so in front of a restaurant full of people would cause a sensation from which this town would never recover.

"Knox, please let me out," she asked quietly.

His curt "I'm sorry" was grudgingly given and barely resembled an apology.

Had Chloe not interrupted, Spring might have teleported anyway. "Please stay, Miss Spring. He promises to be nice. Right, Knox?"

"Sure," he agreed.

Left with no choice because Knox didn't intend to budge from his spot anytime soon, Spring nodded and kept her eyes glued to the menu. With false cheer, she asked, "What are we thinking about for dinner?"

"Knox said we can get dessert first. I want a hot fudge sundae with extra fudge and sprinkles."

Spring's laugh was genuine in the face of Chloe's enthusiasm. "Good plan. Monica's hot fudge sundaes are most excellent. I'll have the same."

A cute brunette server showed up at their table. Her covetous dark-brown gaze was drawn to the beauty of Knox. "What will you have?" The huskiness in her voice was pure invitation, as was the flirty hand on his bulging bicep.

Spring white-knuckled the plastic menu in order to keep from zapping the woman's ass into next week. When she lost the battle to control her jealousy and contain the bolt of magic, salvation appeared in the form of her Uncle Alastair.

*a*lastair's cold "you're dismissed" worked better than any witchcraft Spring could've summoned. The skank scurried away as if her butt was alight.

"Uncle Alastair. To what do we owe this pleasure?" Spring asked formally as she laid the worn menu flat on the table, aligning it with the table's edge, then straightened the bottom edges of her already perfectly aligned eating utensils.

She glanced up from her place setting to see three sets of eyes staring at her; Alastair's in amusement, Knox's in stunned disbelief, and Chloe's in curiosity.

A fiery blush started somewhere around the area of her chest and swept to the roots of her hair. Her obsessive-compulsive tendencies had gotten the better of her in her nervousness. The struggle was real and took everything she had to not straighten the rest of the table and wipe the water spots from the glasses and chipped Formica top.

Alastair winked and forged ahead. "Since our last discussion, I have a better idea as to the location of Thor's Hammer. I need you and your young man to retrieve it, pronto."

Her uncle referred to the Mjölnir amulet, also known as Thor's Hammer. Legend stated that in addition to being the God of thunder and lightning, Thor was the God of healing and fertility. The original amulet's setting housed a stone from Odin's ring and had been blessed by Thor himself. The runes on the amulet also contained a spell for healing. Legend held that whoever possessed the amulet would have the power to heal anyone or anything.

She frowned, unsure exactly why her uncle had sought her out for this particular scavenger hunt. She'd have preferred to head to Greece where the final artifact was last seen. "Tommy? He do—"

"No, not Tommy. That boy can't tie his own shoelaces without help," Alastair said with a disgusted snort. He gestured for Chloe to scoot over and took a seat beside her. "I mean you and Knox."

Spring's stomach dropped at such a rapid rate, she thought she might lose her cookies. "Uncle Alastair, Knox isn't m—"

Alastair waved off her objection and faced Knox. In a low voice, he said, "I know you moonlight for the Witches' Council along with Preston. But for my niece's sake, I hope you'll make an exception and assist her in this."

"I haven't—" she started only to be cut off by Knox.

"What do you need me to do?"

"There's no way—" Spring objected, and this time Alastair spoke over her.

"Like we discussed at our last meeting, I need you and Spring to head to South America." Alastair pulled a faded map from inside his blazer pocket and laid it on the table.

She reached for the map only to have it intercepted by Knox. "I can do—"

"I need a little more to go on," Knox told him.

Frustrated at being ignored, Spring slammed her fist on the table, rattling cups, saucers, and silverware. This time when all the eyes turned to her, she was prepared. "Mind your own business," she snapped at the other diners. She added a mental magical boost to her command, and all the patrons ducked their heads to concentrate on their meals.

"Nicely done, child," Alastair murmured approvingly.

"It wouldn't have needed to be done if you'd have actually included me in the conversation," she retorted.

"Are you crazy?" Knox hissed. "The Council frowns on that type of mass manipulation."

Alastair and Spring stared at him for a long moment before they blinked and faced one another again. Neither of them gave a damn about the Council, and their lack of acknowledgment stated it loud and clear.

"As I was saying," Alastair said, easily dismissing Knox's indignant protests on behalf of the WC. "There is a short window to retrieve the object. After this week, it will be out of our hands for good."

"Why?" Knox demanded.

"The last remaining Désorcelers council member won it during a private auction today."

"Zhu Lin? How do you know?" Spring asked.

Alastair's brows clashed together. "Seriously?"

Spring waved a hand. "Forget I asked. You probably have spies everywhere."

"Close enough." Her uncle summoned a server over for a cup of coffee. They all waited to continue until they were alone again. "Or at least I did. With Ryker's cover blown and my back up mole MIA, I'm working blind. The last missive from my source stated that in exactly one week, Lin will take possession of the Hammer. I can't risk letting that happen. We all know how dangerous he is. If Lin obtains a magical artifact with that type of power…"

She nodded. Alastair didn't need to complete the thought. It was easy enough to fill in the blanks. Two of her sisters, Autumn and Winter, had almost died at Zhu Lin's hands. No one understood better than Spring that the man was dangerous. Slowly but surely, Lin had been building a small army to revitalize the Désorcelers organization, who was in direct opposition to the Witches' Council and whose primary goal was to obliterate witches and warlocks from the face of the earth. More recently, Lin had tried to harness the magic of Spring's sister Winnie in order to empower himself. He failed, which only served to make him more desperate and deadly.

"Then I need to get in and get it immediately. Where is it being held?" she asked.

"You aren't going alone," Knox stated as if his word were law.

"I don't answer to you, Knox Carlyle, and I certainly don't want your help."

His eyes narrowed on her face. "But you do answer to the Witches' Council like everyone else does. The council set out an order this week for all witches and warlocks to keep clear of Lin. Last I checked, you fell under that edict."

"Are you gonna run to the WC and tell on me?" Spring scowled her ire. "I expect no less." A blast of power smacked into her side. "What was that?"

"What?" Knox asked with feigned innocence.

She cast a quick look about and lowered her voice. "The blast of energy. It was like a light hit to my side. Did you do that?"

If he directed a blast so easily, then Knox was more powerful than she'd given him credit for. It was a rare witch who could manipulate energy to strike like he had. Was that why the Council had hand-picked him as their watchdog in the first place? Were they keeping the best of the best for their own little army? One didn't get better than a Thorne witch or warlock, but other than Spring's father, none of their family members had been drafted into the WC's ranks, nor did they care to be. The Council was authoritarian by nature, and all the Thornes were rebellious at best. But the Carlyle's tended to be rule followers. They would make the perfect candidates to recruit.

Knox grinned down at her. His cockiness held major appeal. Spring was such a sucker. She ripped her attention from his beautiful face with great difficulty. The man was a walking dream. With his drop-dead good looks and penetrating blue eyes, he had many a woman's heart beating faster. But she was no longer one of their ranks. She could channel self-denial with the best of them.

"Regardless, I don't need Knox's help, Uncle. I've found no legend surrounding Thor's Hammer that indicates it needs a couple to retrieve it. Tell me where it is, and I can be in and out in less time than it takes to blink."

"If you think you are going anywhere alone with that maniac Lin on the loose, then you're crazy," Knox stated. "Or foolish. Either way, you need a keeper."

There had been a time when Spring would've verbally battled him, but now, she decided to hold her tongue and bide her time. Once Alastair provided the rest of his intel, she would be able to slip away with no one being any the wiser.

The flirty server—more subdued thanks to Alastair—returned to take their food order. Spring picked a dessert to share with Chloe, but declined an actual meal. As it was, she'd more than likely only pick at her food under the watchful gaze of Knox.

KNOX FROWNED WHEN SPRING IGNORED HIS NEED-A-KEEPER JIBE. Her failure to rise to the bait was disconcerting. Previously, she'd have gone toe-to-toe with him over a comment of that nature in her quest to prove she wasn't a kid anymore. But now…

He could put his finger on the exact moment she'd stopped challenging him: the last Thorne family meeting concerning Spring's mother and the artifacts needed to revive her. When he'd called Spring out in front of the others, the ever-present spark of fire in her eyes had been snuffed out. Her pride had been stung, and yet, she'd lifted her chin like the fighter she was and gracefully exited the room. It had taken every ounce of willpower he had not to follow and beg forgiveness for being an ass.

He had been a complete jerk to her during recent years in his attempts to circumvent her adoration. Any kindness on his part was interpreted as encouragement by her. Her youth and innocence scared the hell out of him. He didn't want that type of commitment. In his experience, if anyone got too close, saw the real him, then they ran like hell in the other direction. He couldn't bear it if Spring looked at him in disgust. Better to hurt her feelings now so that someday, they might salvage their old friendship.

Surreptitiously, Knox intertwined his pinky with hers and tugged as he had when they were younger. Spring's surprised face turned up to his. As he gazed down onto her stunning visage, he was overcome with a desire to touch, to feel, to bask in the sunshine that was Spring. She was everything perfect in the world. But she was, and always would be, hands off.

Keeping his voice low for her ears alone, he said, "I'm sorry."

Her surprised inhale tempted him to drop his gaze to her chest, but his eyes remained locked with hers. A fleeting look, a clashing combination of hope and resignation, appeared and disappeared in an instant. When Spring dropped her gaze, nodded, and disconnected their pinkies, his stomach flipped. It seemed he'd done his job too well. She no longer held onto aspirations of being with him. And wasn't that a knife to the chest?

He tore his attention from Spring and met Alastair's penetrating stare. The man missed nothing, but then, Knox wasn't trying to hide his feelings from him; he only intended to keep Spring in the dark about his love for her.

Alastair squinted as if he were trying to figure out what made Knox tick. He could've told the guy it was fairly easy to do. He cared about his horses, his cousins, and Spring; not necessarily in that order.

The underlying truth was that he would always be there for the underdog in a fight. Had his Uncle Phillip not taken him in and saved him from a crappy home life at the age of eight, odds were Knox would've turned out a whole lot differently. But Phillip had granted him the gift of compassion and understanding at a young age. His uncle had shown a small boy that there was more to life than a fist to the face. There wasn't much Phillip could do to make him feel worthy, but at least he'd learned that there were people in this world who cared. The very least he could do was to pay it forward.

With a shrug to dismiss the past, he dug into his meal. He watched in amusement as Chloe chatted up Alastair. The surprise came when the older man answered playfully and paid marked attention to her, making her feel as if she were important. The kindness surprised him, and as Knox looked on, Alastair whipped out a credit card and showed Chloe how to palm it and flip it as if she were performing a magic trick.

"Okay, your turn. Let's see what you remember," Alastair said to Spring.

With a wicked laugh, she produced three credit cards—*all in Knox's name.*

"What the hell?" He felt for his wallet and scowled. "You taught her how to be a pickpocket?"

"Not just me," Spring said with a cheeky grin. "All the Thornes are well-schooled in larceny. We owe thanks to our great-great… how many greats were tacked onto our grandparents?" She waved a hand in dismissal before her uncle could answer. "Regardless, we had a very interesting upbringing."

"I'd say," Knox muttered. "I'd like my wallet back now, please."

"Don't fret, Knox, I wouldn't have kept them." She ruined her serious expression when she said, "I'd have returned them after I went shopping."

Alastair's bark of laughter turned heads. Normally, his austere nature kept others at bay. "She's delightful, don't you think, Carlyle?"

"She's a pain in my ass," he retorted.

And in an instant, Spring lost her sparkle. Her expression carefully blank, she said, "On that note, I need to get back to the manor. I still have a few floral arrangements to create for tomorrow."

"Spring, I didn't mean it the way it sounded." He reached for her hand, but she drew back.

"No worries. If you'll excuse me… please."

He would've argued the point, but the coldness in her moss-green eyes said she wouldn't be swayed. It bothered him that her irises had darkened—a witch's emotional barometer and a clear indication of Spring's unhappiness—all because of him.

Knox looked to Alastair. For what, he didn't know. Perhaps some clue as to how to proceed. Maybe to make sure the man wouldn't strike him dead on the spot for being the biggest asshole on the planet.

Alastair's neutral expression told him nothing.

"Will you be there when I come for training tomorrow, Miss Spring?" Chloe asked woefully. She, too, had picked up on the somber current.

"For most of the day. But I do have deliveries mid-afternoon. Perhaps, if you finish up early enough, you can help me. Would you like that?"

Chloe's smile practically split her face in two. She nodded her excitement.

"Good," Spring said with a nod. "I'd love the company."

Knox stood, unable to stall another second when it was clear Spring was ready to go. She bent and kissed her uncle's cheek.

As Spring turned to leave, Knox grabbed her hand, effectively surprising them both. "Thanks for keeping me and Chloe company tonight." As olive branches went, it was all his frantic mind could come up with.

Spring gave him an impersonal smile, tugged her hand free, and turned her attention to Chloe. The smile she bestowed on the child was breathtaking. "It was my pleasure. See you tomorrow, sweet girl."

After she'd left, he felt bereft—just as he always did.

"Wake up before it's too late, son," Alastair advised with a pat on Knox's back. "She's the Thorne treasure. Someone who values her worth will try to steal her soon enough."

3

*L*ater that evening, after Keaton and Autumn returned home to tuck Chloe into bed, Knox experienced a restlessness he couldn't shake. Needing air, he strolled to the clearing in the wooded area between the Thorne and Carlyle estates. He wasn't surprised to find Spring there. She was like a beacon for his soul and lit the way like the brightest of lights.

Knox's curiosity got the better of him when he observed her as she went from tree to tree, touching and speaking to each in turn. "What are you doing?"

"Helping them maintain strong roots and preparing them to come out of their dormant stage when it's their time."

"Have you always done this?"

"Yes, mostly for the trees surrounding the clearing. I feel the magical boost gives back some of what they've provided to us during our ceremonies." She glanced over her shoulder to where he stood resting against an oak tree. "I'll be done in about five minutes, then you can have the clearing to yourself."

"You don't have to leave."

She snorted and turned back to the tree she'd been spelling.

"I mean it, Spring. It's not my intention to run you off."

Spring ignored him and continued to boost the tree's life with her power.

He frowned. Her new cynical attitude pissed him off, but it wasn't her who he was irritated with. No, all the aggravation he felt was self-directed. How many times had he been mean to her since she fancied herself in love with him? *Too many to count.* Yet, he'd done it *for* her. He'd done it to make her see that he wasn't hero material or someone worthy of her attention. But now that her attention was firmly affixed elsewhere, it didn't sit well.

She ended her ceremony with the tree beside his. Without meeting his gaze, she said, "Thanks for your patience. Good night, Knox."

"Don't go." Where the hell had that come from? Some inner desire to torture himself?

"It's late."

"Not that late," he said quietly.

Spring leaned back and rested palms flat against the tree, but she didn't speak or look at him.

"How have you been?"

A tiny frown danced between her delicate brows. "Fine."

"When did you start dating Tommy Tomlinson?"

"You asked me that earlier."

"You never answered." Knox shifted closer to her, and Spring's eyes lifted to reveal her panic at what he assumed was his nearness. She certainly wasn't afraid of him. He didn't stop moving until he stood within mere inches of her. She craned her neck to see his face.

"We've been dating about a month and a half, off and on."

"What does off and on mean, Spring?"

"What does it matter to you?" she snapped. "Why all the questions? It's not like you've ever been interested. You wanted me to move on. I have. Yet, here you stand belaboring the issue." She pushed off the tree and stalked toward the center of the glen. "I promise, I'll no longer be a nuisance to you, okay? You can breathe free. My 'little slut routine' is no more."

He winced. "I never meant that to be as ugly as it sounded."

She released a harsh laugh so at odds with who she was. "Right. Anyway, do me a favor and don't encourage Uncle Alastair. When he pushes you to help retrieve the Hammer, decline."

"I'm going with you," he informed her.

"For chrissakes! Why?" Spring demanded. "What purpose could you possibly have to go?"

"To care for you and protect you."

"You think I can't protect myself? I'm not the pretty little airhead you seem to think I am, Knox. I'm capable of a lot more."

Inexplicably angry with himself and her, Knox stormed to where she stood with her hands on her hips. "You think I don't know that? But I'll be damned if I can turn away. Damned if I can allow you to run off and face Lin or any number of other dangers by yourself."

"I've handled Lin before."

He scoffed. "When? In the park? You didn't face him alone. There were five others to help that day. You haven't seen what he can do, Spring. I have."

"Are you trying to tell me you've fought him?" she asked in disbelief. "Sorry, I'm not buying it."

"He killed my father in front of my eyes."

The change in her was immediate. "Oh, Knox!"

When she moved to touch him, he backed away as if burned.

SPRING SILENTLY SCOLDED HERSELF FOR TRYING TO COMFORT KNOX. How many times did he need to drum it into her head that he found her touch abhorrent? No wonder he didn't think she possessed an IQ over one-hundred. She continued to do stupid shit in his presence. But the rawness in his tortured eyes called to her. It always had. All she ever wanted was to see his eyes light with laughter and warmth as they had on those rare occasions when they were younger and he allowed himself to exist in the moment.

"No one should have to witness that," she said with more reservation in her tone and actions. "I'm truly sorry."

"I didn't say it to garner your sympathy. I said it so you'd know how damned dangerous he is!"

"I *do* know, Knox. My mother has been in a twenty-year stasis because of him. And I've witnessed what my sisters have gone through. Both Autumn and Winnie nearly died at his hand." She shoved her fists in the back pockets of her jeans. The action didn't curb her desire to reach for him, but it reminded her to keep her hands to herself. "But I have Isis on my side. My faith is strong that she will protect me and all her other descendants from his evil. She's invested in the outcome."

"That!" Knox jabbed a finger in her direction. "That right here is why you come across as a foolish child! You are naive to the ways of the world, Spring."

She flinched at the derision in his tone. She'd been condemned in his eyes long ago, and she'd come to terms with it, but damned if it didn't sting. "You seem to think I'm still a teenager, Knox. While you'll always be older than me, it doesn't mean you're wiser." When he would've spoken, she held up a hand. "Yes, I get that you think you are, and I get that you believe you have more life experiences than I do. Maybe you do, but it doesn't make me naive or a child. Quite honestly, I'm tired of you saying so."

His tone changed. "Then please explain to me why you are determined to rush into this on your own."

Had Knox demanded an answer, had he been even the slightest bit challenging, Spring would've told him to go to hell. But he truly appeared to want to understand her reasoning.

"Because being around you is painful in every way," she confessed. At his hurt look, she continued. "I live with the embarrassment of your condemnation. Yes, I wore my heart on my sleeve. I adored the man I believed you to be. And though I've moved on, it's not something you'll ever allow me to live down. To you, I'll always be a starry-eyed kid who can't make adult decisions."

He stared at her, and the fierceness in his gaze made her want to hide.

"You've moved on?" His dark tone scared and excited her at the same time.

"Yes."

"You no longer have any feelings for me? Any desire?" Knox stalked her as she backed away from the purposeful glint in his eye.

"No," she lied.

His long stride ate up the distance between them. When he was mere inches from her, so close that she could feel the heat radiate off of him, he stopped. "I don't believe you."

Her chin jerked up. "Believe it."

Spring wasn't prepared for the strong arms that hauled her close or the forceful kiss he bestowed upon her. She blamed her surprise for the way her body melted against his and the way her arms encircled his neck to hold him close. Obviously, he possessed some magical sexual magnetism that drew unsuspecting women. It was the only explanation why she couldn't pull away as his tongue plundered her mouth and as his large, calloused palm closed over her breast.

She moaned and pressed the flat of her lower abdomen to his budding erection, desperate in her desire. Except her forwardness had the reverse effect. Knox pulled away so fast, Spring just about face-planted in the dirt. "What the—?"

"No."

She stared at him in confusion.

"You're not over me. You can tell yourself you are, date all the Tommy Tomlinsons on the planet, but you'll never erase me from your mind or convince me I'm not the one your body craves." He ran a rough thumb over her swollen lower lip. "The evidence is as plain as the lovely lips on your face, sweetheart."

Spring shoved his hand away. "How do you know I don't respond to Tommy that way?" she said with a lifted brow and a mocking sneer.

Maybe she *was* naive because she had in no way anticipated his swift, violent reaction to her taunt. One moment she was jeering at him, and the next she was backed against the tree, straddling his thigh as his mouth ravaged hers. He'd ripped her top open and cupped the fullness of her breasts in both his hands. As he teased her nipples into pebbled points, she cried out against his mouth.

"Do you want this?" he whispered as he nipped her earlobe.

Hell, yes, she wanted it! That and a helluva lot more if she was forced to be honest. But she'd be damned if she admitted it to Knox. She gasped her pleasure and tilted her head to the side but refused to answer in the affirmative, although every cell in her body cheered him on.

His lips trailed along her throat and down her chest. He scraped his teeth over her exposed nipple. "Tell me, Spring," he commanded.

Her fingers tangled into the thick strands of his white-blond hair and pulled him closer, feeding him her entire breast. He cupped and massaged the roundness as he sucked and tugged. The rush of want straight to the apex of her thighs embarrassed her. He had to feel the wet heat against his well-muscled thigh.

With his other hand, he made short work of her jeans, shoving them down enough to gain access to her core. He inserted one finger into her even as he used his thumb to toy with her clit. She was helpless to protest his high-handedness. Helpless to say she didn't want what he was offering. *Because she did.* Her head dropped back against the tree as her orgasm built.

Right before she crested, he asked again, "Does that tool Tommy make you feel this, sweetheart?"

The waves of Spring's release crashed over her, and she bucked against his hand, riding his thigh as he held her to him. Her screams echoed about the glen and returned to mock her.

Knox dropped a hard kiss on her mouth before snapping his fingers and restoring her clothing to pre-ravished order. "Somehow, I don't think so. Keep telling yourself you're over me, and I'll keep proving you a liar."

"Why?" she asked raggedly. "Why did you do this? Why couldn't you let it be?"

He had no idea what he'd done. No idea of the maelstrom of emotions he'd unleashed within her. How could she ever forget his electric touch? Forget the deep ache he caused with a single kiss?

"I don't know. Maybe I don't like the idea of being replaced in your affections."

His answer surprised her, but she was too tired to wonder what it could all mean. Being around Knox was like riding a rollercoaster of emotions.

"You don't want me, but I'm not allowed to want anyone else either? You can't have it all ways, Knox. You just can't."

She didn't give him the opportunity to answer. She teleported to the sanctuary of her room. Using Granny Thorne's spell, she cloaked herself and soundproofed the room before she gave over to her sobs.

4

*A*s Spring strolled through her hothouse, collecting various blooms for her online orders, a commotion on the front lawn caught her attention. She conjured a jar of water and placed the cut flowers in it before she headed toward the front of the shop.

Knox strolled in, halting Spring in her tracks.

"W-what are you d-doing here?" she stammered and struggled against the blush trying to gain ground on her skin.

"I owe you an apology for last night. I thought you might like to go for a ride with me." With a thumb he gestured toward the door.

She inched past him and saw two horses saddled and ready to go. Her heart melted in her chest to see her favorite mare, Macy, from her childhood days. Unable to help herself, she went out to greet her four-legged friend. "Hello, sweet girl! Long time no see. Nice cone you have there. The sparkle gives it that extra punch, ya know?"

Macy whinnied and tossed her head to show off the sparkling, glitter-enhanced traffic cone attached to her head. Spring laughed and kissed her velvety snout.

"Why does she still wear the cone? I thought the vestibular disease had run its course," she asked Knox.

"Chloe insists Macy likes it. Said the mare is depressed without it."

They'd all recently discovered Chloe had the ability to communicate with animals in the same way Spring's sister Summer could. They received images of the animals' thoughts.

She sighed and stroked the horse's long neck. "Thanks for bringing her by for a visit, but I'm going to pass on the ride."

"You'd reject my apology?" he asked softly.

"No. Your apology is sweet. I'm bogged down right now."

"Come on, Spring. You know you can snap your fingers and fill the orders for your shop." Knox used his thumb and index finger to lift her chin. "What's the real reason?"

She jerked away, feeling branded by his simple touch. "We can't go back to the innocent friendship of our childhood. It's stupid to try. Too much water has washed away the bridge. *And* I have work to do."

"You're wrong. We can if we—"

Out of the blue, her temper erupted and startled them both. "Yes, that's right! I'm always wrong, aren't I? I can't have a simple thought without you contradicting it. Go away, Knox. I have things to—"

He grabbed her shoulder as she started to storm past him. He spun her around and planted his mouth on hers. Before he could obliterate her resistance, she summoned the branches of a nearby bush and created long, winding limbs. They inched their way up his legs and wrapped around his wrists, tugging him away from her. His shocked expression almost triggered her laughter.

She pulled away and made it four feet before Knox's arms wrapped around her from behind and lifted her off the ground. "What the hell are you doing? Let me go!"

"Nope. You have to pay a forfeit for your dirty, little trick," he growled. "A kiss or a ride, your choice."

They both sounded divine, but Spring doubted his "ride" was the same one she had in mind. "Fine. I'll take the ride." When his wicked chuckle sounded in her ear, her insides turned to mush. So maybe his definition of ride *was* the same as hers. She shook off her lustful thoughts and clarified. "On the horse."

Knox loosened his grip enough to turn her in his arms. "Spoilsport. I was hoping for that kiss."

She snorted her disbelief. When he frowned, she twisted free of his embrace and strode over to Macy. In one graceful move, she was in the saddle, reins in hand. "I don't know what's changed suddenly, or if teasing me is a game to you, but knock it off. I'm not interested in someone who can't see me as a person and only sees me as an empty-headed female in a pretty package."

"You have no idea what I think or how I see you."

Her stomach jumped at his words. Why the change of heart? Why the two kisses? What was he trying to prove? Whatever it was, she wasn't buying it. She didn't trust that Knox didn't have a secret agenda on behalf of the Witches' Council. "You're right, I don't. And I don't want to. Can we get this ride over with so I can get back to work?"

Knox paused at Macy's shoulder and ran a hand down the length of the horse's neck. Macy turned her head and nudged his chest. He smiled and rubbed the sweet spot between the horse's ears, careful to avoid her makeshift horn.

Spring had never been jealous of an animal before, but she supposed there was always a first time. When Knox turned his incredible eyes her way, she had a difficult time holding in her sigh.

"I thought this would be a nice break to your day. The weather is mild, and we haven't ridden together in an age." He rested a hand on her calf, and she ceased to breathe. "But if you feel forced, we can call it off."

It took an effort, but she was able to tear her gaze away to study the area surrounding them. Her attention was caught by her sister Winnie, staring down at her from the attic window. They shared a silent communication. It was easy to tell Winnie urged caution.

Mind made up, she glanced down to find Knox watching her. "I'd like the break. The reforestation project I've been working on has been time consuming."

The stunningly white smile he cast her caused Spring to blink in surprise. If she didn't know any better, she'd say he was pleased to spend time with her. Because his behavior unsettled her, she tugged at Macy's reins and headed toward the wooded area of their property.

Knox was beside her in a minute. "This way. I want to show you something."

They rode in silence to the clearing, and when they arrived, Spring had to rub her eyes to make sure she hadn't imagined the table and chairs. Covering a round table was a white tablecloth, and in its center was a potted rose bush already in bloom. It was covered by a glass dome which Spring assumed was to keep the plant warm on the chilly day.

"Is that a Dragon Rose plant?" She urged Macy into a trot to get closer. "Oh, Knox. It's beautiful." And it was. The variegated petals of white and royal blue were gorgeous.

He dismounted and held up his hands for Spring to do the same. She fell into his outstretched arms, confident he'd catch her like he always had when she was younger. For a brief moment, he held her close before he released her.

"I'd hoped you'd like it," he said softly. "It's the least I could do for being such an ass lately."

She wanted to trust this new side of him, but she didn't see how she could. He'd spent too many years keeping her at arm's length and piling on the insults. The about-face was perplexing. "I do. Thank you," she said carefully. "What's all this though?"

"Lunch?"

Spring watched in silence as Knox removed the tack from the horses to allow them to wander the clearing. There was little concern of them running off. His magical connection to the creatures assured his control.

With little fanfare, he held out her chair and waited as she took a seat before he moved to his side of the table.

"Are we conjuring food?" she asked with a half-smile.

His expression was sheepish. "Other than the dessert the other day, I have no clue what you like. I figured we could play it by ear."

31

"I'm a vegetarian, but I'm not picky."

"Italian?"

"Perfect."

With a simple swirl of his hand, Knox morphed their table into a picture-perfect Italian feast. Garlic bread rested in the spot where the rose bush had been. A dark, ruby wine in Waterford crystal glasses was within reach for each of them. A small silver tray with a domed lid sat before Spring with a matching setting in front of Knox.

"Where did my plant go?"

He laughed. "Need you ask? I sent it to your workshop."

Mollified, Spring lifted the lid and inhaled deeply of the lasagna dish underneath. "God! That smells like the stuff your Aunt Keira used to make!"

His deep laugh struck her right in the chest. When was the last time she'd heard him laugh? It must've been close to eight years or more.

"It's exactly the same," he confessed. "I learned to cook it a long time ago. Or in this case, conjure it."

Wasting no time, they dug in. She closed her eyes and moaned her pleasure. "Oh, Goddess! It's better than I remember."

When she looked up, Knox was frozen in place, his fork halfway to his mouth.

"Knox? Are you okay?"

He cleared his throat and chugged the wine he'd conjured for them. "Fine," he barked.

She blinked her confusion over his gruffness. What had she done this time? Knowing she'd never figure out his mercurial moods, she shrugged and went back to devouring her meal.

KNOX SHIFTED IN HIS SEAT. SPRING'S ENJOYMENT HAD CAUSED A visceral reaction in him. Her throaty moan and orgasmic expression were the stuff of dreams. *His* dreams to be exact. Now that he'd seen the real thing, he realized his imagination hadn't come close.

Christ, the fact that she could turn him on with a simple moan troubled him. He didn't want to want her. Certainly, he didn't want to love her. But he'd spent the better part of ten years fighting his inappropriate thoughts and feelings for her, and he doubted it would end anytime soon.

He took another sip of wine as he recalled her words from yesterday. She was right. He'd been treating her like a child for far too long. It was his fallback. A safety measure of sorts. If he thought of her as an adult, he'd no longer have an excuse to keep her at a distance. He might have to do something about his unnatural obsession for her.

Last night, he hadn't been able to sleep. He kept picturing her face as the orgasm took her. Even rubbing one out hadn't done the trick; he'd maintained a semi-hard-on the rest of the night—like the one he was sporting now. It seemed he stayed in a constant state of arousal around her. Thank the Goddess that Spring was too inexperienced to notice.

Knox was tired of fighting the pull. Maybe he wasn't deserving of her, but he wanted her with an ardor that was rivaled by nothing and no one else.

"What are you thinking about so hard over there?" Spring asked softly.

He lifted his gaze from her rosebud mouth. Their eyes connected and held across the expanse of the table. "You."

Surprise lit her lovely face. "What have I done this time?"

She was always quick to go to a negative place. His fault to be sure. He'd spent too many years deriding her at every turn to keep her at a distance.

"Nothing." He set down his glass and moved to squat in front of her. Taking both her hands in his, he tried to relay what was in his heart. "You're perfect, sweetheart. You always have been. I never meant for you to question your worth, Spring. I need you to know that."

She withdrew her hands from his and rose gracefully to her feet. "I think it's time I got back."

He sat back on his heels. "Don't go. Stay for dessert."

"What is the point of all this, Knox? Are you trying to butter me up about the South America trip?" She shook her head even as he opened his mouth to deny it. "This..." She waved a hand. "...is overkill. All you had to do was speak to me like a decent human being for a change."

He rose and crossed to where she stood, arms folded over her chest as if she were hugging herself—or protecting herself from him.

With the tip of one finger, he smoothed a wayward, coppery strand of hair from her cheek. "I've been ugly to you for far too long. It makes you question my sincerity now. I get it. But it never had anything to do with who you are as a person."

"So you're denying this is a trick to get me to cave and accept help?"

"I'm completely denying this is a trick. I only wanted to do something nice for you for a change. An apology."

"Don't play me for a fool, Knox. You may think I'm sweet and innocent, but I swear by all that is holy, if this is a game to humiliate me, you'll wish you'd never set eyes on me."

Spring's anger was palpable. But Knox suspected it was born of desperation and fear. He'd done nothing to earn her trust, but he intended to rectify that. "I'll never play you for a fool, sweetheart. That's my promise to you."

She nodded once. "I have to get back. I'm sorry to decline dessert."

"Thanks for sharing lunch with me."

Still they stood, less than a hair's breadth between them; Spring's confused eyes gazing up at him as if trying to figure him out.

He lowered his head and gently placed his lips to hers. Her response was instantaneous, and her lips clung to his. But Spring—contrary as always—jerked back and scrubbed her mouth with a scowl.

"I gotta go," she muttered.

He stood staring at the space she'd occupied long after she'd teleported away. How did he reverse the damage he'd wrought to their friendship?

"Nicely played, son."

Knox jumped and spun around. Alastair sat at the table and picked through the garlic bread for exactly the right slice. How the hell had Spring's uncle gotten the jump on him? He'd been trained from the time he could walk to be alert to his surroundings. It had saved him multiple beatings.

"I don't need your approval."

"I didn't think you did. All I'm saying is that this was a nice touch as far as seductions go. She'll come around."

"I have no intention of seducing her," he lied to Alastair as easily as he lied to himself.

"Keep telling yourself that, boy. But I think you've reached the end of your proverbial rope where she's concerned. Your suppressed feelings have all ganged up on you, and now you don't know if you are coming or going. Am I right?"

Alastair spoke the truth, but Knox would be damned if he'd admit it. "Why are you here?"

"I miss Keira's garlic bread. Nice re-creation on your part. It takes me back."

"I'm glad I could provide your trip down memory lane. At your age, it must be all you have left."

Alastair lifted Spring's untouched wine and toasted him with a sardonic smile. "Touché." After he took a sip, he carefully set the glass down. "Great vintage. Now, on to things that matter. Have you decided to remove your head from your ass and pursue my niece?"

"That's none of your damned business."

"I disagree. Everything Thorne related is my business." Alastair tilted his head and smiled like a cat that got the canary. "You love her."

Knox didn't dignify the guess with an answer.

Alastair rose and straightened his cufflinks. "What I don't understand is why you won't go after what you want. If I'm not mistaken, she professed her love to you eons ago."

"She was a kid. She didn't know what she was saying."

"Thornes only love once. My dear Summer set her sights on your cousin Cooper when she was barely out of diapers. My family members are blessed to recognize their soulmates with a single glance."

Knox's heart increased its pace, and sweat broke out on his lower back. Somewhere along the way, Spring had said something similar. The memory of that day when she was only eight and determinedly dogging his footsteps flitted through his mind. Her words came back to him. *"Thornes only love once, Knox. I choose you."*

At the time, he'd thought she was a lonely child who dreamed about unicorns and happily ever after, but based on Alastair's revelation, perhaps she'd known her own mind from the start.

It wasn't until she grew into a teenager and became aggressive in her pursuit that Knox had to get firm and deflect her advances.

He had never discussed Spring with anyone after meeting her. Hell, he wasn't sure the others knew she existed. The Thornes didn't remove the cloak from their property or start their pretense of "moving to town" until the older girls were ready to start high school. But he'd always known they lived at the manor since he'd moved in with his aunt and uncle. He'd stumbled across the sisters playing in the clearing once, and from that moment on, he'd made it his mission to find out more about their family.

The first time he'd seen Spring, she'd been a four-year-old, running about the woods unsupervised. He'd stayed to watch over her. As he looked on, she used her magic to change the flowers to the colors of the rainbow. It was the sweetest thing he'd ever seen. In that moment, he understood that she was the Thorne Jewel—bright and precious—and he treated her accordingly.

"She's like a princess, and I'm the equivalent of a stable hand," he told Alastair roughly. "I have no business pursuing her."

"Then you've condemned not only yourself to a life of unhappiness, but Spring as well. Or perhaps you don't feel you deserve to be happy?"

Knox cut the other man a sharp glance. "What's that supposed to mean?"

"Exactly what it sounds like. I know Robert Knox wasn't a good man. I also know your mother, Marianne, was no better. They were two bad seeds, and you suffered at their hands. I'm here to tell you, you can break the cycle. You aren't destined to be a horrible person."

"You have no idea what type of people they were. What they've done," Knox snarled.

"I do, son. I knew them a lot longer than you. You've forgotten more than you've remembered. But answer me this, you don't honestly believe I'd let someone unworthy near my family, do you?"

Knox's shock must've been evident because Alastair cast him a wry half-smile.

"You've done nothing wrong. You've been the model child both to the two half-wits who abused you and then to your Uncle Phillip and Aunt Keira. You've treated everyone around you fairly and always had the backs of your cousins. What more do I need to know?"

Knox was speechless.

"You are the smartest of the lot, son. I have high hopes for you. Don't mess this thing up with Spring. She deserves the very best, and I believe that's you."

So saying, Alastair teleported away, leaving him trapped with his own thoughts and fears.

5

*A*s Spring was ending her workday, a knock sounded on her shop door. The man on the other side of the glass set her heart racing—as he'd always done.

"Knox. What are you doing here?"

"I thought I'd bring you the dessert you missed from yesterday's lunch." He held up a pink and white striped bakery box with a bright white bow.

As far as gestures went, it was romantic as hell. Yet, she couldn't allow herself to hope. She couldn't deal with another rejection.

She stepped back to allow him entrance to her flower shop.

Knox studied the setting as if he'd never seen it before. She didn't need to struggle to recall if he'd ever set foot in her place; he hadn't. He'd never wanted anything to do with her before, and as a result, he'd avoided being in the same vicinity. That included her business.

"This is great."

She lifted a brow. The struggle to hold back her sarcastic comment was real. "Did you think it was only a hobby shop?" she asked instead.

When Knox turned those all-seeing eyes on her, Spring swallowed hard.

"No. But based on your continued work in restoring expired species to their natural habitat, I'd thought the flower shop was an afterthought. I didn't realize you had such a large, viable place. Does that make sense?"

She couldn't help but smile. His reaction was normal. When most people saw the inside of her shop on the Thorne estate, they were stunned. In comparison to her space downtown, this one seemed enormous. "Common mistake if you've ever seen my retail shop."

"I did see it once when I sent flowers. Robin was manning the counter."

He referred to her full-time employee. But what struck Spring was that he'd been inside her business and that he'd sent another woman one of Spring's arrangement. The wind was knocked from her. Talk about insensitive. "I see."

Knox frowned at her tone. "The flowers were for my aunt Keira's birthday."

Color flooded her cheeks, and she ducked her head to avoid his penetrating stare. "It's no concern of mine who you send flowers to, Knox."

"Isn't it?"

The question was delivered as if it were a given that she'd be all up in his affairs, as if she were a stalker who spied on his every move. Her temper flared to life. "No, it isn't. If you want to send flowers to a dozen women, it's no skin off my back." She shoved the dessert box back into his hands. "Please leave."

"You've mistaken my comment. We care about each other. It's only natural that you'd be salty if I sent gifts to someone else."

"I'm not salty. I'm not *anything* where you are concerned. You made your thoughts on the subject crystal clear. This about face? Yeah, it doesn't wash. I'm not a player in your games, Knox." She was careful to keep her voice neutral. The live plants surrounding her were sensitive to vibration and mood. With her magic, an angry atmosphere could shrivel the foliage.

"Spring, I'm trying to tell you that I'm not an asshole or insensitive to your feelings."

She snorted and headed toward the exit. "I'm getting ready to head out, and I'd like you to go. I have a date tonight, and I don't want to be late."

"Who?" he barked.

The hard edge in his tone took her aback. If she didn't know any better, she'd say it was laced with jealousy.

"Tommy is taking me to the movies if you must know."

"I told you, he isn't for you. Why are you continuing to give him hope for the long term?"

"When you figure out who my perfect match is, you let me know. Until that time, I'll continue to enjoy Tommy's company. He's a nice guy."

"He's a non-magical human," Knox stated as if it said it all.

"Witches and warlocks marry non-magical humans all the time."

A dark, dangerous emotion entered his eyes. "You will not marry him."

Her brows shot to her hairline. "Wow! You have a shit-ton of nerve."

"You are being deliberately obtuse. I'm trying to tell you that I care for you!"

Her heart rate doubled its speed. He cared? As in romantically or as a friend who didn't want to see her hurt? It was difficult to tell, and she was too afraid to ask. If she embarrassed herself in front of him again, she'd have to move to the other side of the planet. The best course of action was to remain silent, and she did.

"What about you, Spring?" he asked softly. "Do you still care for me?"

"As a friend, sure. But the silly girl who professed her feelings for you? No, I'm beyond that now, Knox."

Confusion clouded his face before a firm resolve took its place. "I don't believe you. I don't think you've moved on at all." He shifted to stand in front of her. "I think you do care. More than care. I think you love me, and a Thorne only loves once."

"Maybe my feelings were hero worship. You were handsome and different. You treated me like I was important to you. I guess it went to my head. As a lonely little girl, I was drawn to it. But it wasn't love, Knox. I could never love someone who doesn't respect me."

"I *do* respect you, sweetheart. You have to understand, at first, you were too young. As you got older, I didn't trust you wanted me and not this." He waved his hand around his face and down his chest.

"What's changed?" she scoffed. "I'll tell you, *nothing*. Nothing except I've moved on. You can't seem to handle the fact you've tumbled off of that pedestal I'd put you on."

"*That's* what's changed. You finally see me as a *real* person. Not some make-believe hero." He dipped to meet her gaze. "You're seeing me as one grown up sees another."

"Please stop. You're embarrassing us both," she whispered, unable to take another excruciating second of their conversation. Whatever game he now played was flaying her nerves.

Knox stepped closer. He cupped the side of her face and directed her head up so she would meet his gaze. "I l—"

The door of her shop flew open.

Hearing a shocked gasp caused Spring to pull away from Knox and turn toward the entry. With matching expressions of disbelief, Winnie and Tommy stood stock-still in the doorway.

"I'm sorry, sister. He showed up early, and I thought you'd be finished up in here."

"What the hell is with you Thorne sisters and those damned Carlyles? It's like you're all suckers for punishment." Tommy's anger was palpable. He glowered from his position by the entrance, his hands balled into fists and hurt radiating from him.

Spring could only feel sorry for him.

Knox, on the other hand, took exception to Tommy's attitude and stepped forward, ready to do battle.

"Tommy, it's not what it looks like." Spring edged around Knox and gave him a wide berth. "I—"

Any remaining words were strangled off as Knox spun her about and wrapped an arm around her waist. His lips cut off Spring's protest, and she forgot why she'd protested to begin with. Her body melted against his as his arm tightened and the fingers of his other hand wove through her hair to cradle the base of her skull. When the kiss ended, she was breathless and left longing for more. As she struggled to inhale oxygen, her chest came in contact with Knox's with each draw of air. The friction made her breasts ache with her want.

"Not what it looks like, my ass," Tommy snapped. "You're nothing but a two-timing bitch!"

One second, Knox was supporting Spring and her weak knees, and the next, his fist had connected with Tommy's unsuspecting face.

Knox shook Tommy like a terrier with a rat. "Apologize. *Now.*"

The sisters stood in shocked amazement; neither had expected the ugly turn of events. But a secret part of Spring—the part that had never put to rest her infatuation for Knox—was thrilled by his aggressive defense of her honor.

Tommy's "I'm sorry" was grudgingly given, and to prevent further bloodshed, she accepted with grace. She placed a hand on Knox's arm to encourage him to release his hold on Tommy. "It must've been a shock for you to see Knox kiss me, but I swear there is nothing between us."

The disbelieving snorts of the other three occupants of the room brought on Spring's frown.

"It's true!" she exclaimed hotly.

"Give it up, sweetheart. No one believes you. You don't even believe yourself."

Knox's amusement at her predicament grated on Spring's last nerve. "Believe this!"

Putting all her weight behind her swing, she socked him in the gut. Knox's pained grunt gave her a small measure of satisfaction, as did the dropped jaws of Tommy and Winnie.

With a flick of her hair over her shoulder, Spring sailed out the shop door. She only made it fifteen feet when Knox scooped her into a fireman's carry. Her outraged screech echoed around the yard and was met with a sharp slap on the ass. The only thing that kept her from teleporting was the fact that Tommy was surely watching from the porch of her business.

"I swear to the Goddess, I am going to bury you neck deep in quicksand if you don't put me down, Knox Carlyle," she snarled and pounded on his back.

"Oh, sweetheart, save your empty threats for someone who might actually believe them."

KNOX GRINNED, BUT ONLY BECAUSE SPRING COULDN'T SEE HIS FACE. Her body was stiff with outrage. Oddly enough, it turned him on. It seemed he could be as contrary as Spring. The feel of her breasts as they rubbed against his upper back with each step fed his fantasies of ravishment.

Of its own volition, his hand traveled the length of her jean-clad thigh to cup her ass. The slight meep she emitted turned his grin into a self-satisfied smile. The little liar could say she felt nothing, but her physical reaction to him told a different story.

Instead of heading into the house, he took them into the empty barn where Summer's sanctuary used to be housed. Along the far wall was a stack of hay which suited his needs perfectly. He set her on her butt at eye level. "It's time we got a few things straight, sweetheart."

"Like the fact that I'm going to—"

He kissed her. It was the best way to shut down her empty threats. Or wipe her mind of any not-so-empty threats. But as their tongues collided and their hands reached to draw each other close, Knox was the one whose mind was wiped of thought. All he could do was give over to the sensation. It seemed Spring might be innocent when it came to the actual sexual deed, but at kissing, she was an expert.

The realization brought him up short, and he jerked away to glare down at her. "Who have you been kissing? I want a list of names."

"What?"

Her frown would've been adorable if he wasn't so furious at the idea of another man touching her.

"How many men have you kissed?"

Understanding dawned in her eyes, and a wicked gleam brightened the green of her irises. She leaned back on her palms and smirked. "Who said I stopped at kissing?"

Fury—black and all-consuming—flooded him. "That's all you'd better have done. Anything more and I'll kill someone."

She tightened her thighs around his hips where he stood between them. Maintaining eye contact, she edged up the hem of her sweater and drew it over her head. The tank top underneath showed she was braless. Within a second, the last barrier to her skin was gone.

Knox's rage morphed into a raging desire as his attention was caught by her high, firm breasts. Spring took his hands and placed them over the creamy mounds. His reaction was instinctive as he cupped and caressed the nipples there. As he lowered his head to capture her rosy areola, she fisted a hand in his hair and jerked him back.

"This is where I stop."

The little tease! She knew exactly what she was doing to him; working him into a frenzy and calling a halt was close to driving him insane.

"You're playing with fire, sweetheart," he growled and tightened his hold.

She gasped and dropped her head back. "Some guys kiss me here." She indicated the base of her neck.

"Like this?" Knox placed a delicate kiss on her silky skin.

"Mmm."

"Or perhaps like this?" He grazed his teeth along her column of her creamy throat and nipped the skin there.

"Yes," she breathed.

"Maybe they even do this." Knox latched on and sucked. He knew it would mark her as his, but he didn't care. As a matter of fact, he loved the idea that the world would know he was staking his claim.

He pulled back and gazed into her desire-filled eyes. "When you're ready to acknowledge what we have, we'll continue this."

Knox left her and teleported home. He imagined he could hear her outraged scream, and smiled despite torturing himself in the process. At some point, he'd have to deal with her displeasure. But today wasn't that day. Or so he thought until two minutes later when he witnessed the plants in his room shrivel and brown. *The spiteful little witch!*

She'd given him various exotic potted plants as presents when they were still children. He'd had kept them all these years as a reminder of Spring's sweetness.

He looked to where he felt the strongest magical pull. She had to be scrying to know if he had plants in his bedroom. With a wink and a cocky grin, he walked the perimeter of his room and restored each one to life with a simple spell she'd taught him in exchange for her horse-riding lessons. When he was done, he clapped his hands together to obliterate her scrying mirror. *See if she liked having the tables turned!*

6

*S*pring had just found a spell to restore the family's antique scrying mirror when Alastair stepped into the attic. She squirmed at the sight of his lifted brow. While she'd never believe he'd stoop to spying on her, the man had an uncanny knack for knowing things.

"Uncle. To what do I owe the pleasure of today's visit?"

He flashed a half-smile at her formality. "Do I need a reason to visit my beloved niece?"

"Yes."

At Alastair's deep bark of laughter, Spring bit back a giggle. Although rarely used, Alastair Thorne's laugh made everyone around him want to join in. It was hard to believe she'd feared him once. All too soon he turned serious.

"I suspect you know well my reason for popping in today. Thor's Hammer. We need to speak with your young man and devise a plan. I have the coordinates of the artifact."

"Uh…" How could she tell him that she and Knox were in the middle of a war?

Alastair narrowed his shrewd eyes and took in the mirror. "Hmm. His handiwork?"

"Yes."

"What did you do?"

"Why is this my fault?" Sure, she'd peeked into Knox's bedroom, but it was only to get even for his stunt in the barn. In her defense, she had no idea he was a metal element. But either way, Knox had absolutely no right to destroy their antique mirror.

"Because despite your righteous, wide-eyed expression, you can be a little she-devil at times, and the boy doesn't strike me as someone who bends mirrors in half all willy-nilly."

With a scowl at the twisted up mirror, she said, "He's not a boy. And he's quickly becoming a pain in my ass."

Something akin to cackling exploded from Alastair.

"It's not funny, uncle. You did this. You brought him into my life again. I was ready to move on."

"No, you weren't, child," he countered softly. His voice was filled with so much sympathy it made Spring's stomach hurt. "You love him. You always have. And while I understand his perceived rejection stung, Knox had his reasons."

"What reasons?" She desperately wanted to know. Perhaps if she could understand those reasons, she could move beyond the humiliation of the past. Because at the moment, each of those memories was too difficult to swallow.

"Those are for him to reveal. But he's always had your best interests at heart."

"I don't believe you. Or him." She swiped at a tear that escaped down her cheek. "It's a game to you both. You only want the artifacts, and he wants to prove I'm the naive child he always accuses me of being."

Alastair shook his blond head and ran his hand over the mirror to restore it to its original form. "Look, dear heart. What do you see?"

Knox had regenerated all the plants in his room to healthy once more. As they watched, he brushed a fingertip over a leaf of the last one and smiled.

"I see him obsessing over plants. So what?"

"Look closer. Do you remember giving him those same plants?"

Shock made her eyes bug. Long forgotten memories of bringing him the occasional gift flooded her mind. She studied the foliage of each pot. They were the same ones she'd given him! "He kept them? Why?"

"Because they were from *you*, Spring." Alastair clasped her hand and squeezed. "From a precocious little girl who wore her heart on her sleeve. I'll tell you a little secret that few people know."

Her head whipped up. "What?"

"Carlyles only love once as well. They fall just as hard as the Thornes, but they are more stubborn than our clan by far. A little dumber, too."

Spring hugged her uncle. She was helpless not to because he'd given her the most exquisite gift of all: understanding and the knowledge that Knox loved her in return.

"Should I make him suffer?"

"Absolutely. But not too much. Despite looking like a Greek god, the boy's ego is fragile."

She laughed and rested her cheek against the area of his heart. "I was raised to believe you were a bad person. I'm glad you're not. I love you, Uncle."

The heart next to her ear picked up its pace, and the rumble of his deep voice was echoed in his wide chest. "I'm sorry to hear you feared me, dear girl."

"Oh, I was really more fascinated by you." She pulled back to gaze up at his sad face. "You are a legend in this family. Your power. The mystery surrounding your death at Lin's hands. Your resurrection. But I've learned you're human like the rest of us, and I like you more for it."

The dark emotion never left his eyes, but he smiled all the same. "I like you, too. Now, call Carlyle and get him here. We need to discuss your trip."

"I don't have his number."

"Stop stalling. I know you've read the grimoire from front to back. You can call without ever having to dial a number."

48

"How do you always know when I'm lying?" she asked, curious despite herself.

"Your right nostril twitches."

Her hand flew to her nose. "It does not!"

"No, but if I tell you the truth, then you'll find a way to disguise it, and I'll lose the advantage."

Laughter bubbled up and out. "Fine, but promise me, when this is all done, you will take me on a grand shopping expedition in Paris."

"Deal."

Spring gathered her magic to her and called her familiar for the added boost. Her raven landed on her shoulder and nuzzled her cheek.

"Hello, Mr. Black. I need an assist."

The bird answered with a caw.

"Thank you."

Concentrating on Knox, she pushed a telepathic wave in his general direction. *"Knox, I need you to come to the Thorne attic."*

His response was instantaneous, and when he arrived, his expression was not happy. "What the fuck was *that*?" He glowered down at her. "How did you get in my head?"

"Simmer down, son. Spring didn't have your phone number, and I needed you here." Alastair stepped forward and lifted the raven from her shoulder. Spring recognized the protective move for what it was.

"I wasn't in your head," she explained, certain she'd be upset if the situations were reversed. The idea of anyone having access to her thoughts was terrifying. "It was a telepathic call with a boost from Mr. Black. I couldn't hear your thoughts."

Knox stared at her as if to gauge her truthfulness. Whatever he saw in her clear-eyed return stare made him nod and look away. When she met her uncle's gaze, he winked.

"Okay, kids, let's get down to business." Alastair lifted his arm to give the old bird a boost toward its perch. From his pocket he pulled two amulets with the Thorne Family crest: a raven surrounded by the five elements with the words *Honor Reigns* in Latin below. One he gave to Spring, and the other he gave to Knox. "There is a spell on these amulets blessed by Isis herself. They've been in our family for generations, so don't lose them."

Spring slipped hers over her head and immediately felt the ancient magic associated with the piece. "Wow! It's like an electrical charge."

"Exactly."

"What does the spell extend to?" Knox asked, studying the disc at the end of the chain.

"It's more of an early warning system to let you know should things go wrong. Preston and I have worked together in hopes of counteracting the Lin's Blockers and added that little boost, so if you need to teleport, you'll be able to." Alastair paused, then added, "In full disclosure, there was no way to test against the Blockers. It could be hit or miss. However, the crowning touch is the cloaking ability it offers. No need for a spell. Use your thumb to trace an X on the back of the disc, and it will give you invisibility with the added bonus of soundproofing. More than that, and it's up to the two of you to use your wits." Alastair gave Spring a pointed look. "Keep the tanzanite necklace Winnie gave you on you at all times. It allows us to psychically communicate if necessary."

A slight shiver danced along Spring's skin. She frowned, nodded, and sent up a silent prayer in hopes she wouldn't need to use it. "Understood."

"There are only four days left before Lin is scheduled to retrieve his prize."

"Don't worry, Uncle Alastair. I'll get it for you." Her mother's life depended on it, and Spring had no intention of failing the mother she hardly remembered but loved dearly.

"*We* will get it," Knox corrected.

"Fine. *We* will get it. Whatever." She'd done it now; committed to Knox accompanying her to South America. A small part of her thrilled to the idea of spending time with him, but the other part—her bruised ego—was vehemently opposed. "Does tomorrow work for you?"

"Yes."

"There is no time difference, so be ready to leave at nine a.m. sharp." Spring spun on her heel to leave.

"When did you get so bossy?" Knox asked, amusement laced his voice.

"I've always been bossy. I used to hide it better," she quipped over her shoulder.

KNOX SHOOK HIS HEAD AND LAUGHED AS SPRING LEFT THE ATTIC.

"She's a little spitfire. You're going to have a merry chase on your hands, son."

Knox started at Alastair's words. He'd forgotten the man's presence. "Yeah, but she's worth it."

"I'm glad we're in agreement and that you've come to your senses."

"Me, too. Now all we need to do is convince Spring."

"That will be easier than you think." Alastair frowned and changed the topic of conversation. "Something doesn't feel right about this trip. It could be the ease of finding the Mjölnir amulet, or it could be that we know Lin will be there. But either way, something is off."

"I feel it, too. How sure are you about your source?"

"He's never steered me wrong, but there is always a first time. It's not like I've never been betrayed before."

"By my father," Knox stated dully. On the night he witnessed Zhu Lin murder his father, Robert Knox had set Alastair up. And although he'd never learned the specifics, Knox did know his father's scheme had backfired and cost him his life. "I'm sorry he did what he did. But I owe you my life for getting me out of there that night."

"You don't owe me anything other than to take care of my niece should you two decide to make a go of it. Try not to break her heart."

Knox nodded at the stern warning. If he could help it, Spring would never feel unloved a day in her life. He only needed to figure out how to set to rights the wrongs of the past. One of the things he wanted to put to bed was his childhood. Until he understood why things had gone down the way they had, he'd never find peace. "What happened that night? I know my father tried to help Lin capture you, and I know he failed."

Alastair studied him for a long moment. "Are you sure you want to know?"

"Yes. I trust you to tell me the truth."

With a heavy sigh, the older man walked to stare out of the large window overlooking the drive.

"If you'd rather not..." Knox experienced a keen sense of disappointment. He'd hoped Alastair would be honest in all things.

"I'm taking a moment to gather my thoughts, son." Alastair faced him and perched on the edge of the window sill. With an elegance lost to modern-day men, he crossed his ankles and shoved his hands into the pockets of his slacks. "Your mother adored your father. Marianne was obsessed with Robert and would do anything for him. I don't think he held one ounce of affection for her. If he did, he hid it well."

Knox remembered much the same. He nodded and remained silent.

"It was right after the war between the witches and the Désorcelers. When the new war took place only in Lin's mind. When vengeance was his bedfellow. Robert was broke. He'd blown through all of Marianne's money and had decided his new payday would happen when he turned a Thorne over to Lin. He convinced your mother to help him."

Alastair looked up from studying the tips of his brown leather Salvatore Ferragamo shoes and met Knox's gaze head on.

"Marianne didn't care that I was with Aurora. She set out to seduce me. That night, I agreed to meet her. Not to take advantage of what she was offering, but to help her. I intended to try to convince her to get away from Robert and the damaging influence he offered.

"You were there, sitting silently in a corner with a book that seemed too adult for one so young. For that matter, *you* seemed too adult for a child so young. Your solemn little face broke my heart."

"I remember you conjured candy, using a sleight of hand."

Alastair gave him a half-smile. "I did. And although you accepted the treat, you remained serious."

"Why can't I recall you after that moment?"

"Your mother put you into a deep sleep. I guess she had a slight bit of maternal instinct after all. She didn't want you to see anything you shouldn't."

"That makes sense."

"Anyway, I ignored Marianne's overtures and tried to get her to see reason where Robert was concerned. He arrived with Lin hot on his heels. They had intended to trap me, but I was able to teleport before their plan came to fruition."

"The arguing woke me. My mother screamed my father's name, and then a gun went off. I'll never forget Lin's face as he stood over my father. He was so smug, so satisfied by what he'd done." Knox tried to wrap his brain around the sequence of events. "But you got me and my mom out. How did you manage that?"

"I teleported back within minutes with a few members of the Witches' Council as backup. We had hoped to get the drop on Lin, but he managed to escape. Your mother was forced to face the Council, and you were placed in Phillip's and Keira's care."

"I never had the chance to thank you for what you did. But I'm grateful. I want you to know that."

"I know, son." Alastair walked to Knox and placed a hand on his shoulder. "I get the feeling you've always questioned your worth. You shouldn't. Your parents didn't deserve you. Without a doubt they dishonored the Goddess when they mistreated her gift of a child. If I didn't believe you were worthy, I wouldn't send you with Spring."

"Thank you."

Instead of teleporting, Knox decided to walk home through the glen. The need to clear his head was strong. As the cool night air wrapped around him, he lifted his face to the sky and breathed it in.

Tomorrow, he'd start his journey with Spring to recover Thor's Hammer. It wouldn't be easy. Nothing in his life ever was. But at the very least, he could provide the protection Spring needed, whether she believed she needed it or not. He'd keep her safe or die trying.

Once they returned home with the prize, he intended to turn up the heat. To make her understand he was crazy about her. Make her understand his reasoning more fully for rejecting her advances until now. Make her see him as the flawed individual he was instead of the god on a pedestal that he wasn't. And maybe help her to understand the threat that had been associated with him until now. When she did, he intended to be certain she understood how much he loved her.

In the meantime, Knox had plans of his own to make. He picked up his cell and punched in a pre-programmed number. When the man on the other line answered, he said, "I have a job for you."

7

*T*he early dawn light, filtered by the curtains that graced Spring's five-feet tall windows, was relentless in its quest to wake her. She'd been awake half the night as she mulled over the last two days' events. As a result, she was a wee bit groggy and irritable despite the lovely golden light of dawn.

A shadow shifted in the corner of her room. She bit back a scream at the split-second she recognized the shape of the man gliding toward her. How could she not? She'd made a study of everything about him.

"Knox! What are you doing here?" She sat up and rested her back against her heavily upholstered headboard.

"I couldn't sleep." He sat sideways on the bed, one leg bent with his foot hooked behind the other leg. Although he rested an arm on the bent knee with a casual grace, he exuded an air of restlessness.

His inability sleep shouldn't have been cause for him to invade her privacy. If he did so, knowing how much of a stickler Knox was for the rules, he'd have done it with great deliberation. He was here for more than a casual chat. "Why? What's going on?"

"I'm not sure. I feel as if something is off." He sighed and scratched his day's growth of beard. "Alastair mentioned he felt the same last night. Since then, I can't seem to shake this odd sensation."

"You and my uncle are worriers by nature. Everything is going to be fine," she stated with a confidence she didn't feel. In truth, she felt off, too. It was as if the Goddess was gearing up to battle Fate for Spring's future. Maybe she was being fanciful, but she sensed a disturbance in the Force. She drew her legs up and wrapped her arms around her blanket-clad knees.

"I don't want you to go."

The scab covering her wounded heart was ripped away, leaving nothing but a raw, oozing opening. She tried to ignore the ache. Tried to tell herself his reasons for wanting her to stay home might have nothing to do with why he'd rejected her in the past. When she couldn't take another second of his brooding silence, she asked, "Why?"

Knox seemed surprised by her question. "Because you might get hurt. I don't think I could stand it if anything happened to you, sweetheart." He traced a finger along the arch of her brow.

Appeased and more than a little relieved, Spring halted his hand's trajectory down her cheek by turning her head. When he dropped his hand, she said, "You can't protect me from injury, Knox. As you've pointed out, Lin came to our town to cause trouble. The only safe place is our own properties or the clearing, and I refuse to be held captive to fear. Being held prisoner would be the one thing I could never tolerate."

His eyes made a quick study of her face as if he was judging her earnestness. His mouth tightened in frustration. "I know, but I also don't think you should take unnecessary risks."

"You're never going to see me as a grown woman, are you?" The question needed to be asked. Spring needed to hear the final nail driven into the coffin of her DOA unrequited love.

"Sweetheart, if you don't know the answer after that day in the clearing, then you are living in denial."

A shiver of awareness went through her. The deep, husky quality of Knox's voice had the ability to reach in and caress her nerve endings. She wanted to curl against him and purr whenever he was close or spoke to her in those raspy, knowing tones.

Perhaps her sister Autumn had been correct months ago when she suggested Spring should've found another guy to relieve her of her pesky virginity. Until nine months ago, she had wanted that someone to be Knox, but now she understood that in holding onto her girlhood dreams and expectations her own actions had been a deterrent for him. It was only when she confessed to making out with guys that he'd become interested.

This new realization made her sad. "I'm tired, Knox. I think you should go so I can catch a few more hours sleep. We can meet up and discuss it later this morning."

His mouth twisted in a wry smile. "You grew up when I wasn't looking."

"I suppose so, but when were you ever looking other than to see me as some young, innocent pest?"

Again, he frowned. "Confession?"

She nodded.

"I've always seen you as someone desirable. That was part of the problem. I feared if we formed a relationship while we were both teens, you would never have a chance to experience life. You deserve more than what I can give you, Spring."

"In your mind, the times you purposely rejected me were for my own good?"

"It sounds stupid when you say it aloud, but yes, that was my thinking."

She shook her head in wonder. "For someone with an IQ off the charts, sometimes you're dumb as a rock."

"Gee, thanks."

She cupped his face but waited for him to pull away. When he didn't, she said, "If you truly cared about me, treating me like crap and shoving me away was never the answer, Knox. You might have done irreparable damage before we could form any type of lasting relationship."

"Have I?" he questioned hoarsely.

"Are you saying you want to form a lasting relationship?"

"I am."

She dropped her hands and sat in contemplative silence for a moment. *Had* he done irreparable damage? She didn't know the answer. All she did know was her ability to trust his motives was nil at the moment. What if she committed to him and he decided he didn't want her once again? She didn't think she could stand the humiliation a second time around.

"Would you be mad if I said I need time?"

"No, never." He smoothed a stray lock of hair from her forehead. "You take the time you need. I'll be waiting."

"And what if my answer is no?"

His expression tightened and turned watchful. "I'll have to respect your decision, won't I?"

"Thank you."

"Does that mean you're saying no?"

"I still want time to think. Let's get this thing with my mother out of the way and return to normal before we make any life-altering decisions, okay?"

"Fair enough. One more question; may I kiss you before I go?"

"Hell, yes!"

Knox laughed at her enthusiasm, but when she straddled his lap, he was no longer laughing. Kissing Spring was no joking matter. It required his utmost attention. Their gazes locked, and in Spring's eyes Knox could see trepidation. She honestly feared he'd reject her again. But he wasn't sure he had the ability to deny his baser instincts any longer. He'd already touched her. Tasted her. *And now he had to have her.*

Spring said she needed time, and Knox intended to give her whatever she required. But he also held onto the hope that Thorne family legend rang true, and he reserved the right to try to change her mind if she decided she no longer wanted him in her life.

"You are, hands down, the most beautiful creature on the planet, Spring Thorne. One wicked look from your mischievous eyes, one smirk from those delectable lips, or one sassy comeback makes me want to drag you to the bedroom and thoroughly ravish you."

She gasped at his candor. When she would've spoken, he placed a finger over her full lips. He reached for her hips and held her in place as he shifted his pelvis.

"Do you feel that?" He dipped his head and lightly brushed her lips with his. "When I'm around you, it never goes away. You were always too inexperienced to tell." He kissed her more fully. When he pulled back, he said, "I can't ever imagine a day when I won't want you. And one day, when we are old and gray, I'll still be chasing you around the bedroom as fast as my walker will allow me to go."

Spring's smile brightened the still-darkened room. Or maybe it only seemed so, but she beamed her delight at his words. With a not-so-subtle shift of her hips, she said, "You won't need to chase me, Knox."

He growled low in his throat and captured her mouth, plunging his tongue into its warm depths. Spring gave as good as she got. Her fingers wove their way into his hair, and she gyrated her body against his.

He fell back on the bed and allowed her to take the lead. He intended to stop her before things went too far and she did something she would potentially regret in the morning light. But for the moment, he was dog enough to enjoy the sensation of her body flush against his.

He ran the tips of his fingers along the smooth skin of her spine at the same time he pushed a low burst of power from his hands to her back.

She broke their kiss to stare down at him in wide-eyed wonder. "What is that? I feel it all the way to my…" The blush coloring her cheeks delighted him. "Is it normal?"

With a suggestive grin and a quirked brow, he slowly shook his head.

"Can you do that again?" she asked breathlessly.

"I can, that and more, but I thought you wanted me to go."

Indecision was written on her face. Clearly, she wanted to experience the pleasure of magic while making love, but she was still torn about her feelings for him. With a deep sigh of regret, she climbed from atop him and flopped on her back.

Knox rolled on his side and slid a hand under her shirt to caress the full cup of her left breast. "When you're ready, we'll spend a week in bed. I'll show you every trick I know, and we'll make up more as we go along. We'll eat bonbons and drink champagne. We'll make love in every position imaginable."

With one last, lingering kiss, he pulled her shirt down to cover her chest and rose to his feet. "I'll see you later. Try to get some rest, sweetheart."

"You, too," she said softly.

Knox let out a small bark of amusement. "I'm not getting sleep. Not after what just happened here. Besides, I have horses to feed in another hour."

As he stood to leave, Spring stopped him with a hand on his arm. "Knox? Why now?"

"I don't understand."

"You said you were purposely trying to push me away. Why do you want me now when you didn't before?"

"I can't answer other than to say that seeing you with Tommy triggered some sort of primitive, possessive gene within me." He couldn't tell her about his other reasons. Maybe one day he would, but for now, all was as it should be. Or it would if Spring decided to give him a second chance.

The solemn look in Spring's eyes bothered him. Instinct told him to press the issue, but she had already pulled the blanket up to her chin and snuggled down into her pillow.

"Sleep well, sweetheart."

"Bye, Knox."

True to his word, Knox stayed awake after he left Spring's room. Unease had taken over and refused to let him get a quiet moment. A sort of rapid-fire warning repeated in his brain throughout the morning as he cleaned stalls and tossed hay to the stock. As mid-morning rolled around, he concluded that he needed to convince Spring to stay home. The Goddess wouldn't send him these vibes for no reason.

8

"Why are you being stubborn, Spring?" Knox demanded.

Spring sat with her legs curled under her and calmly sipped tea as six feet plus of enraged male paced like a caged tiger in front of her. Knox had regurgitated the same argument for the last twenty-three minutes with no success. Indeed, she had no intention of staying behind. Her goal was to get the damned artifact, plant the near-extinct species she'd been growing for a future trip to Colombia, and get the hell out of South America as quickly as possible.

He paused and glared down at her. "Well?"

"I'm not being stubborn, Knox. I'm being practical. My reason for going is two-fold, *as we've discussed*, ad nauseam. You just refuse to believe your way is not law."

"I had magical warning bells ringing in my head all night. *All. Night!*"

"So you've said, repeatedly."

"And yet you still refuse to listen." He swore under his breath. "Of all the stubborn, irresponsible—"

She surged to her feet. *"Enough!"*

A look of surprise flashed on his face before his lips tightened against whatever additional points he wanted to make.

"Knox, I'm going. You are wasting time and irritating the hell out of both of us by trying to persuade me otherwise. Enough, already," she said on a more gentle note. "Please."

He took the cup and saucer from her hands and placed them on the coffee table beside him. Then, he tugged her closer. For a long moment, he stared at their joined hands. "I'm sorry. I know I'm being overbearing. I can't seem to help myself where you are concerned." He glanced up, and his mouth twisted in a small semblance of a smile.

"You have to trust that I can handle myself. I'm not some fragile flower that needs to be kept under glass in a hothouse somewhere. I'm stronger than you think."

"I know, but it doesn't calm my worry or make me feel any less inclined to protect you."

She loved him for his protectiveness. Not that she'd ever say as much, but it added to her already long list of reasons to love him. "This is going to be easy peasy. You'll see."

"From your mouth to the Goddess's ear," he muttered. He drew her against his chest and kissed the top of her head. "You're killing me, sweetheart. You know that, right?"

"Come on. Let's take a second look at Alastair's maps and then gather the items I need to repopulate the species I'm working on."

"Can the planting wait until a safer time?"

"I suppose it could, but why wait? Once we grab the Mjölnir amulet, we can hand it off to Alastair, and I can pop over to the jungle for a little gardening. You can stand as my bodyguard if it makes you feel better. It will be a breeze."

"Christ, every time you say things like 'easy peasy' or 'it will be a breeze,' I get the heebie jeebies. It's like you are tempting fate."

She laughed at his beleaguered expression and patted his cheek. "Poor Knox. Let's get this show on the road, shall we?"

"There's nothing I can say to persuade you to stay?"

"No."

"And why the hell doesn't Alastair go after these items himself?" The question came out on a low growl. It seemed Knox didn't care to be Alastair's errand boy.

"He won't leave my mother in anyone else's care that long. If he goes on a mission and becomes trapped, he'll lose his shit."

"That wouldn't be a bad thing. He's one of the most powerful beings in existence. Besides, you or your sisters could care for her. That's the much better plan."

Knox's argument was valid, but Spring dismissed it all the same.

"What part of 'he won't leave my mother' didn't you hear?" She grimaced and moved to stare out the window. "It's sweet, but pointless all the same. The chances of reviving her are slim, and yet he clings to hope. She might never be normal even if she does wake."

The air around them crackled, and she wasn't surprised when Alastair spoke. "Does that mean I should give up on her? Perhaps I should hold a pillow over her head and be done with it all." Fury vibrated in his low, cold tone.

She doubted he'd ever expressed this level of rage to any one member of her family before this moment. Alastair never lost his cool. She sighed and faced him. "I'm sorry, uncle. I didn't mean to insult you or my mother."

His blue eyes were the color of a raging sea. Other than the set jaw, it was the only thing to indicate Alastair's rage—if one didn't count the electrified air around them or the boiling liquid in her teacup.

"Don't break my mother's china, Uncle."

Alastair pulled back some of his emotion. "For someone so smart, you know nothing." He ran a hand through his perfectly styled, blond hair. The mussed locks were the final indication of his upset. Alastair was always pristine. "You volunteered for this, Spring. If you don't want to go, I'll send someone else. Say the word."

She moved to where he stood and placed a soothing hand on his crossed arms. She sent a pulse of calming energy through their connection. "I'm going. It was never in any question. She's my mother, and I owe her that."

The brows that had shot up in surprise at her gesture lowered into a frown. "She would never expect you to sacrifice for her. As a matter of fact, she wouldn't want it. You owe her nothing."

"What's with the about face?" Knox moved to stand behind her. She imagined it was a show of solidarity.

Alastair dropped his arms and severed the connection between them. "I don't expect anyone to do what they don't want to. Not for me. Not ever."

"I already said I want to go, and I intend to. Now, you mentioned this was a private auction. Do you have the details of when and where Lin is to pick up the amulet? We need to get moving before he beats us to it." Her hardened tone indicated she meant business. She was tired of the argument, and they were losing their advantage.

Alastair's gaze lifted over her head, and Spring figured he'd shared a private communication with Knox.

Men! They always assumed women weren't tough or resilient. She wanted to express her disgust, but what good would it do? "Well?" she demanded.

"Let's head up to the attic. We'll pinpoint the exact location and bring up the images of the surrounding area for you to teleport." Alastair's anger seemed to be well under control, and his tone was more even. Whatever he'd seen when he glanced at Knox eased his mind.

Once in the attic, they gathered around a map of Colombia.

"Here. Cartagena." Alastair pointed to the city on the north-most point by the coast. With a snap of his fingers, he conjured a folder. "This is all I could gather. It's a dossier on the seller and a map of his property."

"I thought Morty's painting indicated a jungle," she asked, referring to the series of paintings Summer's chimpanzee had created as clues for the magical artifacts. She still didn't get how the damned beastie had the inside scoop, but she didn't intend to question her sister or uncle about the little ape's skills. He hadn't been wrong so far.

Alastair shrugged. "My intel says here. Maybe he indicated the jungle for the country itself."

She nodded her agreement. It seemed like a reasonable enough explanation.

Knox studied the photos for a moment before handing them off to her. "It seems heavily guarded. Should we be concerned he's someone important? The last thing we need is an international incident."

She glanced up in time to notice Alastair's quick grimace.

"I'm not concerned with politics, son. Thwarting Lin and obtaining the amulet are my primary goals."

A shiver of warning ran the length of Spring's spine. She narrowed her eyes. "What do you know of the man who owns this property, uncle?"

"He's a drug lord by the name of Don Carlos Esteban."

"Fuck!" Knox replicated his pacing from earlier. "No! Nope. Not gonna happen. We are not doing this."

"Are there any hotels you deem safe in the area?" Spring directed her question to Alastair.

"I said *no,* Spring! You are not doing this. Let Lin have that damned amulet. We'll find another." Knox's adamant response wasn't a surprise to either her or Alastair, and they both chose to ignore his rant. "Did you not hear me?"

"With your shouting, how can we not? But you're not my boyfriend, my boss, nor my keeper."

"I will lock your ass up in my basement and throw away the key. I swear to the Goddess, I will. You are not going into the house of a drug lord."

She rolled her eyes. "You are being unreasonable. It's a simple matter to disguise ourselves with a glamour spell then be in and out before anyone knows we are there. Once we see the head asshat-in-charge leave, you take on his appearance. I'll be your arm candy. You'll order someone to open the safe, and bam!"

Knox leaned in and spoke like he was talking to a particularly slow child. "Except we don't know what he looks like, sounds like, or how to speak his particular dialect."

She leaned closer and copied his snarky attitude. "That's what magic is for, or did you forget you are a powerful warlock?"

"You're impossible!"

"Why don't you two kiss and make up. I can wait in the other room." Alastair's dry tone cut through the tension, jerking Knox upright.

"I'll tell you what, how about we run this by Spring's father and see what he has to say about her running off into harm's way?" Knox's tone carried a nasty edge.

"How about you stop treating me like I'm a flighty teenager trying to sneak out of the house after curfew?" Spring returned. "I'm an adult with a perfectly functioning brain."

"This is what happens when you don't give into the urge to have sex with one another. Tempers run high. You should probably get that out of the way," Alastair said as he straightened his tie and smoothed back his hair.

Spring lost it. One moment she was angry with Knox's high-handed attitude, and the next, tears were leaking from her eyes in her hilarity.

"What's so funny about having sex with me?" The seething hostility coming from Knox made the situation that much more humorous.

"Oh, Knox!" Another round of laughter shook her. "Your face! It's like you're a tight-assed virgin or something."

"I would've gone with a nun or medieval maiden in a chastity belt, but the tight-assed virgin is probably more fitting," Alastair inserted dryly.

Pure outrage took over Knox's countenance, and even Alastair lost his standard decorum to laugh.

"I'm glad you both find this situation so hysterical."

Had Knox's tone not held a wounded quality, Spring would've continued to tease him. As it was, she sobered and closed the distance between them. Utilizing her sweetest smile, the one she knew could melt even the hardest of men, she cupped his jaw. "If you can't laugh at yourself, who can you laugh at? Stop taking life so seriously."

Their gazes connected, and the hurt fled his eyes to be replaced by a wry humor. "I suppose I did sound like a tight-ass."

She held up her index finger and thumb an inch apart. "About this much."

He surprised her when he wrapped his arms around her and hauled her close. "I just don't want anything to happen to you. Can't you see how risky this is? Even for a powerful warlock and witch?"

She drew back and sandwiched his face between her palms. "You can't keep bad things from happening to me. It's impossible. What is fated will be. You know that."

A DISTINCT CHILL TOOK HOLD OF KNOX'S SOUL AND REFUSED TO LET go. "I have a feeling, sweetheart... I can't put into words."

She sent a frustrated look toward Alastair. Knox wanted to groan due to his own frustration. How could she not see that popping into the home of a drug lord was a recipe for disaster? For that matter, why the hell was Alastair determined to allow it? The man had a screw loose. But maybe he had a point. Maybe Knox should make love with Spring until she couldn't stand upright. He could keep at it until the deadline for Lin to take possession of the amulet.

As he warmed to the idea, Spring separated from him and bent over the table with the photos. Knox's gaze was drawn to her perfectly rounded ass, outlined in her designer jeans. Yep, he liked his new plan of seduction.

"It won't work, son," Alastair stated with his voice pitched low to keep Spring from overhearing.

"What won't?"

"Seducing her to do your bidding. She's a Thorne and as stubborn as they come. Probably more stubborn than Autumn, and that's saying something."

"Thanks a lot, Uncle."

Both men and Spring whipped around to find Autumn lounging in the chaise. Alastair frowned his displeasure, and Knox surmised it was because he'd been surprised. "When did you arrive?" Alastair demanded.

"I've been here all along. Granny Thorne's cloaking spell," Autumn clarified with a cheeky grin. "I really hate missing a great drama."

Alastair waved a hand. The cloaking spell hiding Winnie dissolved. She sat there with a startled look and popcorn halfway to her mouth.

Knox's funny bone was finally tickled. Once started, he found it impossible to stop laughing.

9

"*I*'ve checked us in. We have a premium suite."

Spring jerked in surprise and stared at Knox. When he went off to check them in, she assumed he'd get two rooms. "I... we... we're sharing a room?"

"Is that a problem?"

Yes! How the hell was she supposed to keep from staring at him the whole time? His male beauty melted women's brains and made them do stupid shit. What if she lost her mind and jumped his bones? "No. No problem," she mumbled as she took the proffered key.

With one hand on her lower back, Knox guided Spring toward the stairs. When they reached the foot of the staircase, a small Asian man moved into view. Knox's fingers curled into her hip, but the man only gave them a cursory glance as he came down the steps.

Spring didn't breathe a sigh of relief until he'd passed them. "Think he's one of Lin's?"

"I don't know, but I'm glad we put our disguises in place before leaving the manor."

She bit her lip and nodded.

Earlier that day, they'd spent time glamouring their looks to appear as different as possible to the outside world. Knox had settled on dark brown hair, and golden lion-like eyes. There was nothing he could do to reduce his height, but he was able to make his naturally lanky frame appear more muscular and solid in stature. Spring had morphed into a redhead and changed her eyes to a deep, dark brown. She altered her leaner body to make herself curvaceous and fuller chested. They still came across as Americans, but they were different enough in appearance to pass muster should anyone only send them a fleeting glance. To each other, they appeared as their normal selves.

"After we get settled in, we'll go out for lunch and recon."

Knox's willingness to allow her to accompany him shocked her speechless. Her astonishment must've been apparent because he said, "I'm not comfortable letting you out of my sight."

"I'm cool with that."

Some of her unease made itself known. Confidence exuded from Knox, and he gripped her hand and squeezed to dispel her misgivings. "I intend to do my best to see us home in one piece."

"I'm cool with that, too."

He kissed her knuckles before urging her up the stairs. Once they reached their floor, he guided her to their room and escorted her inside.

The hotel was lovely. Natural plants lined a two-story atrium and sent waves of welcome only an earth element witch could detect. Spring leaned over the wide, white banister and gazed down into the main floor. The terra-cotta tiles and off-white walls gave the place an authentic native-Colombian feel.

Their room was homey and decorated in a manner befitting the rest of the hotel. One wall was the same burnt orange shade as the colorful pottery on the surface of the wood and wrought iron dresser. Spring loved it.

"Um, Knox, there's only one bed." The idea of sleeping with him short-circuited her brain. Positive she sounded like an idiot, she mentally scolded herself.

"Mmhmm." He kicked off his shoes and flopped down on the mattress. "Is there a problem?" He lay there with a casual ease, one arm behind his head while one hand rested palm down on his lower abdomen. A small, wicked smile played about his lips.

The interior of Spring's mouth resembled a desert. There wasn't a drop of moisture to be found. "I... I..." Yeah, she was at a loss. Mind fried. Goddess, he was the most incredible specimen on the planet, bar none. Her sisters believed their half-sister Holly's bodyguard, Quentin, had it all going on, but he was nothing compared to the perfection of Knox. Not that Spring would ever say as much aloud. No, she'd be teased mercilessly for it.

Just as Spring's saliva glands had kicked in, Knox patted the bed, and in a low voice, he asked, "Do you want to join me before lunch? I'm sure we can get one in before we leave."

She choked on her own spit at the innuendo. When she finally stopped coughing, she straightened. "Are you suggesting a quickie?" She couldn't prevent the squeaky pitch.

His deep chuckle reached right in and tickled her lady parts. "What a dirty mind you have, sweetheart. I was suggesting a nap, but if you would rather have a quickie, I'm up for anything."

She kept her eyes pinned to his smirking mouth. She didn't dare glance below his belt to see if he was truly "up for anything." "I think I'll check out the balcony."

He was off the bed and in front of her before she could touch the door handle. Any forward movement was delayed as his hand came down over hers. "No. I'd prefer to have as few people see us as possible."

She gulped and jerked her hand back. "It's a private patio. Who's going to see? Besides, we're disguised, remember?"

He shifted closer. "I have a second reason for not wanting you to run away. I want to kiss you, Spring." His low, gruff voice caused her nipples to tighten and her hot pocket to go nuclear. How the hell did he do that?

"Do you, um, utilize magic to make me, um... like..." She lowered her voice to whisper, "...wet."

His slack-jawed expression told her she'd erred. His resulting laughter at her mistake meant he wasn't getting lucky anytime soon.

Spring stomped toward the bathroom, but again, Knox beat her to her destination. When she tried to shove by him, he captured her hands.

"Don't be mad, sweetheart. I wasn't expecting the question." He drew her close and nuzzled her neck. "To answer as honestly as I can, no, I didn't utilize magic. I *can*, like yesterday morning, and it would make it that much more amazing between us when the time comes, but I didn't. Your response is all you."

That's what she feared. Knox had the ability to simply touch her hand or say a word in a certain tone of voice, and she was panting for him. It didn't bear thinking about when all of the kisses by the men she'd dated in her life left her lukewarm at best. If this was a game to him, if he only wanted her now because of some caveman response to seeing her with Tommy, she'd come out the loser in the end. He'd ruin her for anyone else and leave her cold.

She pushed him away. "This is a bad idea."

Knox frowned, confusion in his sapphire eyes. "Why?"

"You only want me because I'm dating Tommy. It's a matter of wanting what you can't have. I don't feel like being used that way, especially when you couldn't run far or fast enough in the opposite direction until this week."

"I thought we had already gotten the explanations out of the way." The intensity in his stare unnerved her. When he didn't get a response, he said, "I care about you. And I sure as hell have always wanted you." When she remained silent and watchful, he sighed. "I don't want you because you were dating Tommy, Spring. I want you because I can no longer stand to be without you. When you moved on, I realized how lonely my life would be without you in my world."

Sincerity shone from his face, and the truth was right before her eyes if she chose to see it. But as stupid as it sounded, she was scared to trust him, or trust in anything good for that matter. Yes, she had her sisters, but essentially she'd been left to her own devices for a long time. No mother, an absentee father, three sisters who had lives, careers, and loves of their own, not to mention a fourth sister she'd recently discovered who lived in another state. Not that *that* mattered due to their magical ability to teleport, but a bit of the awkwardness was still present when the family would get together. Her only true friend had been Knox, and he had rejected her as she grew into a woman.

She must have delayed too long because he backed away with a regretful sigh.

"Let's get some lunch," he suggested.

"I need a minute."

Spring closeted herself in the bathroom and splashed cool water over her face. She had no idea what to do with Knox's sudden attention. Did she grab onto what he offered with both hands, or did she maintain the status quo? How was she expected to move on if he played these stupid games at her expense? Did she want to? For a long moment, she stared at the woman in the mirror. No answers would come, and she was tired of worrying about it. She'd do what she'd come to do and get the damned amulet. After they were safely home, she'd take a longer look at her feelings on the subject.

THEY WALKED THE STREETS OF CARTAGENA LIKE A COUPLE IN LOVE. Periodically, Knox would take advantage of their cover to hold Spring's hand, or pull her under the shade of an awning to kiss her petal-soft lips. He hand fed her bits of their meal and allowed his fingers to linger on her lips until a flush of color lit her cheeks.

To him, she was the most exquisite woman on the planet. The spark of happiness in her eye when she came across a plant native to the area warmed him. At the same time, the jealousy he experienced when she'd stroke her hand down the leaf of the plant bothered him. He had it in him to destroy anything or anyone he considered a threat; anyone who might steal Spring's affections from him. The strength of his feelings for this one tiny woman were disconcerting. He'd seen what obsessive love had done to his mother. Marianne Carlyle had gone insane when Robert Knox was killed.

Not that Knox planned to let anything happen to Spring, but he worried he'd lose his mind should she ever die or become injured. The strong emotions she evoked terrified him to a large degree. What wouldn't he do for her?

Spring startled him from his musings. "What are you thinking about that has you miles away?"

"You."

"Ah." She tugged her hand away.

Knox entwined his fingers with hers. "Not the way you think."

"How do you know what I think?"

"Your expressive face says it all," he mocked softly. "I believe you've drawn the wrong conclusion."

"I doubt it, but do enlighten me."

"I am worried about how deeply I care for you. I'm afraid there is nothing I won't do to protect you."

"Okay, so I can see maybe you were right and I was wrong."

"I certainly hope someone, somewhere is marking this note-worthy occasion down. I don't think anyone would believe it if they hadn't witnessed this conversation," he teased.

"Oh, shut up, you tool. I'm not that difficult."

Knox pulled Spring to a stop and faced her. He bent his head and rubbed his nose lightly against hers. "No, you're not. And I'm sorry I ever made you feel otherwise."

"Don't start being nice to me now. I won't know how to survive it." Her attention was caught by something or someone behind him. "Oh, look! Cotton candy!"

He laughed as she dragged him along to the nearest street vendor. A hunched old man operated the cart. The down-trodden expression disappeared as the guy laid eyes upon Spring.

Knox felt the need to warn her. "Uh, sweetheart, that isn't—"

"Do you want one?"

Spring practically bubbled with excitement, and Knox bit his tongue, not wanting to ruin her fun. "No, thanks."

A few pesos exchanged hands, and they were on their way. He watched closely as she bit into the pastel fluff.

She gagged and spit it on the ground. "Dear Goddess! What the hell is that? It's bitter!"

"Not the sweet goodness you were expecting?" He fought to contain his laughter, he really did, but the disgusted look on her face was priceless. "I imagine it tastes very similar to a mouthful of *dirt*."

Narrowed eyes pinned him in place. "You did that on purpose."

Hands up, he backed up a pace. "No."

"Yes, you did. You knew it wasn't cotton candy, and you were going for payback," she accused, stalking toward him.

"Uh, yes and no. I did try to warn you."

"Not very hard!"

"Still."

"I feel like I should give you a *taste* of your own medicine."

Knox's laughter disappeared. He didn't relish another mouthful of dirt—Spring's standard revenge on her enemies. Damned earth element witches! "No magic in public, sweetheart. You know the rules."

An unholy light danced in her sparkling eyes. "Oh, but no one would see anything other than you spitting out some soil. They may wonder why you were eating it in the first place, but you know those crazy Americans."

"Spring, I'm warning you. You don't want to do this."

"Oh, but I really do." She smirked and raised a hand, middle finger and thumb pressed together in position to snap.

"You'll start a war you can't win," he warned with a nervous laugh.

"Hmm, that sounds like a challenge."

He surprised a squeak from her when he hauled her close. "I'd rather fill my mouth with the taste of you," he murmured against her lips.

Her body relaxed into his, and her arms gripped his biceps. "Smooth answer."

"Is it too corny to say I'd rather make love, not war?"

"From anybody else, I'd say yes. From you, not so much. You have a way with words."

Her mouth curled against his, tantalizing and teasing. Knox gave into the temptation to kiss her. His tongue teased along the seam of her lips which she graciously opened to allow him to explore the delights of her mouth.

He pulled back and met her desire-laden eyes. "Better than candy?"

"Mmm, much."

"I'd like nothing better than to head back to our room. Do you want to give up the idea of finding Don Carlos and return?" One moment he was holding an armful of willing woman, and the next, Spring was stomping away. "What the hell did I say?"

*T*wo hours later, as they lounged against a tree across from Don Carlos Esteban's downtown home, Knox was still at a loss as to what he'd said to piss off Spring. She hadn't spoken to him other than to remind him to make a cross on the back of his amulet in order to cloak himself with magic. The few times he'd tried to address the problem since then, she shushed him.

"Spring," he attempted for the fourth time.

Once again, she cut him off. "I think that's him." She straightened and peered at the picture in her hand. In the dim light, their visual acuity wasn't great.

"Fantastic," he muttered. He slapped the paper against her chest. "What's your plan, Princess?"

"Murder comes to mind," she retorted.

He scratched the thick stubble along his lower jaw. "That's one way to go about it, I suppose, but I thought I was clear that I'd rather make love than war."

She wadded up the picture and chucked it at his forehead. "You'd rather play me and keep me from doing what I need to do."

"Play you? What the hell are you talking about?"

"Pfft. Don't act like you don't know."

"I don't."

She snorted her derision. "Right."

"You are the most infuriating woman on the planet, you know that?"

"Lucky for you, after tomorrow, you don't need to ever see me again."

His heart stopped. "What the hell does that mean?"

"We do our recon tonight, then tomorrow we make an attempt for the necklace. When we go home, we go our separate ways." The tightness and hurt in her voice wasn't lost on him.

"Is that what you want?" Every muscle in his body tensed as he waited for Spring's reply.

"Yes."

The air rushed from his lungs, and he sank back against the tree. In the low light, Knox could only make out the outline of Spring's set jaw. It was impossible to interpret her expression. "I see."

"Good. Now if you'll pay attention, you can make out what he's saying. Try to imitate the lilt of his voice."

"Let's get closer. Set your phone to record."

After several minutes of listening and recording the conversation between Don Carlos and the man who appeared to be his next in command, Knox joined hands with Spring and teleported back to their room.

"Try to get some rest. I'll listen to the audio tonight and try to mimic his speech pattern. A simple spell will disguise my voice and translate my words into Latin."

"You can take the bed, I'll take the couch," she argued.

"I won't sleep tonight, Spring. Just take the damned bed already."

"I—"

"Can you do one thing I ask without a fucking argument for a change?" he snarled.

Hurt flared in her eyes. But she rallied quickly, and her pointy little chin lifted skyward. Pride and defiance were her boon companions.

"I'm sorry." He found it impossible to keep the gruffness from his voice. "Sleep or not. It's your choice. I'll be out on the patio." He placed a hand over his heart. "Please, don't leave this room without telling me."

"Of course."

"Thank you."

Knox eyed the tiny metal chair on the terra-cotta tiled porch. As he settled his body weight into the seat, he hoped like hell it wouldn't buckle under him. He placed his earbuds in and went to work.

Time and again, he needed to rewind the audio recording for playback because he couldn't concentrate. His mind continued to wander back to the conversation he and Spring shared outside the Esteban estate. From what he could deduce, Spring believed he had tried to manipulate her into forgetting their mission. He ripped the earbuds away from his head and angrily wrapped them around the phone before tossing it onto the mosaic-tiled table in front of him.

What the hell was he supposed to do now? How did he convince her the thought had never occurred to him to seduce her into submission? Hell, his mind hadn't gotten further than the image of her naked and spread-eagled on his bed.

He scrubbed his hands up and down his face. "What a freaking mess!"

"Love always is."

Before the intruder's identity registered, Knox had him by the throat and against the wall.

Alastair lifted a dark-blond brow and crossed his arms over his chest. "You might want to remove your hand if you wish to keep it."

"Sorry. You startled me."

"Seems you startle easily."

"Only when I'm not expecting company while in a foreign land."

"Fair enough."

"What are you doing here, Alastair?"

The other man dangled a necklace containing a tanzanite stone. "Spring forgot this. It gives us a direct link."

Knox stared at the piece of jewelry before he held out his hand. "I'll be sure to give it to her."

"Are you all right, son?"

"Yeah. It's all good."

"Somehow, I doubt that. But you're entitled to your secrets."

He moved to stare over the lights of the city. "Spring misinterpreted my intent earlier today. It's made her a bit salty."

"Why are you out here instead of in there, trying to smooth things over?"

With a short, humorless laugh, he said, "I value my life and dislike the taste of dirt."

"Perhaps all the dragons of our lives are princesses who are only waiting to see us once beautiful and brave."

Surprised, Knox faced Alastair. "Did you make that up?"

"It's a quote from the poet Rainer Maria Rilke. I feel it's appropriate, don't you?" Alastair clasped him on the shoulder. "In other words, man up, son. Are you going to let one small female keep you in terror?"

"Yes."

A deep, dark chuckle was Alastair's response. "Women are terrifying to the extreme. Good luck."

"Thanks."

"How are you coming along on the Don Carlos Esteban front?"

After a nod toward the phone on the table, Knox grimaced. "I have a bad feeling about all this." He met Alastair's contemplative gaze. "I don't like bringing Spring into all this mess."

"Are your feelings based on a legitimate premonition, or is it only your worry for my niece?"

"Both. I worry she is too young and inexperienced. Her temper could get her into trouble."

Upon overhearing Knox's words, Spring backed away from the door opening and shook her head. He would never see her as anything but a child. Somehow, he'd fixated on her youth and refused to see her any differently. The need to escape the confines of their room struck. She was halfway down the stairs when she remembered Knox's request that she not leave the room without letting him know. A pang of conscience struck her, but she shoved it away. She was only going to sit in the atrium. It's not like she intended to leave the hotel.

Once she'd found a seat next to a grouping of palm trees that overlooked the shallow pool, she double checked her surroundings. It wouldn't do if someone saw her conjure a drink. When she was certain she was alone, she closed her eyes and visualized a brandy glass with a double shot of Hennessy's finest cognac. She lifted the glass and offered up a silent toast to the Goddess, who never seemed to have Spring's best interests at heart. The very least her ancestor could've done was pair her with a man who respected her as a woman.

As she was about to take her first sip, the plants around her sent out a vibration. The fine hair on her forearms rose up on end. *She was being watched.* As casually as she was able, she continued the sipping motion, casting a furtive glance over the top of the glass.

There. In the corner of the atrium, blended into the ferns and palms, was the Asian man they'd seen earlier.

Spring closed her eyes and sent a request to the vines along the wall to detain him so she might make good her escape. As she gained her feet to flee, Zhu Lin appeared. At his back were five armed guards.

They studied one another across the short distance. For such an imposing figure, he was at most five-feet-ten. But he possessed a controlled energy. Power radiated from him. Not magical, but a strong air of command. His dark hair held a hint of gray at the temples, but other than that small indication, he appeared ageless with his smooth skin and trim frame. His most disturbing feature was his eyes. He possessed a pair of peepers that were the palest shade of green that Spring had ever seen. As an earth element who dealt with plants for a living, she'd seen every color on the green scale, but those eyes were colder than any she'd ever witnessed.

She absently wondered what he saw.

"Ms. Thorne."

Ten feet separated them. Not enough space for her to bolt.

"You must have me mistaken for someone else," she said kindly as she palmed the amulet disc at her throat. Why had she left home without the damned tanzanite necklace? "I do hope you find whoever it is you are looking for. If you'll excuse me, I'll leave you to your search."

He smirked, and the chilly smile chased an arctic blast down her spine. "How amusing that you and Winter Rose chose the same ploy. It didn't work for her, and it won't work for you."

"Fair enough. In that case, how about we go with this?" Spring made an X with her thumb on the back of the amulet and cloaked herself.

"She wasn't supposed to be able to teleport!" Lin snapped as he strode farther into the atrium. "Get me Grace. I want to know why the Blockers failed."

Spring didn't know who poor Grace was, but she really didn't want to hang around to find out. Closing her eyes, she concentrated all her power to teleport. It was a big nope, nada, zilch in the teleport department. So much for the mighty Thornes' ability to counteract the Blockers.

Someone bumped her side, and her eyes flew wide. *Lin!*

Zhu Lin slowly spun toward her, and Spring backed against the wall.

"She's still here. Fan out."

Shit on a cracker!

She tiptoed through the maze of guards, but the opening was small, and she doubted she would make a clean escape.

"Show yourself, Ms. Thorne. You aren't getting out of this room."

Most probably he was correct, but still, she eyed the distance from the atrium to the second floor. Did she dare attempt to scale it? The vines didn't appear thick enough to climb, but she could take care of that easily enough. On the other hand, her fear of heights might paralyze her if she got too high.

Once, when Spring was younger, she'd tried levitation. It hadn't worked so well for her. Aunt GiGi had found her curled in a ball under her favorite tree, cradling her arm, afraid to tell what she'd done because young witches were forbidden to perform magic without an adult present. From that day forward, Spring possessed a fear of heights.

"I'm losing my patience, Spring. Show yourself."

Not a fucking chance, asshole.

Decision made, she sent a burst of magic to all the vines surrounding the atrium, and grabbed for the nearest one.

"Ostende!" Lin commanded.

All eyes turned to her where she balanced four feet above the ground. Where had that bastard gained the ability to utilize magic? A lesser witch?

"Clever, girl." Lin moved to stand beneath her. He made a slicing motion with his hand, and the vine fell from the wall. Spring landed in a heap at his feet. "But not clever enough."

As she saw it, she had two choices. Allow Lin to abduct and possibly kill her, or scream the hotel down around them. She opened her mouth to emit an ear-splitting scream. The roundhouse kick to her jaw knocked her out.

ALASTAIR AND KNOX JERKED IN RESPONSE TO THE SCREAM ECHOING up from the atrium. The plants around them shriveled and blackened.

"Spring!" Knox shouted as he ran into their room.

"You're too late, son. That scream is a clear indication that Lin already has her."

Not bothering to reply, Knox teleported to the lobby. A wide-eyed maid pointed toward the atrium. By the time he arrived, there was no sign of Spring other than the dead foliage. Cupping his hands over his eye sockets, he fell to his knees. Knox lost his ability to breathe. As he tried to gulp in much-needed oxygen, Alastair appeared in the entry.

"We'll get her back, son."

"I blame you," he said hoarsely. "Everything you touch turns to shit. Do you know that?" Knox poured all his rage and despair into the clap of his hands. The wave of energy he produced slung Alastair into the nearest wall. "You did this. You took a green girl and threw her into the way of that sociopath."

Other than to straighten and adjust his cuffs, Alastair remained quiet.

"If anything happens to her..." Knox's voice broke and he swallowed hard. "If he..." He cleared his throat. "Luckily for you, I have a backup plan."

"*W*hat the fuck do you mean, you lost her?*" Knox bellowed at the man he'd commissioned to protect Spring should it be needed. "You had one job! *One!* Watch Spring Thorne. Don't let her out of your sight." He cleared the closest dresser with a vicious swipe.

"I'm sorry, Mr. Carlyle. They got the jump on us."

He glared at the Witches' Council guard a moment before he let loose a blast of energy. The younger man stumbled backward. The sound his body made as it collided with the chest of drawers didn't give Knox even the merest smidgeon of satisfaction. Continuously throwing the brainless knob against the dresser until the man was a limp, bloody rag doll might help counter Knox's rage, but it wasn't going to help him find Spring. *"Get out!"*

He dreaded the calls he needed to make. It was a toss-up to see who would be the first to tear the skin from his bones: Spring's father or her protective older sister, Autumn. Whatever torture they devised, it wouldn't be enough to atone for the life-threatening situation in which he had placed Spring.

He withdrew his phone and pressed the button for his contacts. Preston's was the first name to come up. It stared back at Knox accusingly. Closing his eyes against the self-disgust and fear clawing at his mind, he hit call. After this, any rapport the two men shared over their mutual work for the Council would be void. Preston would hate him.

"Thorne."

"Lin has her."

The change in Preston's tone was immediate. "Take a picture of your room and send it."

Knox disconnected and did as ordered.

Preston arrived within seconds. "Send a text with the image to Cooper Carlyle with instructions not to tell Spring's sisters. Tell him to come immediately."

Once again, Knox did as commanded. Within two minutes, Coop had joined them.

Preston wore a haggard look while Coop's face held disbelief.

"What happened?" Preston demanded. "How did Lin get his filthy hands on my baby?"

"He must've had men watching the hotel. When she left our room, he grabbed her."

"Why was she leaving the hotel alone? She had to know there was a chance of running into Lin and his cronies," Coop said.

Knox remained quiet in an attempt to form the words that wouldn't put both him and Spring in a bad light. How did he explain that he believed she'd run away because of his advances? Coop would understand; he'd been through something similar. But the Thornes were likely to kill him first and ask questions later.

He took a deep breath and went for broke. "We had a fight. She was upset when she left here. I believe she went to the atrium and probably wasn't aware of her surroundings."

Preston crossed his arms over his massive chest. As an intimidation factor, it went a long way. "What could've possibly upset her enough to ignore the threat of Lin?"

"I believe she thought I was trying to seduce her to get her out of the way," Knox stated, expression hard, daring anyone to say anything.

Closing his eyes, Preston drew a ragged breath. Knox imagined the man didn't want to think of anyone seducing his daughter for any reason. "None of that's important. If Lin has her, he intends to kill her."

"We'll find her, brother. And when I do, all involved in taking her will die a painful death," Alastair promised. "I'm done with Lin's games."

"Games? You think what he's done up to now has been a game?" Coop demanded. "He's shot a boy, tried to kidnap Chloe, thrown Autumn in a dungeon—all the while promising to burn her. He was responsible for the tomb collapse that almost cost my cousin his life. *And* he strangled Winnie." He scrubbed a shaky hand through his blond hair. "I wouldn't call any of those attacks a game."

Alastair nodded. "Poor choice of words on my part. I apologize, son."

"It makes this that much more dire in my opinion," Preston said. "Spring isn't tough like Autumn, or powerful like Summer and Winnie. She's sweet and sees the good in everyone."

Knox opened his mouth, but Alastair, who stood outside Preston's line of sight, shook his head in warning.

Preston gave into his anger and slammed a fist on the nearest surface. "When we get her back, this little scavenger hunt of yours is over, Al. I can't take any more of the stress associated with the endangerment of my children. I'm sorry if that means Aurora pays the ultimate price, but you can't continue to risk the children."

Before their eyes, Alastair's face hardened to stone. "I said I'd deal with Lin."

"What do you need us to do? Where do we start?" Coop asked in an admirable attempt to keep the peace.

Knox shook his head and moved to the bank of windows overlooking the city.

"Pull the mirror from the wall," Alastair ordered Coop. "Knox, is there something of Spring's lying around?" He faced Preston. "You know the herbs we need. Find a way to get them from Spring's garden without the others knowing. The last thing we need is four enraged women on the hunt for Lin's head."

"They could be helpful," Coop inserted.

"Do you want to place your fiancée in Lin's crosshairs, boy?" Alastair snapped. "Because I certainly don't want to see anything happen to my daughter."

Coop's reply was more of a reality check. "What do you think they will do to us if we don't tell them?" His question hung in the air, unanswered. None of them wanted to contemplate the rage fest that would follow.

"We should at least contact Keaton and Zane. They could help," Knox inserted.

"Lin won't make it easy to find her," Alastair warned the men.

A sickening dread unfurled in Knox's gut. The blame for Spring's capture could be laid squarely on his shoulders. How long would Lin keep her alive? Did he intend to try to syphon off her power like he had done with her sisters? If they couldn't save her in time, he would never forgive himself. Regret was a bitter pill to swallow.

"We'll find her, Knox." The quiet assurance in Coop's voice made Knox feel marginally better.

"Thank you," he returned gruffly as he handed over an earring of Spring's. "Can you contact the others? I need some air."

ALASTAIR WATCHED KNOX RUSH FROM THE ROOM. THE YOUNG MAN needed action to keep from going stir-crazy. The feeling was understandable. In the early months and years of Aurora's stasis, Alastair had been the same. Any inactivity felt like a betrayal to the woman he loved. He needed to be doing something—*anything*—toward the goal of returning her to full health.

Across the distance of the suite, he met his brother's frantic gaze with a steady assurance that Alastair hoped conveyed confidence. Losing his youngest would send Preston over the edge of reason.

"I hope the Council won't stand in my way this time, brother. Lin needs to be put down like the rabid animal he is," he said. When the

Council decreed to stay away from Lin, they had also stated that he was still untouchable. Alastair didn't know what the Council thought Lin could be useful for other than as ground fertilizer, but he would no longer follow their mandates.

"I'll make sure you have a free rein, and if they still go against you, I'll side with you. He's come after our family for the last time," Preston agreed.

Although caution was present in Coop's blue-gray eyes, he wisely remained silent. Alastair knew what it cost him. After all, the young man was a small-town sheriff with a clear sense of right and wrong. Talk of murder wouldn't sit well with him.

"You don't need to be a part of this, son. I can understand if you want to step back to claim ignorance when it all goes down."

"You're my future father-in-law. How would it be if I didn't have your back?" Coop asked with an attempt at a smile.

Alastair almost laughed. Had the situation not been dire, he would have. "Fair enough. Let's get scrying before too much more time goes by. Lin has other witches and warlocks on his payroll. He'll block us at every turn. I don't want him to be able to cover his tracks."

"I'll be back in less than two minutes with the Carlyles and the ingredients we need for the spell," Preston promised.

THE GAG HER CAPTORS USED SMELLED OF DIRTY SOCKS, AND THE black cloth sack covering Spring's head lent to her panic. With her wrists encased in Lin's magic-busting bracelets, she was as helpless as a newborn babe.

Rough hands dragged her down smothering-hot hallways. Terrified screams and pleasure-filled moans, at direct odds with one another, echoed around her. The stink of sweat, urine, and sex found its way through the thick hood and into her nostrils. She recoiled from the odor.

Her mind rejected the horrific impressions it received, refusing to believe she was in such a horrid pit of despair and inhumanity. Yet, each step, every muffled or pain-filled cry, along with the malicious energy pulsing next to her, assured her there was no possible way to deny the terrifying reality of her current predicament.

After what being dragged or shoved for what felt like miles, she was jerked to a halt. Her hood was unceremoniously ripped from her head. She had mere seconds to peer around her before she was shoved forward into an eight-by-six room. She backed away from a filthy, full-sized bed in horror, and whirled to run, crashing hard into the massive wall of her captor's chest. Still reeling from the impact, she scrambled to escape.

Her screams were muffled by the gag, and she tore at her mouth to remove the offending material. A cruel hand fisted in her loose hair. Tears burned the back of her lids at the pain inflicted on her poor scalp. The two men who'd escorted her to her new prison dragged her kicking and screaming to the stained mattress, where they pinned her down and attached her shackles to a chain linked around the iron headboard.

"After rich man, we have you," promised the larger of the two. "We *both* have you." If his sickening leer hadn't made his intent clear enough, the painful fingers digging into her breasts did the trick.

Bile rose up in the back of Spring's throat and forced its way out. As vomit filled her mouth, she choked. A little voice in the back of her mind reasoned that dying by asphyxiation was better than whatever tortures awaited her at the hands of these monsters.

Tears for what never would be leaked from the corners of her eyes. She'd never know the loving touch of a man. Never find what her sisters had, or experience the beauty of that type of union. An image of Knox as a young man floated through her mind, his blond hair mussed and blowing in the wind as he beamed up at her where she perched on the wooden fence. It had been her favorite spot to watch him work the horses in the early mornings before school. She closed her eyes tightly and tried to hang onto the beautiful picture as the darkness overtook her and she blacked out.

$\mathcal{T}$he immediate days that followed Spring's disappearance were sheer hell for Knox. His tortured mind refused to allow him to sleep or eat. All he could envision was her in the hands of that mad man, Lin. Both Zane and Keaton had experienced some of what he was going through, but neither Winnie nor Autumn had been missing for this length of time.

On day two, the men had made the unanimous decision to tell Spring's sisters the truth about her abduction. Autumn implemented a round-the-clock scrying routine. Each of the family members took a three-hour shift and would hover over the mirror in an attempt to find any indication Spring was still alive. Preston and Alastair had produced spell after spell to divine a location to no avail.

The Carlyles, not to be outdone, tore Cartagena apart on the off chance Spring might still be in town. She wasn't.

On day eight, Knox broke down. He sat on Spring's bed and held her pillow to his chest. A deep inhale produced the faint smell of her minty shampoo. It was his last connection to her. The very last item with her own personal scent. He could never replicate it if she were gone for good. His mind shied away from the thought. How would he ever survive the loss? Goddess, he'd been such a fool for so long.

Only when it was too late had he realized just how big an ass he'd been. If he thought about the wasted time, he went a little mental.

He rested back against the elegant, light gray upholstered headboard and stared at the far wall. The overwhelming need to do something—*anything*—to get her back had given way to the despair of ever finding her alive. His one hope was that she was clever and resilient. More than anyone he'd ever known. With an IQ that put others to shame and a body that turned men's minds to mush, she had to be able to manipulate her way to freedom at some point, right?

Tears coursed unchecked as he stared at the far wall of her bedroom where the Eiffel Tower was hand-painted in a metallic silver. He hadn't known Spring dreamed of Paris until Summer told him yesterday in her need to talk about her sister. So many things had come to light in the week since Spring had disappeared.

"I'll take you there, sweetheart," he rasped aloud. "You come home to me, and I'll take you on a month-long trip to Paris. We'll eat croissants and drink coffee at a little cafe with a view of the Eiffel Tower. We'll stroll the streets hand-in-hand, and I'll buy you enough souvenirs to fill your room. We'll listen to local poets, drink the finest wines, and consume the sweetest chocolates. Then I'll drag you into random alleys and kiss you breathless. Just come back, Spring. *Please.*" He ended the last on a ragged whisper.

He curled his body in a protective ball around her pillow, imagining he held her in his arms. Exhaustion finally caught up to him, and he dozed.

ALASTAIR AND PRESTON CROWDED THE DOORWAY TO SPRING'S ROOM and watched the wretched figure asleep on the bed.

"He'll never recover if we don't find her."

"I know, brother. I was the same after..." Alastair was hesitant to mention the time when he'd come home from his imprisonment only to find Aurora had married his brother. Alastair had become an animal, only eating and sleeping when he could no longer go on. "We'll find her. Lin hasn't sent a message requesting an exchange for me yet, but he will. When the time comes, I want you to accept that deal."

Preston didn't confirm that he would. He didn't need to. Spring's life was more important than Alastair's any day of the week. Her bright, effervescent personality was the heart of this family. In contrast, Alastair's dark, brooding presence had a dampening effect on one and all.

"I also need you to promise me that you'll revive Rorie. Don't let her linger in stasis." His voice was more gruff than intended, but Preston didn't take offense.

"Of course."

"Thank you."

He left his brother's side to gaze down at Knox. He should've been too large for such a feminine bed, but he wasn't. He seemed right at home. Or maybe it was Alastair's guilty conscience telling him he was right in pairing the two. Had he not pushed the issue, would they have found their way to one another? And had he done more damage with his quest?

Watching Knox sleep reminded him of the time he'd first seen him as a child. Knox had that same lost and lonely quality about him now. The only time his isolated air left him was when Spring was near. His niece was Knox's North Star. While Alastair would never show it, he ached for the young man. He knew all about that type of desolation.

He waved a hand over the general vicinity of Knox's brilliant blond head. "Sleep, son. When you wake, you'll be clear-headed and rested." He strode back to where Preston stood in the entry. The dark circles under his brother's eyes told the tale of his own sleeplessness. "You need to rest, Pres. Come on." The startled look Preston sent him made Alastair smile. "Did you think I forgot your childhood nickname, brother?"

"No. You forget nothing. It's more like I'd forgotten. It was all so long ago."

Alastair gave into the urge to embrace his younger sibling. "We're going to get her back. I swear on my life."

"I believe you, brother. But what will she have been through by then?"

A shiver of unease danced along Alastair's nerve endings. Some would call it premonition. He received them too frequently to call them anything but a portent of things to come. "Hell, most likely."

"That's what I'm afraid of."

"She's stronger than you give her credit for, Pres."

"I didn't spend the time with her that I should have. In my own pain at Aurora's leaving and eventual stasis, I couldn't cope."

"No one blames you." Alastair ushered his younger brother from the room and closed the door behind them. "If anyone is to blame, it's me. If I'd never come back, you'd all be one big happy family."

"No."

He looked up sharply at Preston's vehement denial.

"We were never a happy family. You were always the ghost in our home, Al." Preston rubbed the spot between his brows. "I could never eradicate the sorrow lurking in Aurora's eyes. The only time she'd truly smile was over the girls' outlandish behavior. It was always you, brother. She was biding time with me until she could join you, one way or the other."

They stood in silence, each lost in their own thoughts.

"If you had never have come back, Summer and Holly would never have existed," a soft voice added.

Alastair turned to the newcomer. "GiGi." He opened his arms to his sister, and she surprised him by running into his embrace.

"Don't wish them away," she whispered.

"Never." He swallowed back all the words he longed to say. The apologies he wished to offer her for whatever small part he had played in her breakup with her husband Ryker. But he suspected she understood, and apologies came hard for Alastair. "What are you doing here? Shouldn't you be resting?" They had all kept insane hours in their quest to find Spring. He pushed the others to sleep at every turn.

"I wanted to check on Knox." She held up a vial of pink liquid. "A sleeping potion."

"Seems we all had the same idea," Preston laughed. "I found Al lingering in the hall."

"What can I say? Even I can't stand to see the poor bastard so tortured," Alastair chuckled. "Give the potion to our brother here. It's time he got some rest too."

"No, I—"

He lifted a hand to stem the argument. "Pres, please. You're no good to Spring or anyone if you're dead on your feet."

With a wry smile, Preston took the vial from their sister and downed the shot. "I'll bid you goodnight." In a blink, he was gone.

"How about you, Al?" GiGi asked.

"I'll sleep when I'm dead."

She snorted and rolled her eyes. "I've made up Morty's old playroom with a bed. Go take a nap. No one likes a cranky Alastair Thorne."

He grinned, and she laughed. With a kiss to her smooth forehead, he teleported to the attic.

GiGi MADE SURE THE HOUSE WAS QUIET BEFORE SHE STEPPED ONTO the front porch. She curled one foot under her and sat on the wooden swing suspended from the overhang. With her other foot, she set the swing in motion.

A jolt to the smooth back-and-forth rhythm indicated a second presence.

"Ryker."

"I got your message. What's happening?"

"Zhu Lin abducted Spring. She's been gone over a week, and we've heard nothing."

Her estranged husband swore a blue streak. "Why did you wait until now to tell me this?"

She shrugged but didn't face him. His angry stare burned through her, but she was unable to look directly at him without feeling the stab of betrayal in her heart. "I know you still have contacts in Lin's camp. Will you help us?"

"What the hell kind of question is that? She's my niece, too." He sighed and stood. "Whatever else you think of me, however much you hate me, know that I will always be there for my family."

"I don't hate you." But she should've saved her breath because her words were wasted. He'd already gone.

The phone in her hand buzzed. The text from Ryker read, *"I'll have something for you by morning."*

She didn't bother to respond. He never cared for her feelings anyway.

*B*y now you aren't surprised by the omission of this chapter. But better to be safe than sorry, wouldn't you say? Have you preordered Rekindled Magic yet or explored The Thorne Witches shop?

WWW.ETSY.COM/SHOP/TMCROMER

14

$\mathcal{T}$en days plus, gone. Spring had kept count for the first ten days of her captivity. After that, she'd stopped. Keeping track of the passing time only led to heartache and disappointment. Now, with no idea how much time had passed, she went about her daily routine; she ate what she was given, showered when she was told, and paced her gilded cage.

She ignored the opulent setting around her. While Don Carlos would settle for nothing but the best for his latest plaything, she still preferred to regard her surroundings as the prison it was. After all, she was never allowed to set foot outside the twenty by thirty room. The marigold colored walls made her want to scream. The bright, cheerful color was at direct odds with her constant black thoughts.

She stepped to the vanity where a small metal box taunted her. The only out-of-place item on her dresser. It was aluminum and dented from her fist, where everything else on the smooth marble surface was new and shiny or bejeweled. Yesterday, she swore to herself that she wouldn't use the contents for a crutch. But her body's withdrawal mocked her attempts to stay clean. When she lifted the lid, tears filled her soul. On the outside she remained cold and hard.

With a quick glance at the camera in the upper corner of the room, she tied the rubber tube about her arm. She tapped her abused vein, and injected the measured out heroin that Don Carlos had left for her that morning. In precisely six hours, he'd leave another small dose.

Between her clunky power-stealing shackles and the four-times-daily shots of heroin, he was able to maintain control. The oblivion Spring found made tolerable the tortures he'd devised for each day.

Just once, she wished he'd leave a full syringe so she could end it all, but she knew he never would. He loved the thrill of domination. Loved the ability to mar her perfect skin with a lash, a sharp blade, or the searing-hot cigar tip, only to have her body magically heal so he might start the process again. That was to say nothing about the sexual violations of her body after he'd mentally and physically abused her. Her mind shied away from what had become a daily occurrence.

No, Spring welcomed the mind-numbing drug. She only wished for more of it.

As she lay on the bed under the grunting, disgusting pig of a man known as Don Carlos Esteban, she worked to forget her old life. She never thought of her sisters or their shared laughter. She never recalled Knox's breathtakingly handsome face. And she never, *ever* dreamed of rescue. It wasn't going to happen because no one knew where she was.

In blocking her ability to escape, Lin had layered the magic thick enough to prevent her discovery. No amount of scrying or location spells, no matter how powerful the witch wielding them, would find her. He'd made that clear early on.

She didn't even have a Jolly Olly to spy for Uncle Alastair like he'd done for Autumn and Winter. Ryker had blown his cover in saving Winnie. No one in the enemy camp had Spring's best interests at heart.

A sharp slap brought her back to the moment. "Moan, bitch. You need to moan for me. Tell me how much you like my big cock in you, *puta*."

Spring choked back her defiance. There was no place for it here.

Defiance brought more pain. So, like the good little whore she'd become, she pretended to enjoy Don Carlos's groping, all the while swallowing down the bile that threatened to spew.

"HELLO, MACY GIRL," KNOX MURMURED WITH A STROKE OF THE mare's neck. "How are you today, sweet baby?"

Macy tossed her head, delivering a spray of glitter in the air.

"I see Chloe has been changing up the color of your cone again." He gave a half-hearted smile as he filled her feed bucket. "Let her know to utilize a bit of magic so the whole stall isn't filled with glitter, okay?"

With the spray of glitter he had hoped to avoid, the mare nodded her head as if she understood exactly what he was saying—which she did. He was able to communicate with the animals as easily as Chloe and Summer, although from old habit, he never made his abilities known. The mental image Macy pushed his way showed the loving attention young Chloe piled upon her.

"You're a lucky lady to be so loved, Macy."

A caw from the rafters caught his attention, and he closed his eyes against the wave of pain that always came when it was time to feed Spring's familiar. "Good morning, Mr. Black." There was no need to inform the raven that Spring had yet to be found. The molting feathers and droop of the bird's head indicated he suffered from lack of connection to his mistress.

For the millionth time in the four months since Spring's disappearance, he wondered if she was alive. Ryker's contact had no information other than to say Spring had been sold into a sex-trafficking ring run by Don Carlos Esteban.

Sweet, innocent Spring in the hands of monsters. The thought gutted him.

The Thornes, Gillespies, and Carlyles had teamed up to go into all Esteban's homes and haunts with magical guns blazing. They'd turned up nothing. Other than to disrupt Don Carlos's business on every occasion, there was no satisfaction to be found. Not even Don Carlos Esteban himself. The man had gone into hiding after the first attack on his Cartagena home.

Lin had never made any demands, which had amazed no one more than Alastair. But Knox wasn't surprised. No, Zhu Lin struck the heart of the Thorne family when he took Spring and sentenced her to hell. That wily bastard knew they would eventually either fight amongst themselves or implode. Either way, Lin won.

As for himself, Knox had become little better than a wild animal. When he wasn't tearing apart the jungles of Colombia looking for Spring, he was shoveling shit from stalls or clinging to a pink, mint-scented pillow, drunk out of his mind. No one dared speak to him if they didn't have a lead on Spring's whereabouts.

"The Stones."

A sudden cold permeated the barn, chilling him. He lifted his head and searched for the female who uttered the words. "Who's there?" he called.

"The Stones hold the key." Another blast of freezing air caused him to shiver.

His mouth dried up. Could it be that Isis had given him the helping hand he'd been praying for? "What do I do?"

"Alastair will know."

Of course he will. Alastair knew everything *except how to find Spring*. Knox scowled, stripped off his work gloves, and jerked his phone from his back pocket.

"Thorne."

"I either have a ghost in my barn, or a goddess is trying to tell me something."

"I'll be right there."

The phone disconnected, and within sixty seconds, Alastair strolled through the large sliding doors down the main aisle. "What happened?"

"The air turned frosty and an invisible female told me that the stones hold the key. She also mentioned you would know what to do."

"The Stones? In the clearing?"

"I assumed those were the ones. I don't know of any others."

Alastair opened his mouth to speak but slammed it shut when he got a load of Macy's cone. After a long pause, he asked, "What the blazes is on that horse's head?"

"She likes it. It makes her feel special."

"Fair enough." With a nod to the rafters, Alastair asked, "Is that Spring's raven?"

"Yes."

"Finish up here. Then bring the bird to your attic. Mr. Black needs a magical boost if he is going to help us."

"The bird is going to help us?"

"Do you know anything about familiars, son?"

"Other than they can boost a witch's power?"

"A familiar has a direct connect to its witch. Based on the condition of that raven, I'd say Spring is still alive but worse for wear."

Why hadn't Knox thought of that? He turned his attention to Mr. Black. "Come."

The raven swooped down and landed on his extended forearm. Once it had climbed onto his shoulder, it rubbed the top of its head along his jawline in a rare show of affection.

"You've been trying to tell me, haven't you?" he murmured to the bird. A second, long caw trumpeted the raven's agreement. "I'm sorry. I was too wrapped up in my own misery to pay attention."

Fifteen minutes later, he was ensconced in a chair, searching the Carlyle grimoire while Preston sat across from him, thumbing through the Thorne spell book. Alastair stood at the attic window and studied the clearing between the two properties. Mr. Black took up position on his shoulder and stared at the glen as if he, too, were searching for something.

"I'm not sure what the hell I'm looking for," Knox grumbled.

"Do you know, Spring has the Thorne grimoire memorized? Front to back in all its various languages."

Alastair conversational tone set Knox off. Slamming the book shut, Knox tossed it onto the chair he'd just vacated. "And that helps me how?" he snapped. "She's not here to pull a fucking spell out of thin air, is she?"

A small smile played around Alastair's mouth. "No, but you just reminded me we have the next best thing." In seconds, he had his phone in hand and snapped a picture of the attic room. After a few taps of the keys, he said, "Stay where you are. My son will be here shortly."

Within seconds, the air thickened and shifted as Nash Thorne stepped through a rift in the center of the room. His jade eyes, so like Spring's in color and shape that it hurt to look at him, took in all the occupants of the room then settled on Alastair. "Sperm Donor. You sent for me?"

"We want to draw on the magic of the Stones to find your cousin. Like Spring, you have all the spell books in your possession memorized. I need to know how to boost the signal to cut through a Blocker's magic."

Nash shook his head. "I have a Snowflake Obsidian stone that might amplify a spell, but I believe the Stones in the clearing would do that without any trouble. We would need to call them up, but as always, if you draw from their power, you need something to offer the Goddess in return." He strode to his father's side and lifted the raven to examine it. "He's sick. Man-made. A reflection of Spring is my guess." Nash ducked his head and turned toward the light from the window to study the bird closer. "What can you tell me, bird?"

A hoarse caw was emitted from Mr. Black.

"I think she's being drugged. It's the only reason, other than death, for the lack of connection to her familiar," Preston said.

"I agree." Nash nodded absently as he handed the raven back to his father. "If he's willing, we could use him as the amplifier along with the Stones. With at least seven of our most powerful, Mr. Black, the magic from Isis, and a spell from the book of Carlyle, we should be able to pull this off." He hefted the tome, opened it to the back, and flipped a few pages. "We're going to need a body of water, and someone to channel Spring."

Knox's response was automatic. "I'll do it."

"Actually, I feel like it should be me or Alastair," Nash replied. "Her emotional attachment isn't as strong to us, and she'd be less likely to reject us if she's…"

"If she what?" Knox demanded "Why the hell would she reject me at all. She loves me."

"If she's sick or worse, she may not want you to see her in that condition."

"I don't give a damn. If we can break through the blockers, I'm teleporting in and getting her the hell out of there."

Nash opened his mouth to argue, but Preston cut him off with a wave of his hand. "Of course you'll go, Knox. It should be you."

Alastair nodded. "I agree with my brother. The rest of us will work the spell."

15

*I*n addition to himself, Nash utilized the magic of Summer, Autumn, Winnie, Cooper, Alastair, and Preston. GiGi was hard at work, creating potions to help whatever condition Spring might be in when she returned. Keaton and Zane maintained a short distance from the stones in the event they were needed in a pinch.

"Summer, I'd like you to create a shallow pool for Knox to lie down in, please," Nash instructed, never lifting his head from the thick book he was consulting.

Preston positioned the group in a circle, but stopped and faced Alastair when Autumn asked the loaded question, "What do we have to offer in exchange?"

Knox didn't hesitate. "Whatever it is, I'll find a way to pay it. Let's just get Spring back."

A blinding light lit the clearing. The group as a whole lifted their hands to shield their faces. When the light had vanished, a woman stood in the center of their circle. She wore a white, off-the-shoulder dress belted by a gold rope chain that shimmered with each breath she took. Long dark hair fell in waves down her back. Her exotic, kohl-lined amber eyes scanned the group and settled on Knox.

Isis glided to where he waited. "You are brave to offer up a boon without knowing that which I ask, dear child."

"Spring's life is worth any price."

"I'm happy to hear you believe so. What I require is the *Book of Thoth*. In return, I will grant you the ability to locate your beloved."

Didn't it figure she'd come up with something he'd never heard of, much less knew how to locate? There was no time for a damned scavenger hunt, not with Spring's life in jeopardy. "How does one go about finding this *Book of Thoth*?"

Her light, musical laughter rang out around the clearing. "It's no great journey. One of your own possesses the book." Isis focused her attention on Nash. "Is that not so, son of Alastair?"

"I might be able to come up with it," Nash offered.

"Then we have an accord?" she asked, confident her request would be satisfied.

"We do," Alastair cut in. "*But* we need Spring's location and the ability to teleport through the Blockers, Exalted One."

Isis laughed and swished her way to stand in front of him. "If I give you an inch, you'll take a mile."

His grin was pure wicked delight, and the low bow a shade mocking. "Ah, but you would expect no less."

Narrowed amber eyes studied Alastair for a long moment, then she, too, smiled. "True. All right, you have a deal." As she headed for the center of the circle, she lifted her arm out to her side. Mr. Black launched from his spot in a nearby tree to land on her forearm. "Poor boy. You look a little worse for wear, don't you? It won't do for your mistress to see you in such a sorry state." Isis ran the flat of her hand down the length of the bird, restoring his molting feathers to a thick glossy black. "Much better." She leaned in to impart information to Spring's familiar, produced a fine particulate of silver dust and blew it into his face. She launched him skyward and dusted her hands.

"What did you tell him?" Knox was mildly curious what she had to converse about with the raven.

"Nothing you need to worry about for now," Isis informed him with a brisk nod. "When you find her, I recommend you use your ability to stop time to relay that which you want no one else to see or hear. Do you understand?"

"I believe I do."

"Good. When you have the book, place it on the stone slab and proceed with your ceremony."

After she left, the group turned incredulous eyes on Knox.

"You!" Winnie charged to where he stood. "You were the one who saved me in Malta and then again in the desert."

Winnie referred to the moment when he'd used his ability to stop the bullet meant to take her life, and then again saved the lives of her, Zane, and their other companion in the search for a charmed amulet.

"I was."

"How? Why?"

He offered up a bittersweet smile. "For Spring. If anything had happened to you, she'd have been heartbroken."

Tears flooded Winnie's eyes, turning them to liquid pools of blue. "Oh, Knox."

He wrapped her in a tight embrace. "I'm going to find her, Winnie. I don't care what it takes."

"Thank you," she whispered on a sob.

"You don't need to thank me. I'm doing this for entirely selfish reasons. I simply cannot exist without her," he managed to say.

Other than the occasional sniffle, silence settled over the group with his statement. They all understood how important this spell was.

He turned his attention to Nash. "How much do you want for the book? I assume it's in the collection you hold for the Witches' Council."

"It is."

"You have a decision to make," Knox told him. "But know, if you don't voluntarily hand it over, I'll tear your home apart looking for it."

One arrogant blond brow rose skyward, and Nash never resembled his father so much as he did in that moment. "I'm offended you even have to say such a thing."

"Be offended all you want. I'll stop at nothing for Spring."

Nash's face softened. "Understood. I'll be right back."

As they all waited for him to return, Knox paced the glen. He stopped by the tree where he'd first kissed Spring a little over four months ago. Running his fingers down the bark, he imagined he could still feel her silky smooth skin. Still taste her sassy mouth. Still see the wondrous gleam in her vibrant jade eyes the instant of her orgasm.

Despair threatened to choke him, but he ruthlessly shoved it back. They were closer to finding her than they'd ever been. He couldn't give into the hopelessness now.

The air crackled around them. Nash reappeared and flashed a tight smile while he waved the ancient tome. "Let's get to it."

After the protective circle was cast, Summer took Alastair's hands in hers. "Goddess hear our plea. Assist us in our time of need." They knelt. Keeping one hand joined, they each placed their free hand on the ground. *"Stagnum!"*

The ground shifted, and liquid bubbled up from an expanding hole. Before long, a small, pool-sized body of water had formed.

"Clarus!" Summer commanded.

The water became a clear pool, and Knox appreciated the thoughtfulness. He didn't relish the idea of lying down in a mud puddle.

Coop stepped forward and ran a finger through the water. When Alastair lifted a brow, he gave the older warlock a sheepish grin. "I heated the pool. I didn't want Knox to be cold."

"Very thoughtful," Alastair agreed. "Places everyone." He nodded to Nash. "Please place the *Book of Thoth* on the altar."

The Thornes gathered within the circle, stretching their arms with palms facing outward toward the person on either side of them. After Knox stripped his jacket and shoes, he waded into the water. As a chilling wind picked up around them, he appreciated Coop's thoughtfulness all the more.

Preston started the chant, and one by one, the others joined in.

Bright white light ricocheted from hand to hand and completed the circle when it returned to Preston.

As Knox floated in the water, he could feel the vibration of the stones rising up from their hiding places beneath the earth. Soon enough, massive rock formations towered over the occupants of the clearing. At that moment, Mr. Black swooped from his branch and landed on the bank of the pool. He plunged his silky midnight head into the water at the same instant Knox called to Spring.

He left his body in a sleeping state and focused on Spring. Within seconds, Knox had astral-projected to her location. The sight that met his eyes ripped his soul to shreds.

Naked, she lay on a bed, curled in a ball. Bruises in all shapes and shades covered the entirety of her body. Her lower back and buttocks were darker purple than the rest.

"Spring. Sweetheart?"

Her head came up, and her eyes widened in shock. Twice, she swiped a hand over her eyes as if she didn't believe what they revealed to her. With a wild glance toward the far side of the room, she sat up.

A quick check of the room showed a camera mounted in the corner where her gaze continually darted.

"They can't see or hear me. Only you can, sweetheart." He shifted forward, desperate to touch her. In his ghostly form, it was impossible.

"Am I dead?" she whispered after she carefully turned her head away from the camera.

"No, love, you're very much alive. Your family has been actively looking for you for a long while."

Her dull, forest-green eyes focused on him. "Tell them you couldn't find me. Or better yet. Tell them I'm dead. It will be true soon anyway."

Spring shifted her arm to reveal the tracks.

Knox dropped to his knees before her. "Christ! He's shooting you up?"

Tone barely audible, she confessed, "Me."

"*You?* You're doing this to yourself?" He shook his head in denial. Why the hell would she ever willingly drug herself? "I don't understand."

With one fingertip she traced the runes on the shackle at her wrist. "No escape. Ever. None that isn't death."

"Don't buy into that bullshit, Spring. Don't you do it. I'm coming for you. Do you understand?" He reached for her, regardless of his spectral limitations. Tears burned behind his lids as his hands passed through her.

"You were a beautiful dream," she murmured groggily as she laid back on the pillows.

"I'm as real as you, sweetheart. Hold on for a little longer. For me, Spring? Please?" he begged.

"Don't come back, Knox. Let me go."

16

A whoosh of sound echoed in Knox's ears, then he returned to his human form. The first thing he became aware of was Mr. Black. The raven eyed him with a keen intelligence few animals produced. He didn't need to convey to the bird the conversation that had taken place. The raven had witnessed it all.

Knox stroked a finger down Mr. Black's satiny chest. "I'll keep my promise. I'll get her back," he said softly.

With a distinctive nod of understanding, the bird launched into the night sky.

A large, rough hand appeared in his line of vision. He turned tortured eyes up to Coop. Careful to keep his voice low so the others in the circle didn't hear, Knox said, "It's much worse than I thought." If his voice broke, his cousin wouldn't fault him for it. "But I know where she is now."

"Then we'll get her." Coop shoved his hand closer. "Come. Let's get you dry and make a retrieval plan."

Accepting the hand Coop presented to him was more symbolic than he could've said. The life he'd lived to date had been that of a loner. He hid behind an easygoing persona and helped others from behind a mirrored glass. Other than the time when Alastair had removed him from the hell house as a child and arranged with Uncle Phillip to take him in, Knox had never thought to accept assistance from anyone.

With only the slightest hesitation, he grabbed the hand his cousin patiently held out. Heat transferred from Coop to Knox and warmed his cells even as it dried his t-shirt and jeans. A snap of his fingers replaced his jacket and boots. Another snap produced a detailed map of Colombia. He placed it on the empty stone altar.

"She's here." He tapped a heavily wooded area. "There's a long river that runs through this area, and Esteban's house is on the other side of the summit of this mountaintop."

Spring's three sisters and Nash closed the circle as Alastair and Preston joined Knox and Coop. They'd remained quiet while Knox had traced the route he'd flown.

"I know that area," Preston volunteered. "I was close to there for an antique auction. My contact can have aerial photos in a matter of hours." He glanced skyward. "Or rather just after sunrise."

Knox met Coop's concerned gaze and made an abrupt decision to reveal the truth. "I don't think she has that long, sir." Scrubbing the heel of his palm between his brows, he released a ragged breath. "She told me not to come back. To let her go."

"What?"

Preston's disbelief was understandable. Spring was a fighter. To see her laid low, with no hope or fire in her eyes had been difficult at best. At worst? Yeah, a part of Knox's soul had been peeled open and exposed to all the torments hell had to offer. But it still wouldn't have been a smattering of what Spring herself had gone through.

He launched into a detailed explanation of what he witnessed. "There's the matter of a heroin addiction to deal with when we get her back."

"No. She would never. She could heal herself. She..." Preston looked to Alastair who had remained silent through their exchange. "Al?"

"I don't need to tell you that Lin is a sonofabitch, brother." Alastair faced Knox. "Tell me about the ancient platinum shackles she was wearing. I'm assuming you saw them or something similar."

"Yes. They were about two-and-a-half inches wide and had engraved runes. I'd never seen those particular symbols before, but if I had to guess, I'd say they looked to be of Norse origin."

"I'm deeply familiar with those particular shackles." Face pale, Alastair closed his eyes and breathed deeply.

Knox didn't dare touch the man. It was obvious he was lost in the past. But he needed everyone present to save Spring. "What should I know about them, Alastair?"

"They can only be removed upon her death."

The air escaped from his lungs in a rush. It was what Spring had been trying to say in her drugged state. "And healing herself after... after...?"

Ashen faced, Preston turned to his older brother for answers.

Alastair looked as if he would be ill at any moment, but he answered all the same. "She might be able to outwardly heal, but beatings, rape, drugs, they would all be more difficult to recover from if she's wearing Lin's shackles. They drain the wearer's magic." He powered on. "When I was imprisoned, I felt as if I had a constant bout of the flu. My body was achy, and I experienced a general feeling of overall depression. The continuous drain on her body will do that. You have to remember he is literally pulling the magic from her cells." Alastair met Preston's direct stare. "She can't sustain the drain for long. If Isis hadn't rescued me... I'm sorry."

Preston's fist connected with Alastair's jaw, knocking the blond man into Coop. "Find a way to contact Lin. We'll trade him whatever —whoever—he wants. You or me, I don't care."

"Don't you think I've already made that offer?" Alastair snarled in a rare display of temper. "Don't you think I've offered Isis my own life? Apparently, I'm not the treasured, sought-after commodity I once was."

His words surprised the group. The only person *not* surprised was Knox. The Alastair Thorne he knew was no stranger to sacrifice. He just did an amazing job at keeping his true nature hidden from those around him. Knox could relate. If no one expected anything but the worst from you, it was easy to blend into the background. Easy to become a chameleon and hide any spark of goodness you possessed.

"Thank you."

Alastair's surprised gaze shot to him. "It's my fault."

"No. You may have brought your personal quest to our door, but you didn't make any of us step over the threshold. I was wrong to blame you." He placed a hand on the other man's shoulder and squeezed, as Alastair had done to him years before when they'd first met. "Thank you for your willingness to sacrifice on her behalf. You tried, and that makes all the difference to me."

OBLIVION ELUDED SPRING AS SHE INJECTED THE NEXT ROUND OF heroin. Either the stuff Don Carlos had left for her had lost its potency, or he was playing games and was withholding the purer-quality drugs. Agitation took hold as did her anxiety. What was his new plan?

He had already made her beg. She begged for him to end the torture. Begged to receive an injection of the poison he peddled. Begged for sexual favors when he'd slipped her a chemical cocktail of an aphrodisiac and Rohypnol. He enjoyed playing that particular tape back during her more lucid moments.

Yes, she was sure he'd started a new form of torture. For certain, her achy joints and muscles were a sign of withdrawal. She had tried it on her own in the first month. The cramping, sweats, and vomiting were more than she could bear. Especially when Don Carlos had left a syringe of heroin on the dresser in plain view. Spring had attempted to get clean twice more, but the tortures he put her through made her turn to the one thing that would obliterate her pain.

The newest trick to conjure a Knox look-a-like was the worst torment yet. She had little doubt Zhu Lin had assisted with that little stunt. A warlock on his payroll could very easily glamour himself to resemble Knox. She'd revealed too much to his spy.

"I hate you!" she screamed. Who exactly she was speaking to—herself, Don Carlos, Lin, or Knox—she didn't know. Perhaps a combination of all of them.

Anger, humiliation, and a sense of betrayal filled her from the center out. All the emotions she'd suppressed until this exact moment erupted. How had Knox not come for her? And Alastair? Of all people, she believed her uncle would make an attempt to save her. Unable to control her spike of temper, she went about systematically demolishing her room. She ripped the sheets from the bed and tore at the threads. She yanked the drawers from the dresser and scattered the contents about. With one arm, she cleared the dresser's surface of the sickening perfumes and oils Esteban insisted she wear. If it was breakable or smashable, her rage helped her to destroy it.

"I hate you! I hate you! I hate you!" The refrain wouldn't stop repeating in her mind or from her mouth. "I hate you!" she sobbed as she sunk into a heap.

A jagged shard of glass caught her eye. Leaning back against the overturned box spring, she stared at her salvation. It was time. As her hand closed over the triangular piece of her perfume bottle, the door to her room burst open.

"Spring!" Knox stood panting in the doorway, all lanky, six-feet-one male. Or at least the faux Knox did anyway. He was thinner than her Knox, not as vibrant.

"You're not real," she said conversationally as she positioned the sharp edge over the exposed skin of her arm.

"Sweetheart, please. Put the glass down," the imposter begged. "Please."

"I'm done with the games. Tell your bosses. I'm done. I'm no one's plaything."

Fake Knox inched closer as she pressed the sharp, raw edge of the glass into her arm. "Baby, this is not a game. I need you to see me. Hear the truth in my voice. *Please.*"

The blatant desperation in his tone lifted her head. She met his dark gaze and sneered. "Knox has eyes the color of the sea on the purest day." The glass went deeper and scored her skin. "You're not him. Your boss fucked up."

"Spring, sweetheart, if you know anything about our kind, you know when we are upset or sad, our irises darken. Remember? If you look in the mirror now, you'd see yours aren't your normal green."

His statement gave her pause, and she lifted her gaze to his frantic dark gray eyes. As she watched, he crawled toward her across the debris she'd littered about the room in her destructive tantrum.

"I hate you," she whispered. "You left me here with him. That monster."

Anguish flooded his face. "I've been looking for you for a very long time, love. We all have. Come with me now. Let me get you out of here."

"I can't leave." She turned her attention back to carving up her arm. "I can never leave."

"You can!" he practically shouted, capturing her attention again. His hand closed over hers and stopped the opening of her vein. A surge of his magic healed the gash she'd made. "Just try."

"Why did you do that? Why?" she cried. "He'll be here soon."

"I'm not letting him touch you again. I don't care if I have to guard this room for the rest of our lives."

With a dispassionate stare, she watched as he conjured a robe and wrapped it around her. "Am I ugly to you now?"

"What? No!"

Knox was appalled by her behavior. He prayed that Spring didn't see the horror he tried so hard to hide. Somehow, he suspected she did. For sure, she felt the trembling of his hands.

Spring stood, dropped her robe and slowly spun around, allowing him to see her damaged body for the first time since he'd found her hunched over on the floor. "What's the matter, Knox? Isn't this what you expected?"

"Stop it," he rasped. Her scars ranged from cigarette burns to lash marks to jagged marks that he could only assume were from a knife.

In the crease of her arms were tracks from needles. "Cover up, Spring."

A derisive sneer curled her lips as she snapped her fingers and glamoured away all the evidence of the abuse she'd suffered. The image before him was pure perfection. "Is this better? Does it tempt you more?"

"No."

Spring's harsh laugh sickened him. "That's right, I've never tempted you. Not with my innocence, and certainly not now that this vessel has been all used up." Another snap of her fingers clothed her in a stunning emerald evening gown. Its neckline plunged to her navel.

Vessel? Why had she phrased it like that? Was he to assume she only viewed her body as a means to an end? As if it didn't belong to her? He didn't like the turn his thoughts had taken. "It's not like that," he protested.

How did he explain the sight *did* turn him off, but not for the reasons she assumed? All he felt when he saw her now was a gut-churning guilt he was unable to rid himself of.

"You know what? I don't care how it is. I don't care about anything."

Knox could see the truth of her statement in her dead, dark eyes. He mourned the loss of their light. "Spring—"

"Go away, Knox," she said tiredly.

"I can't." He scrubbed his hands through his hair in his frustration. "I can't leave you like this. Not here. Not in this place."

"If you ever held an ounce of affection for the girl I used to be, you'd go."

He imagined he caught a fleeting sorrow in her gaze before she ruthlessly tamped it down.

"Don't ask that of me, Spring. Let me take you home. Please." The last word came out rough and raw. He needed to help her, if only to help himself deal with what had happened. Even if she hated him, he needed to see her to safety.

Her cold, mocking smile told him she knew *he* was now the

tortured one. "Home? I have no home. Tell them Spring Thorne is dead. That she died in a hovel in the Colombian jungle. Or better yet, tell them she couldn't kick the heroin that had been forced upon her and finally welcomed. You won't be lying. That poor unfortunate girl *is* dead."

He hadn't realized tears streamed from his eyes until she lifted a box of tissues from next to the overturned vanity. She whipped the box at his head without blinking an eye. "Don't mourn, Knox. She was only ever a nuisance to you anyway."

He let the box rest where it landed. "Don't."

"Don Carlos will be here any moment. I don't want to be on the receiving end of his tantrum should he find you here."

The mention of her drug-lord captor had Knox seeing red. He intended to kill the scum with his bare hands the first second Spring was free of the bastard.

"I don't give a rat's ass about Don Carlos," he ground out. "I'm not leaving you here."

She spun on him in a fury. Marching to within inches of his face, she growled her rage. "You don't fucking get it, Knox. *I hate you.* The sight of your face makes me want to smash it in. If it wasn't for you, I would never have been taken. Have you thought about that? Have you lain awake nights, recalling *that* ugly little detail?"

"What are you talking about?"

"I worry she is too young and inexperienced. Her temper could get her into trouble," she intoned in a passable imitation of his voice. "You tried to play me. To seduce me so you could have the upper hand. So stupid little Spring would fall right into whatever plan you decided would be best to get her out of the way."

It was as he'd suspected; she'd overheard his conversation with Alastair that night. Oddly, her furious words centered him. In her eyes, strong emotions blazed, but not a one of them was hate or blame. She was trying to drive him away on purpose. A small bit of his confidence returned along with the hope for the two of them.

"You're leaving with me now." He latched onto her arm and spoke the words that would teleport them home.

Nothing happened.

Her hollow laughter unnerved him.

Knox attempted a second teleport, to no avail.

"This room is warded against me leaving," she explained tone-lessly. "Another little goody in Lin's bag of tricks. He didn't want to sell me to the highest bidder only to have them come after him when I escaped. I tried to tell you that earlier."

"Then we'll step out in the corridor."

"Don't you think I tried to escape when I first got here?" She chuckled without humor and held up her wrists. "I can't step over that threshold."

Something akin to horror filled him. His skin turned cold and his head spun. *He couldn't save her!* She was well and truly trapped.

Her expression softened marginally, and she cupped his cheek. "It's okay, Knox," she whispered with a slight catch to her voice. "You've done all you could. It's time for you to go home. I'm past saving anyway."

"I can't leave you, Spring." Heart weighted as heavily as lead, he released an uneven breath. "I love you."

She rapidly blinked away the sheen of moisture that came to her eyes. "When this all started, I'd have given anything to hear those words from you. Now, they only serve to make *you* feel better. Forget I ever existed."

The sound of booted feet rushed toward their location. At any moment, they would be interrupted. But still, Knox was unable to leave her.

"Go. I don't care to have your death on my conscience." The hardness was back in her tone.

"I'm coming back for you. I swear it," he promised. Hand fisted, he halted time and leaned his forehead against hers. "Tell me you understand. Tell me you know I'll be back, and that a thousand Lins and Don Carlos Estebans won't keep me from you."

"Hope is an ugly thing, Knox. I can't afford it."

It was the closest she'd come to a concession.

"I'm never going to stop," he said.

Her hopeless, wide-eyed stare eviscerated him. But he could delay no longer. Time would snap back in the next ten seconds. It gave him seven to kiss her and make a run for the room down the hall. Knox took advantage and poured all the words he could never say into the soft, lingering touch of his mouth on hers. He pulled back and pressed his lips to her temple. "I'll be back with reinforcements soon. Be ready."

17

*S*pring had two seconds to process Knox's departure before an enraged Don Carlos glowered from the doorway with seven hulking guards at his back. His expression left little doubt as to the severity of the beating she was about to receive.

Lin had only left her the ability to glamour and make herself beautiful for her captor. All other magic had been stripped away with spells, charms, and amulets created by the witches and warlocks on his payroll. Spring didn't have the ability to protect herself from the vicious blows Don Carlos liked to rain down upon her. Nor could she defend herself by fighting back. If she lifted a hand to him, excruciating pain wracked her entire body.

She pasted a submissive half-smile on her face and immediately dropped to her knees as a sign of supplication.

"Where did he go?" His accent deepened with his heightened emotions. "The man who touched what was mine, where did he go?"

Spring closed her eyes in resignation. Maybe she would get lucky this time. Maybe he would kill her and put her out of her misery. "He left, master."

His hand snagged her hair and jerked her head back. "*Puta!*"

The first blow split her lip. The second shattered her eye socket. The third bounced her head off the wall. Everything that followed was a blur. Blissful darkness embraced her, and Spring prayed to the Goddess who no longer listened that *this* time she would never have to return to the mortal plane. She also prayed Knox would never find his way back here. That he'd take her advice and write her off as a lost cause.

———

KNOX REAPPEARED IN THE THORNE DRIVEWAY AND JOGGED UP THE steps to the attic. When he stepped through the door, it was to a shocked and solemn group. Preston's gray face looked ghastly, and Alastair had murder written in every line of his tense body.

"What happened?" Knox demanded. Terror began an invasion of his mind. What had he missed in the short time since he'd left?

"Spring," Coop rasped out her name. "The block has been broken."

Their sorrowful expressions finally penetrated. A broken blocking spell meant one thing. "No. I just left her." Knox shook his head in denial. *"No!"* His shout shook the foundation of the house. *"No!"*

He rushed to the scrying mirror and swiped his hand across the glass. Spring's battered and broken body lay on the ground. Blood pooled around her head. Her glazed, vacant stare left no one in doubt as to her condition.

His precious love was no more. She'd gone on to the Otherworld and left him in hell without her.

Esteban's men discussed the disposal of her body as if she were no better than an insect they'd stepped on that needed to be scraped from their shoe.

"No!" Knox's aching cry echoed off the walls surrounding them and shook the windows in their frames.

Without thought to his own safety or the eight men he would face, he teleported back to Esteban's jungle mansion. He ran full speed down the corridor until he got to the room where Spring had been held captive.

The collective surprise of the group gave Knox the advantage. Fisting his hands, he drew on his metal element to heat and melt the gun barrels pointed in his direction. Outraged cries and gasps of fear echoed about the twenty by thirty space.

In mere seconds, Knox had manipulated the bars from the window frames and bent them inward, removing them from their moorings. They floated mid-air as he melted and reshaped the tips into sharp spears. When the three men closest to the door would have run, Knox used the sharpened bars and drove one through the center of each of their chests, effectively pinning the guards to the wall. Their screams of horror and agony were only marginally gratifying. The gurgle of dying breaths slightly more so.

Knox turned his attention to the remaining men who all stood in stunned horror. Don Carlos, the first to recover, shoved two guards in front of him as if to encourage the soldiers to attack.

Knox lifted the guards with a twist of his wrist and flung them against the far wall.

"Don't move!" The harsh crack of his voice echoed throughout the chamber as if it were the voice of God. The lethal tone struck fear in all who were present. But just in case Don Carlos took it into his head to be brave, Knox snapped the necks of two remaining guards with a flick of his fingers as warning.

"You..." He pointed at Don Carlos. "*You* will die a slow, painful death. And if you pass out, I will wake you. And if you die, I will revive you." He moved closer like a tiger stalking its prey. "You will feel what she felt a hundred times over, and you will beg for the end before I am done with you."

But Don Carlos was better prepared than Knox anticipated—not that it mattered. The drug lord drew a gun from behind his back and aimed.

"Seriously?" Knox sneered.

Don Carlos saw his own death in Knox's face, how could he not? The need to kill vibrated through every fired-up cell in his body. A cry was wrenched from Don Carlos at the same time the gun was ripped from his fingers.

The air crackled, heralding the arrival of others. Knox had no idea if they were friend or foe, and he couldn't drum up the extra energy to care one way or another. Once he'd done what he came for, he'd be happy to die. Hell, he welcomed it if it meant joining Spring in the afterlife.

From his periphery, he noted a figure bending over Spring. Like an animal protecting its mate, he snarled and moved to intercept the newcomer. He miscalculated. Nothing told him that so much as the sharp blade plunged deep into his back. It felt like a hard punch to the kidney. No sting, no searing burn. For that, Knox was grateful; his revenge hadn't been satisfied. He did no more than grunt before turning his full wrath on Don Carlos.

First, he harnessed his magic to stem the flow of blood from his wound. Then, he concentrated the complete force of his power on Don Carlos Esteban. Knox went to work dislocating and breaking his enemy's fingers—the bones, then the joints—systematically moving from finger to finger, reveling in Don Carlos's agonized screams. Each terrified scream fueled Knox's rage as he imagined Spring's cries from the torment she had received at this deranged monster's hands.

As Knox moved to the man's wrist, Alastair spoke. "While I can understand your rage and pain, son, you need to finish this. We shouldn't delay."

"Go!" Knox yelled. "What do I care what you do?"

"Knox," Alastair said. There was a wealth of compassion in the way he spoke Knox's name. The shimmering brightness in the other man's eyes indicated he fought back strong emotions.

"Just leave me alone," Knox seethed. "If you'd have trusted me to get your precious artifact instead of dragging her into this... she... she would..." He bent double in his grief. Spring was gone. No amount of self-righteous indignation or blame was going to bring her back. Hadn't he been the one to say it wasn't Alastair's fault?

And although Knox didn't want to see Spring in such an undignified position, he couldn't stop himself from staring. His eyes were drawn to her still, sightless form. He knelt beside her and smoothed back the matted strands from her pale, colorless skin. The blood had pooled and now began to congeal.

"What am I going to do without you?" he whispered. Agony was suffocating him, and he found it difficult to breathe. "How do I continue to exist?" he choked out. "Ohmygod, Spring." Silent sobs shook him as he cradled her head in his lap. "Spring."

He didn't move as arms encircled his shoulders from behind. Coop's grave voice came to him as if from a distance. "I'm sorry, cousin. I'm *so* sorry."

The ground beneath the building shifted, and a loud rumble filled the air. Plaster dust fell down on their heads, and the windows popped as they shattered in their casings. All the occupants of the room froze in fear, even the mighty Thornes.

"Knox, stop!" Alastair shouted over the roar. "You'll kill us all!"

Knox slowly shook his head, never taking his gaze from his beloved's frozen features. "It's not me."

From the corner of his eye, he saw Don Carlos crawl along the wall toward the exit. Rage boiled over from the steady simmer it had been the moment before. "Your reign is over, Esteban," he growled and raised his fisted hand skyward.

Don Carlos's body was suspended three feet above the ground. He clawed at his neck with his deformed fingers, as if to remove the invisible noose strangling away his life force.

Preston Thorne surprised Knox when he sent a flaming ball to eliminate the two remaining soldiers huddled in the corner. The room exploded with fire even as the walls and ceiling crashed down around them. "They didn't deserve to live."

No one challenged Preston's swift administration of justice.

"I'll bring her home." Alastair shifted to lift Spring's body from the floor but jumped back as she gracefully rose from her prone position.

"What the hell?"

Knox had no idea who uttered the question they were all thinking, but it seemed loud in the silence after the earthquake ended.

Dumbfounded, they all looked on as Spring touched a single finger to one bracelet and melted it from her wrist. She repeated the action for the second shackle. Next, her exposed skin transformed from bloody, bruised, and scarred to flawless and smooth. Lastly, a wave of her elegant hand brought with it a stunning Grecian dress of the purest white to encase her body. She flicked her fingers in the general vicinity of her hair. The matted, bloody tresses lengthened and brightened to shining, clean, and healthy once more.

"Much better, don't you think?" Spring said with a satisfied sigh. *Or who should've been Spring.*

"Who are you?" Knox barked the question, enraged that another witch would defile Spring's body by possessing it.

Her image shimmered and another momentarily took her place.

"Isis," Knox gasped.

"Exalted One." Alastair bowed and the others followed suit with the exception of Knox.

"I want her back," Knox stated with an edge of demand. "Spring. You made me believe we could save her. *You lied!* I want her back."

Isis walked to where he stood. Pained sympathy filled the glowing amber eyes she focused on him. "She doesn't want to come back, child."

"Make her!" Knox flung Don Carlos's limp form against the wall as if he were a child's rag doll. *"You make her!"*

A hard light entered her eyes. All affection disappeared in a nanosecond. "You would *dare* to order *me?*"

"He is out of his mind with grief, Goddess," Alastair cut in as he came to stand beside her. "He knows not what he says. You should understand. You knew grief once… when your husband, Osiris, was taken from you. You of all people should know what he is going through."

Any indignation left her, and she nodded regally. "Yes, I have known grief. It is a powerful emotion that clouds the mind." She gave a delicate shrug. "But even I cannot change Fate's design, Knox Carlyle. Your woman has moved on to the Otherworld."

Knox dropped to his knees. "If you require me to beg, I will beg. *Please.*" His voice cracked, and his vision blurred. "Please."

"What would you do for her return? What would you give up?"

Alastair's hand came down hard on Knox's shoulder—a warning of sorts.

"What wouldn't I do?" Knox returned, effectively ignoring Spring's uncle. A small ray of hope lit his soul.

A contemplative light entered Isis's eyes. "If I were to bring her back, I would need something in return."

He opened his mouth to agree, but the Goddess held up a hand. "Before you accept, you should know that in order to restore her, her memories will be lost. She will wake as if she were a babe."

Knox frowned and met the concerned stares of the other men. A babe? Would she have to learn to walk and talk? "What does that mean?"

"She will not know you. Nor will she know her family, or indeed, anything from before her rebirth. Her memory will be wiped clean and will *never* return."

"She won't know her sisters? Her father?"

"No. I'm sorry."

"Why?"

"This vessel's brain was damaged. To heal it, I will need to start from scratch."

Vessel, there was that fucking word again. Spring was more than a vessel, she was his everything.

"But other than the memory loss, she'll be whole in every way? She'll be happy?"

"She will be whole again. No scars, no broken bones, and no addiction. It will be as if she was born anew," Isis informed him. "Happiness is never promised, but she will not suffer the memories of her time here."

"Do it." Knox swallowed hard. "What do you ask of me in return?"

The Goddess smiled and caressed his cheek. "Nothing more. You've given it."

"I don't understand." Surely, it couldn't be as simple as all that?

"You sacrificed your love. There is no stronger sacrifice and no other requirement."

Sacrificed his love. Yes, he'd certainly done that with his stupidity. He looked at the woman who wore his beloved's body. The exact same body that had housed Spring's soul. And yet, he felt nothing for the woman before him. The spirit of Spring was gone and no substitute, no matter how exact in looks and voice, would be able to replace her.

A long, lonely existence faced him without her. But what about her future? Could she love again? Would she pick him? Could she? "It's said Thornes only love once. Is it possible she will fall in love with me again?" he asked hoarsely. "Is all hope gone?"

"Stand, Knox Carlyle."

He complied.

"It is possible for her to meet and fall in love with you again. It is also possible she could meet and fall for another. There are no guarantees. Spring's new path is her own."

"What about her abilities?" Preston asked.

The smile Isis turned on the other man made Knox blink. It was as if the Goddess held a special affection for Spring's father.

"She will retain her magical abilities. However, she will need to be reminded of the ways of the Goddess for any rituals she performs. Those memories will be gone with the others."

"Thank you, Exalted One. You are beyond generous," Alastair said.

She nodded her head at Alastair. "You are welcome."

To Knox, she said, "Your sacrifice doesn't go unrewarded."

*S*pring wandered around the sprawling manor until the walls closed in on her and she could no longer stand to be inside. With only one destination in mind, she took off toward the east side of the property. Once she saw the gardens, she calmed somewhat. The full green foliage greeted her like a long lost friend, and she pulled soothing energy from the warm dirt beneath her bare feet.

When she'd first gained consciousness two months ago, she had basic motor skills. She could speak and go about her standard everyday needs with a type of muscle memory. A simple spell from her father gifted her with the power to read, and she did so voraciously.

To avoid her overbearing, but well-meaning family, she'd poured herself into relearning magic with a vengeance. Every day, she had marveled as some new skill came to light. But even with all the discoveries, there was an underlying pallor over her life. It was as if the Thornes mourned the old Spring. As if she'd truly died. Yet wasn't she still the same person? Granted she didn't have any recollection of the past, but surely she wasn't so different from who she'd been?

Because she didn't know enough about who she was before, she didn't know if their sadness was justified. Wouldn't it be grand if they all accepted her for who she was today? She sighed her resignation. Maybe with more time, they could all find a comfortable co-existence. One where she didn't feel like an intruder in their perfectly ordered world.

As she stepped around a tall wall of rose bushes in the garden, she felt the presence of another. "Come out. I know you're there," she called as she ran a finger along the outer rim of the closest rose petal. Not bothering to look up, she pushed a little magic into the flower to brighten the yellow color and give it a longer lifespan.

"How did you know I was here?"

She glanced over to see a man step from behind the wide base of an old oak. He was tall with blond hair to his shoulders and a full beard covering the lower half of his face. The scruff was neatly maintained along his cheeks and neck. From just above his right temple ran a thin, white scar that disappeared into the thick growth of hair. The scar had come so close to his eye that the skin tugged down slightly. Although it ruined the perfection of his face, she found him more interesting for it.

He was dressed casually in a pale blue t-shirt and gray cargo shorts with a pair of beat-up flip flops on his feet. The laid-back look fit with their surroundings.

"I've found the earth puts off a vibration when there is another person in my general vicinity." For a long moment, she studied him, hoping for recognition of any kind. Disappointed, she asked, "Who are you, and what are you doing on Thorne property?"

"You really don't remember?" he asked softly.

Based on his reaction to the negative motion of her head, she should've. "I'm sorry," she said, unsure why.

"I'm Knox Carlyle."

She nodded once. "Coop and Keaton's cousin. I overheard one of my sisters ask them about you."

A bitter smile twisted his lips. "Yes. Coop and Keaton's cousin."

"I'm sorry," she said again.

Knox strode to where she stood and gazed down at her face.

While his overall intensity might intimidate some, for Spring, it had the opposite effect. Oddly, she felt protected and comforted by his presence. On the other hand, his incredible blue eyes, which seemed to search her soul with a simple glance, truly made her uneasy. They weren't quite the color of the Caribbean Sea, maybe a few shades darker and more sapphire in color, but the shade was one she'd never forget now she had seen it. Spring didn't fear him so much as she was disturbed by his draw.

"You shouldn't be out here alone." His voice held a raw, rough edge, and her toes curled as the deep sound reverberated inside her.

She smiled softly. "I'm not afraid."

The powerful energy radiating from him was disconcerting to a degree. It was as if he expected something more from her and was waiting for her to recognize his need. In a move of avoidance, she turned sideways and ran a hand along the tops of the roses beside her. "This garden called to me from my bedroom window." She glanced back and noted his frown. "It must seem stupid to you, I guess."

"No. You're an earth witch. I'd be surprised if it didn't."

Inexplicably pleased by his understanding, she changed the subject. "Why are you here?"

"To check on you."

"Check on me? Isn't it a bit late? I've been home two months. This is the first time you've expressed an interest. Excuse me if it seems awkward and weird."

"I wanted to come sooner. It was ill advised."

Unable to find the proper response, she moved farther down a gravel path toward the center of the vast garden. Knox fell into step beside her. It never occurred to her that he might wish her harm. Indeed, for some odd reason, she was happy he walked with her.

"So, how are you?" he asked.

Hesitant to answer, she shrugged. What was she supposed to say? That she felt uncomfortable most days because she didn't know her own family, and yet, they all exuded an air of hope that she would recognize them at any moment? Or maybe she could say the daily inactivity they'd forced on her was driving her insane? None of this was appropriate to dump on an unknown visitor.

"Talk to me, Spring. Tell me what you're feeling."

"I don't know you. Why would I tell you anything?" she snapped, her patience strained due to other people's constant expectations.

Halting, Knox placed a light hand on her forearm. A warm current drifted between them and fired up her cells. Since she'd not experienced such a disconcerting sensation with anyone else, Spring jerked away and glared.

"You don't have to tell me a damned thing, sweetheart. But I can sense you're upset, and I'd ease your mind if I could. Sometimes it's easier to talk to someone who isn't in the thick of things."

Again, she was drawn in by his vibrant blue gaze. Unbidden, the words poured from her. "I don't fit in here. They are virtual strangers, and every time one of my family speaks to me, it's like they are expecting me to suddenly remember everything. Expecting me to throw my arms around them and shout my joy at being here in their world. It's stifling."

"Have you told them that?"

"Not in so many words." She stared at the bare toes she burrowed into the rich, dark soil. "I don't want to disappoint anyone."

"Ah. Now I see." In a sudden move, he hooked his pinky with hers. With a little tug, he gained her complete attention. "There's plenty of Thorne land here. Create your own home."

"What?"

The warm night wind had blown strands of Spring's hair free from its ponytail holder, and Knox let go of her to casually tuck the stray lock behind her ear. She didn't question or object to his touching her. There was something non-threatening and right about having him here with her.

"There is nothing written that says you have to live in Thorne Manor. Or for that matter, on this land. You can go anywhere as long as you make sure there are protection spells in place to guard your home."

Why hadn't she thought of that? Slowly, she nodded. "That's a good idea. Thank you."

"My pleasure."

They fell back into rhythm as they continued their stroll.

"May I ask you something?"

His brows lifted in encouragement.

She drummed up the nerve to ask, "You and me. From something I'd overheard, I got the impression... were we ever... an item?"

She heard his sharp inhale and wondered at the reason. After another long moment, he spoke. "Yes. But probably not in the way you think."

"I don't know what I think," she muttered.

He chuckled. The sound resonated within her. "You were a force of nature growing up. But in a good way. Everyone loved you. You were bright, bold, and curious by nature." He stopped and stared into the inky night. "Every afternoon at precisely three-thirty, you would show up at my family's barn. You had on your pink cowboy boots and your long hair in a topknot. You'd insist on riding Macy, the sweet young mare we owned, and afterwards, you would prepare her stall with shavings for the night." Knox stopped and grinned down at her. "I looked forward to your daily visits."

"We were childhood sweethearts?"

"Not so much. Around your fifteenth birthday, you decided you wanted a relationship with me. I shoved you into a pile of manure."

"What?" She gasped and laughed. This was the first horrible thing anyone had told her to date. Mostly, her family walked on eggshells around her, fearful she might break if anything too terrible were done or spoken in her vicinity. "What a horrible thing for you to do!"

"It didn't dissuade you. Or if it did, no one could tell. You did, however, wait until you were a little older to start your pursuit again. By that time you'd filled out and telling you no took all my willpower."

"Why willpower? If I was abhorrent to you—?"

His snort cut her off. "You were *far* from abhorrent. But I had to maintain the pretense that you were. Or that's what I told myself anyway. I was an idiot. Knowing what I know now, if I could go back, I would definitely have taken you up on your offer. I'd never have let you go."

"You let me go? What does that mean?"

"I thought I was being chivalrous. I thought by waiting until you were older, less innocent, that you might better know your mind. I worried you were only infatuated and when you matured, you might have a change of heart. Taking advantage of you didn't sit well with me."

"Wow! You were an arrogant fucker, weren't you?"

Knox broke into laughter, long and loud. When he got control of his hilarity, he swiped the tips of his fingers under his lower lids. "I really was."

She grinned up at him. "I can see the attraction."

He tilted his head, and a small smile played upon his lips. "Can you?"

There was a suggestive, playful quality to his tone; one that pulled Spring in and made her want to tease him in return.

"Will you kiss me?" Where her request came from, she'd never know. Perhaps it was the need to connect with someone who was not her immediate family. Or maybe it was the luminous light he put off. From what she gathered, only magical humans put off such a light. His was pure. It made her want to crawl into his warmth and stay forever.

"Is that what you truly want?" he asked huskily.

In the short time since she'd awakened to find her life in chaos and her memory gone, Spring couldn't remember wanting anything more. This man eased the constant restlessness that had taken hold. "Yes."

Knox leaned in to brush the tip of his nose to hers before he buried his face in her hair. With his lips next to Spring's ear, Knox whispered, "You'd better be sure you want to go there, sweetheart, because once I taste you again, I'll never stop."

When Knox backed away, acute disappointment ate at Spring.

TM CROMER

Without conscious thought, she grabbed the front of his shirt. Her feelings were jumbled, and she was uncertain as to what she truly wanted, but having him pull away filled her with desolation.

Their gazes locked, and the air stilled around them. A sense of anticipation filled her. It was as if this scarred stranger held the key to her future, and she was able to recognize that fact even when she knew nothing else.

"I want to go there," she whispered past her dry lips.

Without a by-your-leave, he hauled her into his arms. Arms that were like hard steel bands as they encircled her.

She didn't protest. Instead, she placed her palms flat upon his well-muscled chest and ran her hands up over his rounded shoulders. "You're beautiful."

Knox snorted his disbelief and ran a finger down his facial scar. "Even with this?"

"Yes." She cocked her head to the side to study the mark more closely. "Maybe because of that."

The beatific smile that lit his face shocked her into silence.

"I should've known you'd like it."

She frowned and drew back slightly. "I thought we knew each other. You said we did. Why would you not know if I liked it before? It doesn't look new."

When Knox dropped his arms, Spring felt forlorn, but remained silent.

"Because of this." He skimmed his index finger along the scar, and as it moved down the length of his temple and cheek, the mark disappeared as if it had never existed. His face was perfection.

Spring gaped at the stunning visage before her. *"Oh."*

He said nothing as he continued to stare at her, gauging her reaction. She had the distinct feeling he was waiting for something. What, she couldn't say.

"Have you always kept this hidden? Even from me?"

"Yes."

"Why?"

"It's a gruesome reminder of my early childhood."

136

"I'm sorry."

Temper flashed briefly in his eyes, and he spun away. "I don't want your pity," he grumbled.

"I don't. Pity you, that is. I may hurt for the small child who was injured, but I don't pity you because you have a scar." She stepped forward and laid a hand upon his back. "I'm sorry you felt the need to hide it from me before. If I'm being honest, I like you better with it."

He pivoted back and pinned her with an incredulous stare. "Why?"

Spring couldn't prevent the grin taking hold. "Because it adds character and you're far too gorgeous without it for any woman's peace of mind. How many times a day do you get hit on by women?" Knox's wicked delight triggered a hitherto-unknown jealousy in Spring. "Never mind. Don't answer that."

His teasing smirk widened. "I'm going to kiss you now."

Anticipation curled in her stomach and made her nerves jump. "Yes, please."

Strong arms gathered her close, and for an instant, Spring felt a shiver of fear. It was as if his touch triggered something forgotten within her. Then his lips closed over hers. She, who couldn't remember her life before eight weeks ago, and who was aimless and lost, finally came home.

*S*pring was responsive in ways Knox had only dreamed about. She curled into him and opened to allow the seductive attack of his tongue. The passion she expressed, the deep, throaty moan, the little mewl of contentment, all made his body tighten with desire for her.

Because he wanted nothing more than to throw her down and make love to her with wild abandon, he pulled away. He'd learned the hard way; timing was everything. Spring might seem ready, but she still needed to discover who she was before she committed to him.

Her unique scent drifted to his nostrils, and he inhaled deeply when he could draw an even breath. Goddess, he wanted to eat her up.

"Wow! I suppose that could be classified as my first kiss," she laughed.

"I have it on good authority—*yours*—that you kissed a lot of frogs before me," he teased.

"Is that an indication that you're some type of prince?"

"If the crown fits."

Like a balm to his ravaged soul, her light laughter took away the burning pain of their separation. He'd gone too long without talking to or touching her. Now, all he wanted to do was scoop her up and lock her away.

But someone had already done that. Someone else's obsession had led to horrendous actions against her. She didn't deserve what had happened. Knox had to find a way to make this new way of life work for them both. If it meant her permanent freedom, that's what he'd provide for her.

"I think I can understand why I was attracted to you, Knox Carlyle."

"Only think? Hmm, maybe I should've kissed you longer and wiped every other thought from your mind."

Unsure whether he was teasing or poking fun at her expense, she stopped short and glared. As a show of goodwill, he ducked down to kiss the tip of her nose. Her ingrained sense of humor took hold, and Knox released the breath he'd been holding when she smiled.

"Funny," she murmured. "But I'm surprised you'd make jokes at a handicapped person's expense."

He snorted his disbelief. "Handicapped? How do you figure?"

"I'm working blind here."

A bark of laughter burst forth. "I see what you did there. Handi-capped, blind. Good one."

They walked in companionable silence for a while. "You seem easy to be with," she confessed.

"I tend to take life as it happens."

"How so?"

Knox gave his answer some thought and tried to decide how much background he wanted to dump at her feet. He'd learned from an early age never to expect anything good from life, but when it came his way, he treasured the rare moments.

"You don't have to tell me if you don't want."

Her voice sounded small and distant. It helped him to make up his mind.

"I don't mind. I'm trying to find the right words to tell you about me. About my past."

When she curled her pinky finger around his, his heart stuttered to a stop and then kicked into high gear.

"Come on. I want to show you something."

"I've been told I'm not allowed to teleport yet," she warned.

"Second thoughts about trusting me?"

"No. Not at all. But I don't want to upset my family. They've been kind to me."

The confession had been grudgingly given, and Knox had a better understanding of her discontent.

"Would it help if we sent your father or one of your sisters a text?"

Now, it was Spring's turn to hesitate. "It's late. I probably shouldn't."

Using the knuckle of his index finger, he lifted her chin. "Spring, look at me."

Her lids slowly rose until she locked gazes with him.

"What do *you* want to do?"

"I like what we're doing. Walking and talking."

The forthright quality in her bright jade eyes pleased him. They held no guile, no fear, but a healthy caution he could respect.

"Then that's what we'll do." There was always time to show her his estate and explain his dysfunctional immediate family at a later date. Neither of them was going anywhere anytime soon. "Lead the way, sweetheart."

They followed the path to the outbuilding she used for her planting. "Have you been to my workshop?"

"Once."

She frowned but remained silent.

"Have you been planting? I noticed your little magical boost for the roses when I initially walked up. Nicely done."

Spring seemed to welcome the change of subject. "Yes. My first week back, I read the Thorne grimoire from front to back. There were all sorts of wonderful spells. It seems I kept a journal on all my replanting projects." She faced him and skipped backwards. "Apparently, I was working on an almost extinct species before my accident. Do you know if I ever replanted any in Colombia?"

The question was unexpected and slammed him right back to the horrific memories he wanted to forget. The air went heavy, and he couldn't catch his breath.

"Knox?" Spring's delicate hand rested on his bicep. "Are you okay?"

"You said accident. Do you know what happened to you?"

With a heavy sigh, she shifted away. He mourned the loss of warmth from her small hand.

"No. But I've overheard a few things on occasion."

"Pfft. Accidentally overheard or intentionally spied?"

Her arched look told him all he needed to know.

"You listened at keyholes," he laughed. "Well, I'll say one thing; your personality didn't change."

"I was abducted?"

"Are you asking or telling?"

"Don't play coy now," she ordered. "It doesn't fit with who you are."

He wrapped an arm around her and gripped the nape of her neck with his free hand and massaged the tightening muscles. "Yes."

She trembled within his embrace, and her eyes dropped to his lips. "What happened?"

"You and I were on a mission to pick up an artifact for your uncle." Her expectant gaze caused him to correct his speech. "Okay, we were going to swipe an amulet from a private collection before it fell into the wrong hands."

"Do you know who the wrong hands belonged to?"

"A man named Zhu Lin." Shoving back the spontaneous blast of anger generated by the mere mention of Lin's name was impossible. The surge of power ran through him into her. It wasn't enough to hurt her, but it was enough to gain her attention. "Sorry about that. Anyway, Lin runs the last known faction of a group called the Désorcelers. Their one goal in life is to wipe all witches and warlocks from the face of the planet. His hatred borders insane."

Knox bent and pressed his forehead to hers.

"Was he the one who took me?" she asked softly.

"Yes."

"What happened?"

"Christ, Spring! Are you sure you want to know? The whole thing... it... he..." Knox released her and walked away. The remembered pain was slicing him in two. How could it not hurt her to hear what had been done to her?

Her cool fingers entwined with his, and she tugged him to a nearby bench. "Please."

Closing his eyes, he nodded. "Just give me a minute, okay?" After he'd collected his thoughts and emotions, he shifted to face her and gathered her hands in his. "Lin sold you to a Colombian drug lord who ran a sex trafficking ring."

The words came out rushed, but she heard them clearly all the same. Her surprised gasp was swallowed by the night. "How... how did I... what...? I don't know what to say."

Unable to stem the flow of words, he explained most of the sordid trauma.

Her hands flew to cover her mouth. "Ohmygod," she whispered.

"That's why your family is so protective of you right now. You could meet Lin on the street and not know who the hell he is."

"That's why you were out wandering the property, isn't it? You were guarding me."

"Promise not to think badly of me?"

She nodded warily.

"I cast a spell, similar to an early warning system, that lets me know when you leave your home. I can teleport to your location in a split second. In other words, yes, I was guarding you." He scrubbed his hands up and down his face. "It's impossible for me not to."

Once again, she nodded, her bottom lip caught between her pearly white teeth.

"Does it freak you out?"

Spring's tawny head popped up, and she met his gaze squarely.

"A little. But I understand why you would." An awkward silence filled the space between them. "Was tonight's meeting staged?"

"No. You looked lost and lonely. I couldn't stay away from you another second."

SPRING TOOK HER TIME AND MULLED OVER ALL THE THINGS KNOX had revealed. What did he see when he looked at her? Was she damaged goods in his eyes? Was that why he waited two months to approach her? Was it why he pulled away from their heated embrace earlier?

"Am I... uh, do you... *view* me differently now? Like I'm damaged?"

"What? No!" He cupped her face between his large hands. *"Never!"*

His vehement response gave her a semblance of relief. A peace of mind she wasn't aware she needed.

"What happened to the drug lord you talked about?" She wasn't sure she wanted to know, but he'd been forthcoming about everything else.

"I killed him."

The brutal truth of his words slammed into her and alarmed her like nothing else tonight had. She jumped up from the bench and backed away. "I-I've got t-to go."

She was halfway to the garden's exit when his strong hands halted her forward progress and whipped her around to face him. His tortured expression hurt her stomach.

"I'm not a murderer, sweetheart. What he did to you... seeing you lying on the floor, lost to me... I went crazy for a bit."

When she remained silent and watchful, Knox released her.

"You should get some sleep," he said gruffly.

The charming bubble he'd created around them earlier had burst. She didn't know what to think, only that she needed time to process all he'd told her.

He walked her to the wide porch then paused by the bottom of the steps she ascended. "Spring?"

She turned to gaze down at him.

"I'm not the one you should fear." Love shone from Knox's troubled eyes. The raw emotion shocked her to see. "But know, I would do it again if I thought it would keep you safe."

A part of her wanted to run to him. To fling herself into the arms she suspected would open to her the second she approached him. Ruthlessly, she tamped down the urge.

"It's a lot to take in for one night." The small, sad twist of his lips spoke to her as nothing else had. Coming to an abrupt decision to show him her absolute trust, she said, "I've been thinking about exploring the glen. The one I've seen from the attic window." She pointed up inanely.

Knox didn't speak or offer to escort her, so she changed tactics.

"My sister Winnie makes these incredible cinnamon rolls most mornings. There's always plenty left over. You could come over tomorrow and join me for breakfast. Maybe afterwards you could take me to the clearing?"

He gave a sharp nod.

The impulse struck to kiss him, but Spring settled for a friendly buss on his scarred cheek. "Thank you."

Long after she'd climbed between the cool sheets of her bed, she thought about their meeting. Knox had drawn her in with ease. Or it was more like she'd thrown herself at him. *Who asks a complete stranger to kiss them like she had?* But he hadn't seemed to mind. And oh, that kiss. The brief glimpse of heaven she'd experienced in his arms tonight would taunt and beckon her until she was able to capture it for her own.

She smiled in the darkness. He was like her very own guardian angel—or based on his recollection of the events in Colombia, her avenging angel. Either way, when she was close to him, her constantly churning mind calmed even as her heart kicked into high gear. Tomorrow couldn't arrive soon enough.

Spring awoke with her first real sense of anticipation. Until today, she'd dreaded mornings at Thorne Manor. The side glances, the wary looks, the sadness lurking in the gazes around her, they were all too much to bear.

Until Knox.

She stretched and smiled.

A shadow shifted in the corner of her room. She swallowed her instinctive scream as her visitor's identity was revealed.

"You couldn't use the front door?" she laughed as she whipped back her coverlet.

Knox stepped into the beam of light coming through her window and gave her an embarrassed shrug. "I couldn't sleep."

She stepped to him and placed a hand over his sculpted left pectoral muscle. His heart rate increased by her nearness. She smiled softly because hers did the same when he was close. "Because the Colombia incident was fresh in your mind?"

"Yes."

"It's okay." In a gesture of comfort, she patted his chest. Or maybe she just liked the feel of his rock-hard muscles. She turned away to head to her ensuite bathroom. Before she reached the doorway, she tossed her hair back and grinned at him over her shoulder. "But you do realize it's creepy to hang out in the corner of a sleeping chick's bedroom without her permission, right?"

Her cheekiness had done its job and chased away the darkness that had clouded Knox's gorgeous, expressive eyes.

"I'll remember that for future."

"Have a seat, I'll only be a minute. Then we can get some of those cinnamon rolls I smell baking." She inhaled deeply. "Do you know one is the size of a dinner plate?"

"I do."

"Confession: I can eat a whole roll all by myself."

His deep chuckle pleased her, and she winked before disappearing into the bathroom. As she splashed water on her face and gazed at her reflection in the mirror, she wondered about her lack of apprehension where Knox was concerned. Had any other man been as forward or shown up in her bedroom while she was sleeping, would she be so blasé about it? Yet, the haunted quality about him whenever he gazed at her was unsettling to a large degree. Knowing what they'd both gone through, what he'd suffered—possibly still suffered—due to the incident allowed her to forgive the trespass. And of course her body's insane attraction to him didn't hurt his cause.

A short time later, they descended the stairs, their pinkies joined. Knox's face was a perfect mask, no scar, no indication he'd ever been injured in the past. She got the sense the old wound bothered him more than it would bother anyone else who might view it.

When they got to the foyer, Autumn and her step-daughter Chloe had arrived. Surprise lit both their faces when they saw Knox by her side.

"Knox!" Chloe cried as she raced forward.

He scooped her up and hugged her tight. "Hey, midget."

"I miss you since you left."

"I've missed you, too, kid."

Spring frowned and glanced between them. Since he'd left? She had gone off the assumption that he resided at the Carlyle estate.

"What are you doing here, Knox? Do you live with Spring now?" Chloe pulled a pout. "I thought if you married her, she would come live with us."

"I *knew* you were trying to set us up in the restaurant!" He laughed and blew a raspberry on her cheek, causing the child to dissolve into giggles.

Once again, Spring felt excluded from a family moment. It was as if she stood on the outside, looking through a glass window at all the happy people. The disconnect was strange and unsettling.

When Knox turned his happy gaze to her, she wanted nothing more than to remember their past. She wanted to know how many times she'd been the one to put that look on his face. Wanted to know exactly what precocious little Chloe had done to throw them together. But the memories were gone. Never to return. There was a melancholy attached to her situation, one she pushed back daily.

Her thoughts must've been reflected in her expression, because everyone sobered. Unable to stand another second, she abandoned them in the hall and raced for her workshop.

"Spring! Will you hold up a second? For a small woman, you run like a damned gazelle." Knox caught up to her at the entrance to the garden. He tilted her chin up. "Want to tell me what that was all about?"

"I think it was obvious. Everyone was giving me the 'poor Spring' look again."

"No, they weren't."

She gasped at his obliviousness. "As the person on the receiving end, I know what I saw."

"And as the person on the giving end, *I* know what I was thinking when I looked at you. It wasn't poor anything. You looked like you swallowed a lemon. I don't know what the hell you were so pissed off about, but that scene back there..." He jabbed a finger in the direction of the house. "That was on *you!*"

Disbelief at his arrogance boiled through her veins, heating up her cells. She wanted nothing more than to stuff his mouth with dirt to shut him up. Concentrating on his mouth, she lifted her hand—

which Knox promptly grabbed. He used her struggle to pull her close.

"Don't you dare," he warned.

"Don't I dare what?" she snapped.

"I know that look. I've seen it for quite a few years now. You were going to stuff dirt in my mouth. I warned you once before, if you did it again, there would be hell to pay."

Color high and eyes blazing with fire, Knox was breathtaking.

Any irritation dissipated, and her gaze dropped to his mouth again, but not to contemplate a mouthful of dirt. No, instead she wanted to feel those firm, warm lips on hers. She wanted a taste of what she'd experienced last night.

They locked onto one another, each searching for a clue to what the other was thinking. When Knox's bold gaze dropped to Spring's mouth, she smirked. "That's the great thing about no recall. I don't know what you threatened me with or not."

"Yeah, well I also told you I know the perfect way to quiet that sassy mouth."

Her smile widened as she leaned in. "You don't say?"

"Oh, sweetheart, you're playing with fire."

"Mmm. Maybe."

Without warning, but not unexpectedly, Knox plunged his fingers into her hair and angled his mouth over hers. A hairsbreadth away, he paused. "Christ, I want you. Sassy mouth and all."

She closed the distance and became the aggressor. She wrapped her arms around his middle and fisted the material at his back. Without hesitation, she met his descending mouth and moaned her pleasure at the contact. Their heated kiss lasted forever, with them pausing only long enough to gasp for air before they dove back in. His tongue caressed hers. Its erotic exploration made her want to latch on and suck to capture whatever power it possessed to make her hungry and wanton.

"Yo! There's a kid watching you from the kitchen window. You two want to keep this PG please?" Winnie called from her vantage point.

"Looks like there are some things you remembered, little sister. Nice going! Reminds me of the Hallmark channel." Autumn's amused voice penetrated their lust-hazed brains.

"Oh, for the love of the Goddess! Not you and that damned Hallmark channel again," Winnie shouted. "Tell Keaton he needs to occupy your time better."

Spring laughed. It was a deep belly laugh that doubled her over and lifted the oppressive thoughts she'd had since she woke without her memories. This was the first time her siblings were free around her. The first time they opened up and joked without being worried how she would respond. And while Spring couldn't say what was normal, the situation felt right.

Winnie's sky-blue gaze held an approving light. "Cinnamon rolls are ready, sister. Bring that delicious eye candy of yours in for breakfast." She directed one word to Knox. "Bacon."

In a flash, Knox had scooped Spring up and teleported them to the Thornes' homey kitchen. He dropped her into a chair at the head of the old, scarred, wooden table, then dumped a half dish of bacon onto his plate.

As he bit into the crispy meat, he closed his eyes in ecstasy. "I'll be honest, Spring, if you decide you don't want me, I'm making a play for your sister. *That woman can cook.*"

The edge of the Winnie's dishtowel connected with Knox's thick bicep. "It's hard to screw up bacon."

"Stop macking on my woman," Zane ordered in his deep baritone right before he stepped into sight. With a long-suffering look at Knox, he asked, "Why is everyone always trying to steal her from me?"

Winnie's essence brightened, and a wide, welcoming smile graced her countenance. "Zane."

"Hey, babe."

They shared a sweet, loving kiss while the others unabashedly stared.

Spring hadn't been aware of her heartfelt sigh until Knox linked his pinky with hers under the table.

"For the record, I don't care if you can't make perfect bacon or plate-sized cinnamon rolls," he whispered in her ear.

"Good to know," she murmured. "Eat up so we can explore that clearing. They won't let me leave without a bodyguard."

The sound of speeding wheels crunching the gravel drifted through the open window above the sink. Knox craned his neck to see who the newcomer was. A flash of exasperation came and went across his features, and he cast a side glance at Spring. "I'll be right back."

Spring rose only to be gently shoved back into her seat.

"I think it's best if I handle this," he informed her as he strode away to answer the front door.

"What's going on?" No one else in the kitchen would meet her eyes. They were back to trying to protect her. The high-handed behavior set her teeth on edge. "Fine. I'll go see for myself."

"Sister, let Knox handle it," Winnie cautioned.

"In case you all are too obtuse to understand, let me spell it out for you. I don't need you to run interference for me. Last I checked, I'm a grown adult in possession of a capable mind. Just because I've forgotten…" Spring inhaled deeply in an attempt to get her temper under control. "…forgotten a few things, doesn't mean I'm an invalid. Stop treating me like one."

She raced for the door to find Knox arguing with another male approximately his same age. The other guy was shorter than Knox by roughly three inches but outweighed him by a good thirty pounds. He might have been nice looking, except at the moment he was flushed in fury. The red complexion made his round face look like an over-ripe tomato.

Once his eyes alighted on her, his demeanor changed. "Spring!"

The happy cry confused her. "Do I know you?"

The man's mouth dropped open in his surprise. "It's true then?"

She looked to Knox for understanding. The watchful stare told her nothing. "I'm afraid I've had a bit of an accident," she hedged as she stepped closer to Knox's side. "My memory was affected."

The newcomer's mouth opened and closed like a landed trout. "You don't remember me?"

"I'm sorry." She seemed to be saying that a lot lately. "Who are you?"

"I'm your boyfriend."

Spring reeled back in shock. The heel of her shoe caught on a loose board behind her. If it hadn't been for Knox's cat-like reflexes, she'd have fallen.

LARGE, BETRAYED EYES TURNED ON KNOX. "BOYFRIEND? I THOUGHT you... you made me believe you and I were..."

Spring's horrified expression cut deep. Coldness permeated his soul at the same time outrage took control. She'd immediately taken the little dweeb's word for it.

"You and I *are*," he assured her with a little shake. He turned on Tommy and shoved him toward the steps. "Get a clue, Tommy. She's not interested."

A fist connected with his back. "You aren't in charge of who I see."

Jealousy clouded Knox's vision and his good judgment. "You know what, you're right," he growled. "You want to date Tommy, be my guest. It's no skin off my back."

Fury pounded in his temples, and reason took a vacation. He knocked into Tommy and sent the other guy into the dirt on his ass. With a disgusted grunt, Knox headed for the clearing.

He couldn't believe history was repeating itself. He'd fallen for that spoiled-rotten brat just as he had the first time around. And just like before, Spring was determined to lead Tommy on when it was Knox she wanted.

He was halfway to his destination when a second set of footfalls registered. Menacing energy tried to wrap its ugly tentacles around him in a distinctive attack against his psyche. He just about snorted his disbelief. Of all the Carlyle clan, he was the strongest and the most advanced warlock. It would take heavy magic to bring him down, and it certainly wouldn't happen in his current location. The land between the Thorne and Carlyle estates was charmed. Granted, it didn't mean an enemy couldn't attack the old-fashioned way with a man-made weapon, but not with magic unless they were a blood relation to one of the two families.

Calling on the five elements, Knox pivoted on his heel, ready to strike. Shock brought him up short. "Mother."

Two days ago, when he'd last checked, she was locked up in a containment unit at the WC headquarters. The wards on the center made the place impenetrable. No one could get in or out without an express invitation from the Council. And Marianne Carlyle was no exception. She'd been sentenced to life imprisonment for her crimes in assisting the Désorceler Society. She'd been Zhu Lin's little spy for years leading up to the incident that took Robert Knox's life.

"How did you break free?"

"I served my time." The sly, oily expression she graced him with was only relieved by sheer hatred.

"You're a liar," he stated flatly.

A movement in his peripheral vision snared his attention. He darted his eyes around the woods as if he were bored with the conversation and the woman in front of him. A glimpse of tawny hair identified the new arrival.

Spring.

"Go back." He'd meant it for Spring, but he hoped his deranged mother would assume it was directed at her.

Marianne cocked her head and studied him. Knox was careful to reveal nothing. If he showed any sign of vulnerability, she'd strike. It had become her M.O. Marianne Carlyle despised weakness in any form.

One arm behind his back, he gathered the power of the elements he'd mentally summoned.

"Come out, girl," she called. "I know you're here."

"There's no one here but you and me, you crazy hag," he scoffed. "The voices in your head must be confusing you again."

Madness burned bright in her pale-gray eyes. Eyes once the color of his but now practically leached of color from her depravity and inability to find happiness.

"I won't hurt her. I want to see the pathetic fool who holds your affections, my darling son. I feel it's only right to warn her that you bring death and destruction to everything you touch."

Old insecurities rose up and tried to dig their claws into him. Hadn't he done just that to Spring? Brought death after her destruction? Ruthlessly, he shoved aside his negative musings. His mother was a master of manipulation and mayhem. If he let her inside his head, he was done.

His heart skipped a beat when Spring stepped from behind a wide oak and moved toward them. "Don't!" Panicked, he'd been unable to hold back his shout.

Spring paused when Marianne cackled.

"Go back," he called. "Do it now."

"I'm not leaving you," Spring argued, starting in motion again.

His general dismay morphed to full-fledged alarm at her stubbornness. With his head turned toward her but his eyes locked on his mother, he affected an ugly tone. "Don't you have a date with your boyfriend," he sneered.

"I do," Spring answered. Four steps closer, she said, "He's supposed to explore the glen with me this morning."

When Spring's words sunk in, Knox's heart spasmed. Still, he couldn't soften. "Go home, Spring. I have better things to do with my time than waste it on little girls who don't know their own mind."

Marianne's grotesque, mocking smile widened with each word they uttered. She saw through his pretense. "Always the hero, aren't you, my boy?" Her focus on Spring, Marianne raised her hands.

Knox reacted without thinking twice. The burst of electricity flew from his fingertips and hit his mother center mass. The lightning bolt he emitted slammed into her at roughly two million miles per hour and fried her with close to one billion volts.

She didn't have time for any expression of surprise or pain to cross her face, and as such, her face was frozen in a mask of hatred and evil intent. Forever.

21

*A*s Spring stood deeply shaken and paralyzed by shock, Knox sagged against a nearby tree. The power it took to electrocute his mother must have been staggering. His tormented look spoke of a deeper issue. Because of the action he took to save Spring's life, he would be forever forced to deal with the knowledge that he killed his own mother.

She couldn't imagine the weight of that burden.

There had been no doubt Marianne had planned to harm her. Intent was in every line of the other woman's body and in every nuance of her voice. Knox had tried to issue a warning, tried to make it seem like he was an asshole who didn't care one whit for Spring's feelings, but leaving him alone was impossible for her. She could no more walk away from him than she could let him walk away from her.

In the short time they'd spent together yesterday and today, she noticed one thing; Knox's light shone brighter and bolder than anyone else she'd met since waking. While she hadn't appreciated his caveman attitude where Tommy was concerned, watching him storm away had triggered a pain in her chest. She'd become short of breath, and her heart rate went into overdrive.

In her family grimoire, beneath the family crest with its motto, had been a jotted note. *A Thorne will only love but once. They shall know their other half by the warmth of the light emitting from their soul's mate.* Those words had resonated with her when she'd read them. And when Knox had stepped from behind the tree in the garden, he lit up the night with his aura. Maybe that was why she'd given him her immediate trust. Yes, trusting a stranger had been foolish on her part, but she felt as if she knew him. As if he were part of her very DNA. Ignoring their connection would be too painful.

Earlier, when Tommy had claimed to be her boyfriend, Knox's extreme reaction had forced Spring to ask herself how she would've responded should the situation be reversed. She would have snatched a bitch bald. With the realization came a wild urgency to find him.

Now, here they stood. Twenty feet separated them, but it could've been twenty thousand. Expression closed off and hardening by the second, Knox was creating an expansive distance between them.

Skirting his mother's still form, Spring stepped up to him. "Knox."

His gaze was locked onto his mother.

"Look at me. Please."

Violently, he shook his head, causing his blond, shoulder-length hair to catch on his beard. With a trembling hand, Spring smoothed the sweat-dampened locks back from his face. Still, he stared at the same point beyond her shoulder. She wove her fingers into the thick hair at the base of his skull and, with great care, applied pressure until he faced her. She pressed her lips to his in a gentle kiss.

"Thank you for saving me."

He blinked. She imagined she saw a lessening of his pain. She kissed him again. This time, his lips clung to hers.

"You did the right thing. She was intent on harm."

"I could've done something else," he rasped. "Frozen time, bound her. Anything but kill her."

"You went with your instincts."

Wrong choice of words. Knox zeroed in on his mother, and his eyes became glacier-like.

"I have the instincts of a monster." He jutted his chin toward the body on the ground. "*That* monster. Between her evil genetics and those of Robert Knox, I'm—"

She placed her fingertips gently against his mouth. "You are not the product of your birth. You are more. You're better."

There was a glimmer of hope in the eyes he lifted to search her face. He sought her honesty, and Spring let her true feelings on the matter show. "You saved me. It's not the first time either, is it?"

"No."

"How many times have you made sure I never stepped into her crosshairs over the years?"

"Too many to count," he murmured and closed his eyes. "Too many damned times to count."

"How?"

"I kept a constant watch over you both. Sometimes in person, sometimes scrying. But I swear I wasn't stalking you."

"Go on."

Knox swallowed and leaned into the hand she pressed to his cheek. "The day I shoved you into the manure? She was watching from beside the barn. I sensed her presence. It's like a black pall over my soul."

"So you didn't reject me because I was too young?" Because she hadn't experienced the incident firsthand, or at least not that she could recall, Spring could remain detached about the whole situation.

"Maybe in small part." He nodded toward his mother. "But mostly because of her. When I was a young child, if I showed any type of interest or affection for anything, my father would destroy it. He convinced her to do the same. My best guess was that they wanted to mold me into someone as hateful and evil as themselves."

In a blindingly fast move, Knox jerked her into his embrace and buried his head in her hair. She wrapped her arms around his neck and returned to him the comfort he needed.

"She realized early on how much I cared about you. It took a warning from my aunt Keira to make me see the futility of starting anything with you. My aunt and uncle monitored Marianne's every move while I was under their care. They knew how twisted she was."

With the tips of her fingers, Spring wordlessly burrowed her fingers under his long hair and stroked the nape of his neck.

"When I was old enough, they tasked me with the chore of policing her." He exhaled a ragged breath and continued. "The day you stopped coming around was the best and worst day of my life. The knowledge that you were safe kept me going. Kept me from seeking you out and begging you to love me as much as I loved you."

"Oh, Knox."

"A little over a year ago, with the help of your father and my Uncle Phillip, we were able to convince the Witches' Council to put her away for good." Knox's hold tightened, and although a little uncomfortable, Spring didn't complain. In his arms was the only place she wanted to be. "The day you disappeared in Colombia, I initially feared she'd escaped her prison. Seems my fears weren't completely unfounded. As you can see, she did eventually escape."

"She can't hurt either of us now."

"SHE CAN'T HURT EITHER OF US NOW." KNOX ALLOWED SPRING'S words to sink in. For the first time in years, he was free. Free from the evil of his deranged mother and his reprobate father. Free of the darkness shadowing his every step.

"Thank you." His voice was rough and raw. It matched his emotions to a T. Yet, he suspected she understood. In his need to see her expression and judge her sincerity, he pulled back to gaze down into her face. Her clear eyes stared up at him. No fear. No recriminations. Only a gentle understanding for what he'd done. Goddess, he loved this woman. Even without her memories, her spirit remained the same. Open, good, honest, and compassionate. "I love you, Spring. I always have, and I always will. You don't have to love me in return, but I want you to hold on to that, okay?"

Lifting up on tip-toe, she pulled his head down to hers and touched her mouth to his. His control snapped. He lifted her against him and ravaged her mouth. She offered up her innocent passion in return. The soft moan of desire she released set him afire. Wanting nothing more than to lay Spring down on the soft grass and make love to her, Knox pulled away and lowered her feet to the ground. The timing was shit again. There was still the matter of his mother's demise—at his hands. He needed to speak with Coop, Alastair, and Preston to find out what type of punishment he would face in the non-magical world and with the Witches' Council for his crime of murder. And no matter how he wanted to sugarcoat it, that's what he'd done. He had murdered his own mother.

"There is no cell phone coverage here in the clearing to call Coop. I need to get you home and clean up this mess. Is it all right if I pop over later this afternoon?"

With a smile and a nod, she clasped his hand and tugged him toward the Thorne estate. He noted she was careful to place herself between him and the body of his mother, a protective gesture on her part. While Spring needn't have bothered, Knox appreciated her thoughtfulness. He'd stopped feeling anything but disdain for his parents long ago. How could he not? And he experienced no regret Marianne was dead. Maybe that made him a horrible person, but he couldn't drum up even an ounce of remorse.

By some unspoken agreement, Knox and Spring took their time strolling through the woods. Through the canopy of leaves, the sun shone brightly on the path. Here or there, she would stop and caress the grayed bark of a tree, restoring vitality to the old hardwoods. As Knox watched her interact with nature, he experienced a swell of pride. Other than to give voice to her feelings of emotional suffocation, she had taken her whole memory loss in stride. The speed at which she relearned to use her magic was a testament to her intelligence.

"What are you thinking about so hard?"

Her voice startled him from his musings. He squinted upwards at the mid-morning sun and let the rays bathe his face in their warmth.

Spring tightened her hand in his, and he smiled at her impatience. Yeah, some things would never change.

"You." He faced her and let her see the love he felt for her, allowing himself to be open and honest for the first time in a long while. "I was thinking about you." She ducked her head, but not before he witnessed her pleased smile. "What were you thinking?"

"That I could live out here. Among all this." She waved a graceful hand to encompass the trees and bushes on either side of the path. "I…" She halted and cocked her head.

"Sprin—"

She reached an index finger to cover his lips as she frowned over her shoulder. "Someone else is here," she whispered. "The energy is very bad."

Trusting her instincts, he wrapped an arm around her waist and pictured the front lawn of the Thorne Estate. Nothing happened.

Fucking Blockers!

Wildly, his head spun left and right, trying to gauge the best route to run. "Can you get a sense of where they are?"

"Close. To the left, I think."

"That means we're cut off. Head back to the clearing as fast as you can. You'll be protected there."

"I'm not leaving you, Knox."

"Why can't you ever do what you're told?" he growled. "Let's go!"

"Wait!" In a move that surprised him, Spring faced him and gripped his hands. "Goddess hear our plea and assist us in our time of need. *Praesidio!*"

She'd requested protection from the Goddess. And as the morning sun disappeared, the entire wooded area was encased in inky darkness. Had Knox not been holding onto Spring, he'd have panicked because he couldn't see six inches in front of his face.

"Conlumino!"

A faint trail of light appeared. It reminded Knox of small solar lights along a darkened walkway. Careful to keep his voice pitched for her ears alone, he asked, "Can anyone else see this but us?"

"No."

"Clever woman. Let's go."

They hightailed it for the clearing where they knew they'd find the protection of the Goddess and centuries of their ancestors. Roughly ten yards out, Spring pulled him to a halt and ducked into the forest.

"Find them. Conjure flashlights if you have to. They can't have gotten far."

Zhu Lin. Why wasn't he surprised? The only question that remained was if his mother had set him up. It wouldn't surprise him if she had. The underhanded action fit with her previous behavior.

"Who is that man?"

For a moment, Knox had forgotten Spring had no knowledge of Lin other than what he'd told her. She had no way of knowing what Lin looked like. "Zhu Lin."

She straightened from her crouched position and stepped forward.

"What the hell are you doing?"

"It's time to end this."

The steely determination in her voice chilled him to the marrow of his bones. It was as if she were someone else. *Someone other than Spring.* Was there a remnant of Isis left in her?

22

*W*ith a simple snap of her fingers, Spring restored the light to the forest. The surprised gasps of Lin's small army of nine alerted Knox to their assumption that magic had been suspended by the Blockers. He toyed with the idea of another teleport attempt.

Together, Knox and Spring stepped from behind the lush foliage of the forest concealing them. The secondary gasps almost made him laugh. Most witches didn't have the brass cojones to come out of hiding and confront Lin.

"Mr. Lin, I presume?" Spring asked pleasantly, as if she didn't already know the man had sold her to a drug lord to be his sexual plaything.

Lin frowned. Knox reasoned the man was confused as to why Spring didn't know him.

"Spring Thorne."

A lift of Lin's hands shuffled his soldiers into a semicircle around them. "I know who you are, Miss Thorne. We've met before. I also know the name of your companion."

"Excellent. Then let's get straight to the point." She squatted and lifted a handful of dead leaves from the frozen ground, threw them in the air, and blew a kiss in the direction of the clump of leaves before they burst apart. *"Addormio."* The leaves simultaneously fluttered into the faces of the soldiers surrounding them, and one by one, Lin's army dropped to the ground.

"What did you do to them?" Although there was mild curiosity in his tone, Lin's face showed no emotion.

"I put them to sleep so the grown-ups can talk."

As Spring spoke, Lin's hand crept toward the interior of his blue suit jacket. Knox had a good idea what he was reaching for. Knox concentrated on the gun's barrel and folded it in upon itself. Lin would get a surprise when he tried to use his weapon.

"I've been informed that you're an old enemy of the Thorne family." She didn't wait for his confirmation. "You'll have to forgive me for stating what might be obvious to you, but my memory appears to be faulty. Regardless, I believe it's time you left us all alone."

"I will not stop until your entire family is eradicated." The fierceness behind his statement was proof as to how deep Lin's hatred ran. "Serqet demands it."

"I see."

Spring strolled closer to Lin, making Knox's heart rate shift into overdrive. *What the hell was she doing?* The man could physically strike her down in the blink of an eye. "Spring." He voiced his warning with her name.

He placed a hand behind his back and began gathering the elements as he'd done to strike down his mother. If it worked once, he had faith it would work again.

"Here's the thing, I've done my homework these last two months. I've read all the little notations in my family's spell book. There's one thing I know for certain. Serqet now lives in the Otherworld. And if I'm not mistaken, so does everyone in her line with the exception of *you* and a small handful of others. Do you really believe in that honor your ancestors crap? Because from everything I've learned, she sure as hell wouldn't honor you."

Rage began to gather on Zhu Lin's countenance. His eerie, green eyes turned icy.

Spring paid him no heed. "I've read your family history, Mr. Lin." She continued on as if they were girlfriends sitting down over a cup of tea. "Your ancestor wasn't a very nice person. She tried to poison her lover's new bride. Did you know that? No, not honorable in the least if you ask me."

Okay, that was news to Knox, but then he wasn't as fascinated with the past as Spring seemed to be.

"Those are the lies passed down from your family," Lin spat. "The Thornes and Carlyles only know about lies and deception. Ask Mr. Carlyle." A sly expression slithered over his smooth, ageless features. "Did you know he left you to your fate at the hands of Don Carlos? He left you to die."

All pleasantness left Spring's face. A blank mask replaced her previous animation. "I did not."

"Spring..." What could he say? He *had* left her to her fate. Granted it was to find a way to break the spell attached to her shackles, but he'd abandoned her all the same. That desertion had gotten her killed.

A small tremor shifted the hard-packed ground beneath his feet. Had Spring done that?

Lin continued with a sick glee. "Did he tell you what Don Carlos did to you? How he drugged and raped you repeatedly? How he tortured you with every weapon at his disposal?"

"Spring, it wasn't like that." If Spring believed Lin, Knox would lose the most precious part of his world. "I—"

She held up one elegant hand to halt his words. "What proof do you have?"

It was as if she played right into Lin's hands with that question. Within seconds, Lin produced a smartphone and quickly queued up a video. It didn't take a rocket scientist to figure out what that video contained.

"Spring, sweetheart, please." Knox wasn't beyond begging. If she saw that he'd left her to die, she'd hate him. There would be no hard reset of her memory banks this time around.

Spring accepted the phone and pressed play. As the scene unfolded, he could hear his own words. *"I'm coming back for you. I swear it. Tell me you understand. Tell me you know I'll be back, and that a thousand Lins and Don Carlos Estebans won't keep me from you."*

Triumph flared to life in Lin's eyes as horrific sounds of fists on flesh filled the air around them. He wore his smugness like a cloak. "He is little better than an animal, Miss Thorne, this man you've chosen. Like his father and mother before him, he will turn on you, as he turned on his mother. Yes, I did see her body. Perhaps he'll rip your beautiful body apart as he did Don Carlos? You seem to attract the violent sort."

Bile rose up in the back of Knox's throat when he saw the shift in Spring's expression. All warmth faded away as she turned her darkening green eyes upon him. He wanted to throw back his head and bellow his agony for what he'd lost.

With her hard stare locked onto Knox, Spring addressed Lin. "So what is it you suggest I do?"

"Come with me. Serve me. You will receive great financial reward for your loyalty." Lin stepped closer to Spring. "You owe these people nothing."

Her eyes dropped to the ground, and she affected a bored tone. "You would use me against my family?"

"Yes."

"You'd freely admit to using her?" Knox asked, incredulous.

Lin shrugged. "Why lie?"

"Okay."

Both men whipped their heads in Spring's direction.

"What? Spring, no!"

"Why should I listen to you?" Her tone was chilly and scathing— the perfect match to the cold fury in her eyes. "You left me to die."

"I won't let you go with him."

"You don't have a choice."

Knox surged forward, determined to save Spring from her reckless decision, and kill Lin in the process. Her next words stopped him in his tracks.

"There's only one small thing before we go." She bent and ran her hand over the surface of the ground at their feet. "I want you to call off your Blockers and let Knox leave."

"If he lives, he will come for you."

"He's right, Spring," Knox rasped. "I will always come for you."

Because her face was turned away from Lin, the other man missed the small smile that twisted Spring's lips. Knox didn't. He also bore witness to her wink. Her mischievous expression almost made him give into a shocked laugh, but he was careful to keep the look of grim determination upon his face. Whatever she was planning, he wouldn't give her away.

"We'll deal with him if that happens," she said as if she were unconcerned one way or the other. "Call off your Blockers."

Lin's indecision was short lived. "No."

"Well, you can't say I didn't try." She slammed her fist against the ground. *"Terrae motus!"*

The earth directly beneath their feet shook with the force of an eight-point-five magnitude quake. A crack opened, roughly three feet wide, and ran toward Lin at the speed of a freight train. Without a thought for his own safety, Knox dove for Spring. Over and over they tumbled as they rolled to the right of the earth's gaping hole, coming to a stop at the base of an old oak.

Lin cried out. He gripped the edge of the crumbling opening, his fingers clawed for purchase. His frantic gaze sought them out. "Please, help me."

Spring stood and stumbled forward. "Not a chance, you bastard." With a thunderous clap of her hands, the shelf of ground Lin clung to dissolved into dust. His terror-filled scream echoed through the trees.

Kneeling, Spring placed her palms flat on the ground. *"Desino."* The trembling earth ceased its motion and let out a soft sigh as it closed the hole Spring had created.

Knox leaned back against the base of the tree trunk, his gaze transfixed on the spot where the ground had encased Lin. When Spring rose and dusted off her arms and legs, Knox's attention snapped to her.

"Are you okay?" she asked softly.

"Okay?" He didn't know what he was. Okay probably wasn't top of the list. "You buried him alive."

She cast a frown over her shoulder to where Lin no longer stood. "Do you think I was too lenient?"

Inappropriate laughter bubbled up, and once it started, he found it impossible to stop. Tears leaked from the corners of his eyes as his hilarity took hold. "Lenient? I'd hate to see you truly pissed off, sweetheart."

Spring flashed him a delighted smile. "You should pray that never happens." Focusing her gaze on a point somewhere beyond him, she called out, "You can come out now."

As one, the Thornes stepped from behind the trees: Autumn, Winnie, Summer, and Alastair.

Autumn reached Spring first and wrapped her in a tight embrace. "That was kickass, little sister."

"It was, wasn't it? Do you suppose now you'll let me teleport?" Spring quipped.

Winnie and Summer each took a turn hugging her.

"How did you know to come?" Knox stood and faced the women.

The four sisters shared a look and a grin. "Hallmark," they said in stereo.

Alastair's light chuckle died out as he walked to the freshly turned dirt where Lin had been buried. He stared down in quiet contemplation before his somber gaze shifted to Spring. "Never for a moment doubt you did the right thing, child."

SPRING MET HER UNCLE'S INTENSE DARK-BLUE EYES. "NEVER. HE got what he deserved." As Alastair nodded and turned his attention to the remaining soldiers who hadn't been taken by the earthquake.

She swallowed hard. She wouldn't ever let on, but the video of her own death would endlessly haunt her. As would Knox's unnatural scream of anguish when he returned for her. With single-minded precision, he'd maimed and killed Don Carlos's men, and then Don Carlos himself. She couldn't say she was shocked or appalled. No, instead she'd felt a large measure of satisfaction hearing the drug lord's bones popping. He'd never hurt another living soul.

Knox's warmth enveloped her from behind. With his cheek against her hair, he asked, "Are we good?"

As if he had to ask! It hurt her heart to think he might be worried about her reaction. For goodness' sake, he'd watched over her and saved her countless times. She hated that the one time he couldn't help should be the reason for his self-torture. And there *would* be self-torture on his part, of that she had little doubt. Instinctively, she knew he heaped too much blame on himself.

She twisted to face him. "Yes. One-hundred percent."

"I thought when you saw—"

She shushed him with a soft kiss. "Don't go there. You're not to blame for the actions of Zhu Lin and Don Carlos. Don't put that upon yourself, Knox. Promise me."

The struggle to absolve himself was written on his face.

With a palm resting on either side of his face, she gave his head a small shake. "Promise."

"I promise," he said gruffly.

"Good. Now let's figure out what to do with all these bodies."

Autumn kicked the closest one. "Are they dead?"

"Just a deep sleep," Spring assured her.

"Too bad." Autumn gave a shrug and delivered a second kick.

"Your whole family is savage," Knox murmured in Spring's ear.

"Yeah, I'm starting to like them."

His bark of laughter caused heads to turn in their direction. She noted the silent approval. In a way, it validated her choice.

23

"*I*'m surprised you allowed one of your own to perish, sister."
Serqet stood on the edge of the clearing, invisible to all but Isis, watching the Thorne sisters pat one another on the back for Spring's successful murder of Zhu Lin. A boiling rage churned below the surface, but she'd never allow anyone to see, especially not her sister, traitorous bitch that she was.

"He was no longer of use to me," Serqet stated. "He'd become obsessed with his own agenda."

Isis glided to her side. "But still, he was one of your line. I'm sorry for your loss."

"Do you think I care for your condolences?" Serqet turned on her. "You, our father Ra's favorite. You, who could do no wrong. You, who spoiled my revenge and had my power stripped from me?"

When her sister didn't step back from the venom in her words, Serqet experienced a smidgeon of respect. Not many would face down her fury, knowing she was as devious as the day was long.

"What I did wasn't out of malice, sister. It was to prevent you from doing what you would later regret."

"I regret nothing except trusting you."

Sadness entered Isis's amber eyes. "How long do you intend to hold on to your hate? All these lost centuries aren't enough?"

"My hate is all that holds me together now. Don't look for the woman I used to be. You stole that from me. Stole from me that which I loved the most."

"And you didn't do the same to me? You didn't orchestrate the death of my husband, Osiris?"

A ping of something long forgotten echoed beneath her breast. Even before Serqet had cursed the piece of jewelry she had intended for her lover to give to his bride, her intentions had never been pure. But Isis had forgiven her for the part she played in Osiris's death, as she had forgiven their brother, Set.

"Knox Carlyle shall die as the Thorne witch's punishment for killing one of my line," she declared. When Isis didn't issue a challenge to the decree, she faced her. "You do not object?"

"If you feel you must take a life, you may take his."

"We are in accord then."

Isis remained silent, her sorrowful gaze locked on the embracing couple.

Serqet stepped in front of Isis's line of sight. "I want your word you will not interfere."

"I will not interfere in his death."

"Good."

"What brings you to my temple, sister?"

Isis stepped into the light and approached her sister, Nephthys, as she lounged during her repast. Where Isis was curvy, Nephthys was willowy, almost ethereal. She wore her mass of loose, black curls piled high upon the crown of her head, letting it partially cascade down her back. Nephthys favored shades of pale coral to give her skin an added glow. Her kohl-lined eyes were the turquoise color of the Caribbean Sea.

As Isis watched, her sister popped a succulent sweet into her mouth. "Gods, I love chocolate!"

Isis chuckled before she turned serious. "I have a favor to ask, sister."

Nephthys rose from her chaise and hugged her. "Didn't I already grant you a great boon when I allowed you to revive your Thorne Witches at will?"

"You did. But this I ask on your behalf. The Carlyles are your descendants. I have news that Serqet plans to take misguided revenge against Knox Carlyle. I ask that you stop her."

"What did he do to upset her?"

"Nothing. She's upset with one of mine: Spring Thorne."

"The one you recently revived?"

"Yes."

"Tell me all."

Isis relayed the generations-long fight between the Désorcelers and the Thornes. She explained how Serqet had created the Désorcelers after her powers had been stripped by Ra. "Their sole purpose is to destroy my family, and now by extension, yours and Set's."

"Show me."

With a nod of deference, Isis glided toward the life-size mirror across from the chaise. A simple swipe of her hand over the surface replayed Serqet's machinations throughout time. "She has schemed and lied to get what she wants. More recently, there was this." Isis fast-forwarded the playback to the day Spring was taken. She allowed the reel of events to continue without interruption until today. "As you can see, Zhu Lin's demise was, without question, justified."

Nephthys nodded thoughtfully. "I'll allow her to take revenge and kill him."

"Sister, you cannot!" The crafty smile on Nephthys face stopped Isis from any further protest. "What is your plan?"

"I'm ruler of death, sister. I have the power to restore life. After she is finished, I will gift him life."

"When? When will you gift him life?"

"After a century or two, when our sister has had a chance to calm down."

Isis stalked to where Nephthys had settled back on her chaise. "You want Knox for your consort!" she charged. "Carlyles and Thornes only love once. If you take him, you will sentence him to a life of misery. Just as you would sentence Spring to that same misery!" When her sister's brow rose in challenge, Isis reined in her temper and sighed. "Of course you will do what you must, but I ask you to remember, they have both been through enough pain for three lifetimes. I beg you, sister, have mercy on their souls."

"I would have a favor of you, then."

"What?"

"The one you call Alastair. I want him for my consort."

"He is not mine to give. I allow all my children choices."

"Ah, but you've asked him to join you, no?"

"I have."

"And you favor him above all others."

It wasn't a question, but Isis nodded anyway. "I favor him," she lied. Her true favorite remained locked in her heart, hidden from the world. Alastair could take care of himself so she need not worry if others targeted him for being the one she favored.

"Why?"

"He's clever and amuses me. His humor and fighting spirit are rivaled by none."

"He has denied you your fondest wish, and yet you still grant him boons. Why?"

"Love is unconditional, sister. You should know that. The affection I hold for him is not sexual in nature. I love him for who he is. As such, I wish him to rule by my side."

"I see." Nephthys sighed and contemplated the tray of chocolates before her. "Then I shall grant your request on the basis of unconditional love."

Tears stung Isis's eyes and gratitude filled her. It had been a long while since there had been any closeness between any of the siblings. Their history had played a part in their separation. But the olive branch Nephthys extended warmed Isis's soul. "Thank you, my beloved sister."

"Come, break your fast with me. There is time enough to save the Carlyle man."

24

"*I* honestly don't know how to spin this." Coop paced the confines of his office. As town sheriff, he saw things in black or white, depending on the letter of the law. More recently, he found himself in the gray area. Currently, he referred to yesterday's incident with Knox's mother.

Knox was profoundly grateful Coop hadn't locked him up on the spot. He understood better than anyone the position he'd thrown his cousin into. There was a dead body on the Thorne estate. That body happened to belong to Marianne Carlyle, the sheriff's aunt. Rules dictated he investigate the murder, but since Coop had discovered he had latent powers, the standard rules didn't apply to their family anymore. But more importantly, she couldn't be buried in the family plot without some type of explanation. Not that Knox was bothered if she wasn't. They could teleport her body to a swamp in Florida for the alligators to eat for all he cared.

"What about a lightning strike?" All heads turned toward Spring who, until now, had let Knox handle the explanations. She shrugged. "That's essentially what it was. Knox fried her ass."

Because the odd desire to laugh overcame him, the man in question ducked his chin and rubbed the center of his forehead. If he didn't hide his humor, he'd come across as an unfeeling bastard. While Knox had stopped caring about his mother as a person a long time ago, he didn't want to seem as if he'd intentionally set out to kill her.

"And how do we explain a lightning strike in the middle of the woods on a perfectly clear day?" Coop snapped.

Knox lifted his head and stared his cousin down. Coop heeded the warning and apologized for his nasty attitude.

"You don't need to explain it," Spring stated in a calm, prim tone. "We're witches."

Without needing to be told, Knox could see the general consensus of the room was that Spring was a few flowers shy of a full bouquet. By the amused gleam in Alastair's eye, Knox suspected her uncle knew where she was going, but he wanted to see if everyone else grasped what she was saying.

She sighed her frustration. "We're witches," she stressed. When the room remained clueless, she threw up her hands. "*Hel-lo! We can conjure the weather.*"

A slow, appreciative smile curled Coop's lips. "Brilliant."

"Of course." Zane smacked himself in the forehead and faced Winnie. "Ready to conjure some storm clouds, babe?"

Winnie winked at her youngest sister. "I can do that." She sent an inquiring glance to the room at large. "Who wants to conjure the rain? Summer? Uncle Alastair?"

Summer rose to her feet. "I'll do it. I'm sure Dad needs to get back and check on Mom."

"I have someone caring for her. She'll be fine for a little longer." Alastair straightened from where he lounged against the corner of Coop's desk. "I'll assist Knox in creating enough lightning strikes to make the storm look believable." He straightened his tie and gazed down at Spring from his imposing height. "Well, done, child. You may not remember, but you're a Thorne through and through."

"I'll accept that as high praise coming from you, Uncle." She gracefully gained her feet. "What happened to Lin's little army?"

Knox shared a look with the men in the room. "We dropped them off in the woods by the monastery. With any luck, they'll freeze."

"What monastery?" Spring glanced around in confusion.

Autumn stepped in with the explanation. "It's in the Himalayan mountains. Keaton and I went there to retrieve one of the artifacts to save Mother. It's where we first met Zhu Lin."

Spring nodded thoughtfully and hung back as the rest of the family filed out the door.

"Are you okay?" Knox wasn't sure what she was thinking or feeling when she went into her quiet, contemplative mode. Her face would maintain a detached air as she studied the people around her. Prior to the loss of her memory, Spring never had that type of expression. She had always been bright, laughing, and curious.

"I'm good." She graced him with a warm smile. "I was wondering if we managed to get the artifact you and I went after."

"No. I don't know if Don Carlos ever had it or if Lin ever received it, but I suspect that Thor's Hammer is lost to us."

She frowned and rubbed a spot under her shirt. "Thor's Hammer? What is that?"

"It's a Mjölnir amulet said to have healing powers. It contains a stone from Odin's ring and was blessed by Thor himself."

"What does it look like?" Spring laid her palm flat against her chest.

"It's rustic really. Some runes carved into metal that resembles an old war hammer. It would have Odin's stone gracing the handle."

Slowly, she drew a necklace from beneath her blouse. "Like this?"

"Jesus, Spring! Where did you find that?" How had she come to possess the necklace? When they'd found her in Cartagena, she'd been only dressed in the gown and... his mind shied away from her death scene. But none of them had taken the time to search the wreckage of her gilded prison.

"I had a dream last night. A goddess named Nephthys came to me and told me to never take it off." She glanced down at the amulet. "Or at least I thought it had been a dream until I woke wearing this."

175

She frowned again. "No wait, that's not what she said. Her exact words were 'Keep this on you at all times. The day will soon come when you will need its power.'"

A warning of that magnitude from a goddess bordered on terrifying. "She didn't say why?"

"No."

He lifted the amulet and studied it a moment. Rudimentary craftsmanship for such a powerful piece. Carefully, he tucked it underneath her clothing. "Don't let anyone know you have this for now."

"I can do that." She squeezed his hand. "Let's go create a storm."

LATER THAT EVENING, MEMBERS OF BOTH FAMILIES GATHERED around the dining table at the Thorne estate. Winnie had insisted on cooking for everyone, and there wasn't an unappreciative person in the lot. Wine and laughter flowed around the table as if no one had a care in the world. Yet, Spring couldn't shake the little niggling sense of unease. Yes, Lin was dead. That was one enemy off their plate, but were more milling about, waiting for their chance to take on the Thornes and Carlyles? It seemed naive to think there weren't. Both families had been around for centuries.

Spring touched the amulet beneath her shirt. She'd read the name Nephthys in the family grimoire, but other than being listed as sister to Isis, that particular goddess had never played into the Thorne family's history. That she'd appear now was curious at best and, at worst, disconcerting.

Before dinner, Spring had done a little more research on the goddess. Wikipedia hadn't turned up much other than Nephthys was known to protect the souls of the dead. How any of this would play out was anyone's guess. She was certainly clueless.

Twice she caught Knox observing her. Although he didn't say a word, his furrowed brow indicated his concern. Other than to cast him a reassuring smile or two, she was at a loss as to how to ease his worry. She was worried enough for the two of them but refused to show it. Knox had been through enough today; he didn't need an over-excited girlfriend on his hands.

Girlfriend. The thought brought her up short, and she couldn't prevent the pleased smile curling her lips. Neither had defined whatever this thing was between them, but the love was alive and thriving.

As if he guessed her train of thought, Knox reached out to her and curled his pinky with hers. They sat that way through the rest of dinner and dessert. Their connection strong and unbreakable. In the sea of uncertainty where Spring lived, Knox was her anchor. *And she was his.*

"I propose a toast."

The group faced Autumn where she stood at the head of the dinner table. The dark purple grape juice in her glass was in deference to her protruding belly. "To our brainy, badass sister. Spring, thank you for ridding the world of Lin. The death of that evil asshat was long overdue."

A few echoed her sentiment with "Hear, hear!"

Spring basked in their praise, once again feeling as if she was part of this family she didn't remember. Tears threatened and her fingers tightened over Knox's. He lifted her hand to drop a kiss on her knuckles, and she became lost in his proud gaze.

"You really were a badass."

"I was, wasn't I?"

"For a minute, you had me worried you might really hate me."

"Am I so different from who I used to be?" It bothered her to think she might be. While she wanted to be closer as a family unit, maybe those around her viewed her as an interloper, a false Spring. Her attention turned to the quick-witted interactions between her siblings and their spouses. They were a solid unit. Each knew they could tease the other and get the expected reaction in return. But from her, they didn't know what they'd get. The exclusion gave her a deep sense of loneliness.

"You're not."

She whipped her head back around to face Knox.

"You're not so different. I don't think your personality was altered with your memories, sweetheart. You're almost exactly the same."

"Then why would you ever believe I'd hate you?"

He shook his head and looked for answers in the chocolate cake before him. It took Knox time to form the words he wanted to say, and Spring waited, watching him push the frosting around and instinctively knowing he'd speak from the heart.

When he finally did, his tone was low and somber. "I learned a long time ago the love doled out to me was conditional, whatever the source. How could I expect yours to be any different? I walked away and left you to your own devices, Spring. It cost you your life."

She ached for him. The loneliness he must've suffered over the years had to have a detrimental effect on his psyche. "No. You went to find a way to get me out, if I'm not mistaken. The rest can't be laid on your shoulders." She gripped his knee. "Besides, you promised."

"Promised?"

"That you wouldn't blame yourself."

"It might take me a little time to sort it out in my head."

"We have time."

Knox opened his mouth to respond, but whatever he would've said was lost when Summer slapped her hand on the table. "Why the long faces? We should be celebrating."

"What do you suggest? Dancing?" Coop teased.

"Exactly that!" She glanced at her sisters. "Who's up for a little bouncing around in Nashville?"

Spring leaned in close to Knox. "What's bouncing around?"

Autumn's wicked laughter rang out. "Little sister, we have so much left to teach you!"

"Going to bars. Doing some dancing and drinking," Knox answered her. "It's been a long day. Are you up for it?"

Spring looked into the sparkling eyes of her sisters and then at the more laid-back expressions of their significant others. It seemed

178

the men were inclined to indulge the women in whatever they wanted to do.

"Yes. I believe I am."

A cheer went up, and Autumn grabbed her by her hand. "Come on, let's figure out what to wear." With a stern look at Keaton, she said, "Make sure your mom is okay to watch Chloe before we just take off." She fixed a stern eye on Zane and Coop. "You two are on clean-up duty."

"What about me?" Knox shot her an engaging grin.

"You're fine the way you are, good looking."

"He gets out of more work that way." Coop lobbed a spoonful of potatoes at Knox's head.

Spring gasped and tried to choke off her horrified laughter as the mashed potatoes dripped down Knox's face and landed in a soft plop on his slacks.

"Oh, shit." She thought maybe it was Winnie who swore.

"If you boys are going to have a food fight, your asses better be cleaning up the mess when you're done. Keep in mind those chairs in the corner are late seventeenth-century—*ohmygod!*" Autumn's speech was abruptly cut off.

Spring sat frozen to the spot as Autumn wiped off a blob of potatoes from her forehead. Her older sister turned a violent shade of red, and Spring couldn't be sure, but she thought maybe steam had escaped from her sister's ears.

Knox proved he was smarter and faster than everyone else by scooping Spring up and teleporting to her bedroom. "You don't want to be there for the bloodbath. Autumn will kill Coop, Summer will kill Autumn, and then Keaton will be forced to avenge her. The whole family is about to become unraveled." He flicked a finger down the remaining potatoes on his face and licked his finger. "Damn, your sister can cook. I hope Winnie makes it through the war."

Laughter bubbled up inside her, and Spring was certain this was the first real joy she experienced since waking. "Do they do this often?"

"Often enough."

"And you're smart enough to always make good your escape?"

"Someone needs to live to tell the tale." He licked his finger again. "Do you think the secret ingredient is garlic? I'm certain I taste real butter."

This playful, funny side of Knox appealed to her. Unashamedly, he stood there—all six-feet-one of pure brawn—hiding and cracking jokes.

"Some might think this is cowardly," she taunted.

"Some might face the Carlyle wrath for questioning my bravery." His hot eyes promised retribution of the slur against his manhood.

"Yet somehow, I'm not afraid." And she wasn't. The man she'd come to know in the short time since he'd shown up in her garden wasn't the type of guy to hurt her. "But you're welcome to do your worst."

"She creates one major earthquake, and she thinks she's a match for me. Pfft."

Her laughter was pure wicked. "Oh, I think she's more than a match for you."

Knox's grin flashed, and he dove for the bed she was sitting on. Having anticipated his move, Spring teleported to the pink chaise in the corner of her room.

As she watched, he rolled onto his back and tucked a pillow under his head. His shirt rose and provided a glimpse of his perfect six-pack. She found it impossible to look away from the smooth, tan expanse of skin that narrowed to a V and disappeared into the waist-band of his belted pants.

Just when she would've taunted him a second time—or maybe jumped his bones—a knock sounded at the door, and Autumn peeked her head in. "I've dispatched those weakling Carlyles. I'll be back in five minutes to help you pick out an outfit after I've changed." Her sparkling amber eyes darted between Spring and Knox. "Unless you want Studly to do it. Then I can give you about a half hour or so."

Knox rose. "Studly needs more than a half hour to do *it* properly. I'll make sure the cleanup downstairs has been done right." He pulled Spring to her feet and kissed her, light and lingeringly. "I'd love it if you wore something short and sexy."

"We'll come up with an outfit that would make a man sit up and beg."

He groaned at Autumn's response, evoking a giggle from Spring.

"You are a cruel woman, Autumn Thorne-Carlyle, but I adore you for catering to my inner pervert," he told her sister.

"Don't I have a say in what I wear?" Spring asked haughtily.

"No," Autumn and Knox chorused.

Knox cast a quick, discerning eye over her body and snapped his fingers. In his hand was a stunning green dress. From the lack of material, Spring feared it might not cover all her assets.

He leaned in and bussed her forehead. "All kidding aside, if you choose to dress as conservatively as a nun, that's *always* your call. But I think this might work well with your beautiful eyes if you decide you like it and want to wear it tonight."

Spring and Autumn watched as he sauntered out of the room, admiring the way his ass filled out his gray slacks. They sighed in unison.

"Marry that man, sister. Marry him like yesterday, then tell me how amazing the sex is, because somehow, I know he has the moves."

Laughter exploded from Spring. Her sister's pregnancy hormones were alive and well, trying to escape.

*W*ithin fifteen minutes, the women were laughing as they descended the staircase. They made an incredible picture. Autumn wore a fluid, gold, haltered maxi dress gathered high under her breasts. The empire waist allowed a cascade of material to cover her baby bump. With each step, her shapely leg played peekaboo through the side slit that ran to mid-thigh. For a heavily pregnant woman, she was sexy as hell.

Summer emphasized her compact, curvy body in a blue sequined mini dress with a plunging neckline. Her outfit guaranteed Coop was going to have fun running off lecherous men tonight.

Winnie was decked out in an off-the-shoulder glimmering amethyst top and billowing silver palazzo pants. Her own baby bump was barely visible in the flowing outfit. The combination of dark hair, rosy complexion, and the long lean graceful lines of her body made her an incredible sight.

Yes, each woman was beautiful in their own right, but Knox's attention was drawn to Spring. With her upswept, tawny hair and wide, happy smile, she was loveliness personified. Wearing the backless jade mini dress he'd conjured, she was simply stunning. His body was quick to react to the sexy expanse of skin, and he found himself shoving his hands in his pants pockets to disguise the building thickness in his groin.

She paused two steps from the bottom. A soft, shy smile graced her lips, but her twinkling eyes belied her innocent expression. No doubt about it, she understood her effect on him. More than anything, he wanted to tell the group to go without them. Then he could rush her right back up the stairs to make love to her until dawn and possibly beyond.

He met her at the staircase and simply stared.

"Hi." Spring's light greeting wrapped around his insides and wrung him out. She was genuinely happy to see him. Somehow, against the odds, Spring had woken, taken one look at him, and fallen in love. This was their second time around, and he'd gotten a fresh slate. He didn't plan to make any mistakes if he could help it.

"Hi. You ready to party?"

"I think after today, we have a reason to celebrate, don't you?"

"I do."

"One thing first." Spring turned to her family. "We'll meet you outside in just a minute."

They received a few curious looks, but no one objected.

Knox didn't know where she was going with this, but he'd indulge her if that's what she wanted. "What is it, sweetheart?"

"I needed to clarify a few things first."

His stomach flipped over. Maybe he'd gotten it wrong. Maybe she hadn't fallen in love at first sight like Thorne lore foretold. Maybe he'd come on too fast and strong. "Like what?"

"You and me, are we officially a couple?"

"That depends."

Her dark frown thrilled him.

"Depends on what?"

He asked the hardest question he'd ever had to ask. "Do you want to be? No expectations of the past, no feeling as if you owe me anything. Just *you* wanting to be with *me*."

"When I saw you in the garden for the first time, I sensed you were someone important to me. Your light hurt my eyes, it seemed so bright. And when you touched me, when you spoke, there was a sense of familiarity." She waved a hand. "Not that I remembered you; I didn't. But in my world where everything is topsy-turvy, you make me feel secure."

Refusing to allow hope inside, he asked again, "Do you want to be a couple, Spring?"

"I do."

"Good. Because I'm yours as long as you'll have me."

"Earlier tonight, I had the thought that I might be considered your girlfriend..." She shrugged.

"You're so much more than that, sweetheart. You're my everything."

He appreciated that her mouth was level with his. It made kissing her that much easier. Dipping his head a mere inch, he paused to meet her gaze. "You'll always be my everything," he whispered just before connecting his lips to hers.

Like all she'd mastered since awaking, Spring seemed to excel at kissing. Her lips parted, and her tongue zipped across his lower lip, then snuck in to caress his. The steady, sensual stroke and suck shot straight to his groin.

The door swung wide behind them. "Oh, good grief. If I knew you were only after a little slap and tickle, I wouldn't have left you two alone."

Autumn smacked Knox upside his head.

"What are you, my chaperone?" Spring snapped as she rubbed his abused skull. "Last I checked, I was a consenting adult."

"My little flower has grown thorns. It makes a big sister proud." Autumn pressed a palm to her heart and batted her lashes as if to stem off tears. In the blink of an eye, she became all business. "Now get your asses in gear. I was promised a night on the town." She patted her protruding belly. "In another month or two, I won't be able to go anywhere but the Piggly Wiggly for pampers."

THE NIGHT WAS MAGICAL. FROM THE MOMENT THE GROUP DESCENDED on the booming club in Nashville, the family as a whole laughed and danced. Periodically, they forced Autumn to take it easy for Keaton's sake. The poor man looked as if he believed his wife would have their child on the dance floor.

Spring, out of breath from dancing four straight songs in a row, held up a hand. "I need a drink," she shouted to Knox over the thumping bass.

He smiled and nodded his agreement, although he didn't look winded in the least. She had to admire his stamina. Or at least she hoped to later that night when she intended to put a whole different set of moves on him.

Coop stopped them with a hand on her arm. "I need to take a break, too." He looked to Knox. "Switch partners for a bit? The Energizer Bunny here is still going strong."

Summer laughed and accepted Knox's hand. He spun her and proceeded to tear up the dance floor with her as his partner.

"I'm the youngest in the lot, and yet I can't keep up. Where the hell do they get the energy?" Spring asked.

"Beats the hell out of me. Let's get that drink and hang our heads in shame." They pushed their way to the bar and waited until one of the harried bartenders leaned across the wood surface with an ear cocked in their direction. "Margarita on the rocks for her, and an Imperial IPA for me, please."

Once they had their drinks, they made their way to the table where a winded Winnie was being fanned by Zane. She glanced up at their arrival and grinned. "I'm glad I'm not the only out of shape one in the group."

"Out of shape?" Coop growled. "Your sister is relentless. Besides, I have to conserve energy for later tonight. I'll be doing the bulk of the work."

Summer's laugh rang from behind them. "Bulk of the work? Puleeazzz!"

Coop's unabashed grin flashed as he swept her in his arms and kissed her. Spring loved watching them interact. Their love was pure and sweet, with a spark of sassy, just like Summer.

Mind on love, Spring's eyes drifted to Knox, who stood to the side. Their eyes locked, and she drew in a deep breath from the sheer force of the emotion she witnessed in his soft gaze. She stepped into him and rested her cheek against his chest.

"Ready to call it a night?"

"After this drink, I think so." Spring glanced around. "How about everyone else?"

The group as a whole looked ready to depart. Five minutes later, when Autumn and Keaton strolled up hand-in-hand, they all headed for the exit. The family laughed and traded good-natured jibes as they strolled down the side alley by the club.

They'd just rounded the corner when a prickle of awareness struck Spring. A quick glance around showed nothing. Maybe she was jumping at shadows, but the sensation was real all the same. Like a million little beetles crawling under her skin.

Knox, attuned to her every need of late, asked, "What is it, sweetheart?"

"I'm not sure. A bad feeling."

Her unease transferred to the others, and each of them searched the darkness around them. Knox stepped in front of her, providing a shield against whatever might be lurking in the night.

After a moment or two, everyone relaxed, and Knox spun to face her. "Nothing seems amiss." He leaned down to rub his nose to hers. "You okay?"

"I'll be happier when we're home in bed," she admitted.

His grin turned decidedly wicked. "Me, too." Shifting to whisper in her ear, he said, "Balls deep, buried inside of you."

A gasping laugh escaped her. "That's rude, crude, and socially unacceptable! Your place or mine?"

His bark of laughter was cut short, and his body jerked against hers. The happy light taking up residence in his gaze gave way to surprise, then regret. Finally, the light died from his eyes altogether as he sagged against her.

It happened in an instant, but she was sure she'd replay this horrific moment for the remainder of her days at this torturous slow-motioned pace. Hysteria clouded her brain as she fell under his heavy weight. "Knox!" Disbelief warred with terror. She couldn't seem to catch her breath to scream. The chaos around her was muted as she stared down into Knox's beloved, still face. "No! No! No!" She couldn't seem to say anything else. Couldn't seem to grasp what was happening or form a coherent thought.

Rough hands grabbed her and tried to lift her from where she rocked back and forth.

"Spring, we're not safe here. We have to move, love," Coop urged. "I'll come back for him. I promise."

"Go!" she screamed. "Just go! I—" A warm throb started mid-chest. Her hand flew to the spot and encountered the shape of the amulet underneath her dress.

"What the hell is that glowin—" Coop's question was cut off as his body was slammed backward into the wall. His hand flew to his shoulder and came away coated in blood. "Jesus! Everyone, get the fuck out of this alley. Now!"

Another bullet slammed into his leg and took him down. Summer screamed.

Sound stopped. No traffic clamor, no low thud of music, no distant sirens, or noise of any kind penetrated the night.

"Teleport before time snaps back," Winnie shouted. *"Hurry."*

Spring wrapped herself around Knox and visualized her garden. Her cells heated to the point of burning, but when she opened her eyes, the two of them were beneath the tree where she'd first seen him.

The amulet was setting fire to her skin. A memory penetrated her grief-stricken fog. *"Keep this on you at all times. The day will soon come when you need its power."*

Wasting no time, she tore open Knox's shirt. The initial bullet had pierced his heart. How she was expected to heal the wound and bring Knox back was a mystery. Acting on instinct, she removed the amulet and placed it over the wound. "Goddess hear my plea and assist me in my time of need. Restore what was taken from me."

The runes carved into the small sphere glowed a fiery red, and a single beam of light shot through the inky night, straight toward the sky. Once again, she gave rein to her instincts and curled against his side. "Come back to me, my love. Please, come back to me." She pressed her lips to his and infused all the love she felt for him into the gentle kiss. "Please, Knox. Don't leave me in a world without you."

"Spring!" The sound of hurried footsteps thumped against the path. "Spring! Where are you, sister?"

Spring didn't have the energy to answer Autumn. Didn't have the will to do more than rest her head on Knox's oddly still-warm chest. She swiped at the tears rolling down her face and touched the ancient disc. "For all the good you did us," she whispered.

The light on the amulet's runes shifted to a deep amethyst. Spring frowned and sat up just as Autumn reached her.

"What the hell is that?"

"Thor's Hammer." She shook her head at her own stupidity. "I've been praying to the wrong entity."

For once, Autumn seemed at a loss for words.

"Have you ever heard of a book called the *Chronicles of Wōden,* sister?"

"I can't say that I have." Autumn moved closer and bent over her as far as her bulbous belly would allow and placed a hand on her shoulder. "Let us bring him to the house now, Spring." She spoke as if Spring were out of her mind with grief. As if she were guarding a body that no longer needed protection.

Spring shoved her hand away, enraged to her very core. "Don't talk to me like a mental patient. I had enough of that when I first woke. I can save him. I just need that damned book!" Inhaling a deep breath, she forced herself to calm. "Nephthys came to me in a dream. She told me what I needed to do, and until this minute, I'd forgotten. I need that book, Autumn. Someone in the family has it or she wouldn't have mentioned it, I'm certain."

Indecision was plainly written on Autumn's troubled face. "Nash or Alastair, *maybe*. I've never seen anything in Father's library by that name."

"It would be written in the Norse language."

Autumn's dark eyes narrowed in thought. "I think I know which one you're referring to. Be right back." She teleported, leaving Spring alone with Knox.

The light from the Mjölnir amulet dulled, but remained a soft pulsing purple, and she worried they might be losing their window to bring him back to life. "Hurry, sister," she urged on a whisper.

The plants and trees around her picked up on her distress. The roots of the old oak vibrated beneath her. She welcomed the tree's attempt to help her. If only she could utilize all the magic her garden contained. She jerked upright and smacked herself on the center of her forehead. Of course! The Gods of the Old World believed life was contained within the elements around them. For that matter, Spring and her sisters did, too. They were elemental witches for crying out loud.

"My beautiful babies, I need your assistance." All the trees and plants in the garden leaned toward with rapt attention. "Once I have the spell, I will need your magic."

The quiver of the plants and ground signaled the agreement of the living foliage around her.

"Thank you."

The atmosphere took on weight, and a crack echoed through the garden. Alastair stepped through a seam in space with another blond man by his side. The two looked enough alike to be brothers.

"This is your cousin, Nash," Alastair said by way of greeting. He squatted beside Knox's lifeless body. Other than a tightening of his mouth, he revealed no other emotion. "Nash and I will assist you with the spell. My sister, GiGi is with Winnie healing Coop. The shooter struck an artery in his leg. Autumn should be here any moment with the book you requested."

As if on cue, her sister reappeared. Excitement radiated from

Autumn, and she waved the old, leather-bound journal as if she'd won it at the town fair. "I've got it!"

Nash grabbed the book. *"Illuminate,"* he murmured. The space around him lit up and provided the light he needed to see the writing. He thumbed through the pages with a speed that made Spring's head dizzy. "We need an air element."

"I'll grab Winnie." Autumn was off again.

Spring smoothed back the shoulder-length blond hair from Knox's face and neck. "What else to do we need, cousin?"

"According to this, we need broadleaf plantain, comfrey, and burdock root."

She was loathe to leave Knox's side. With a hard look in Alastair's direction, she said, "I'll be right back."

He nodded his understanding. If she came back and they'd moved Knox, there would be hell to pay. She flung open the door to her workshop. She gathered the necessary plants in live and dried herb form. Her return coincided with Winnie's arrival.

"What do you need me to do?" Winnie asked.

"Stand here," Nash directed. "Alastair, you're here." He took a few steps to his right. "Autumn, right here." He then moved to take the northernmost spot of the circle he'd created.

"What about me?" Spring asked. She needed to be useful. Needed to have at least a small part in the ceremony.

"You need to pull from the Earth from beside Knox. The rest of us will do our part to create the circle and pull from the elements." He glanced around. "Everyone be ready. Spring, make a paste of the broadleaf, comfrey, and burdock. Then place it over the wounds in the front and back."

Once she did as he'd instructed, she set the amulet into the paste. "Like this?"

"Exactly so." He turned another page. His lips moved in time to what he read as if he was memorizing the words. With a short nod, he closed the book, and placed it on the ground at his feet. "Here we go. Repeat after me..."

Spring had no idea what was being said. She repeated the Old

Norse spell with the exact pronunciation and inflection as Nash, trusting he knew what the hell he was doing. All the members of their circle joined the chant.

"Pull from your elements and direct it toward the amulet," Nash shouted over the rising storm-force winds Winnie had created.

Spring placed one hand over the root of the oak and held the other about six inches above the amulet. "Odin, I trust in your magic," she whispered as she drew the healing energy from the earth. The ground rumbled and lightning cut across the night sky. One by one, her cells fired within her until she felt as if she were a giant fireball ready to explode. Still she drew from her garden as her beloved plants gave their life source for her cause.

She stared so hard at Knox's chest, she was afraid she imagined the movement she saw. His chest expanded a second time, and his mouth fell open. The light emitting from the amulet was now a blinding blue-white, and its heat seared into her palm. Although tears of pain raced down her cheeks, she held strong. Twigs, leaves, and dirt whipped around and stung where they struck.

The four elements were frenzied, circling and plunging into the disc beneath her hand. She wanted to scream her agony, but she bit her lip. If she let loose her tortured cry, she would kill the struggling garden around her.

The chanting stopped, and as one, the elements fused and slammed into the amulet. The light went out. For one terrifying moment, she thought they'd failed. When a guttural cry was wrenched from Knox's lips, she bowed her head and allowed silent tears to fall. That life-affirming scream was the sweetest sound she had ever heard.

For the span of five heartbeats, her family looked on, but then they all surged forward. Autumn and Winnie wrapped her in their loving arms and cried their relief alongside her. Alastair clasped a hand on his son's shoulder before he squatted beside Knox. "Welcome back, boy," he said softly as he smoothed a hand over Knox's head. "Welcome back."

Alastair helped Autumn to her feet and hugged each sister in turn.

"I can't thank you enough," Spring said to him, her throat raspy and sore. "Can you help me transport him to my room so I can have Aunt GiGi take a look at him?"

"Of course."

She faced Nash and hugged him. "My plants need help."

He gently turned her palm over. The shapes of the runes were burned into her flesh. "So do you."

"I can wait. Knox and my garden need the most attention right now."

"I'll take care of it." He hugged her a second time. "Go on."

"Thank you."

26

*K*nox woke to the smell of cool mint and rolled toward the source. A sharp tug of discomfort pulled at the muscles on the left side of his chest and back. He grunted at the pain but continued to seek Spring's scent. When his nose connected with her hair, he breathed a sigh of relief.

He wrapped an arm around her and drew her back against him, spooning her. She murmured incoherent words and wiggled her ass to get comfortable. Had he felt the least bit human, he'd have been aroused. As it was, he was content to hold her and wonder what the hell he drank last night that gave him this type of hangover.

A soft knock sounded at the door. He mentally cursed whoever was on the other side. It seemed whenever he finally had Spring to himself, someone was always interrupting.

The door cracked open, and Winnie peeked her head inside. When she saw him, awake and scowling in her direction, she grinned. "Welcome back."

"Did I go somewhere?"

Her gaze turned somber. "You did. My sister was having none of it and pulled you back."

"Would it be awful of me to say, I don't know what the hell you're talking about?"

"I'd be surprised if you remembered anything, in all honesty." She stepped farther into the room and approached the bed with the tray she held in her hands. "I brought you some herbal tea and a hearty breakfast. I'd hoped that after a thirty-two hour nap you'd be awake."

"Thirty-two…" He jackknifed into a sitting position and grabbed at his chest. He glanced down to where the skin above his heart was slightly puckered and red. "What the hell happened?"

Spring rolled in his direction and placed a hand against his lower back. "You were shot."

He stared down at her, aghast and unable to pick one question from the seemingly hundreds crowding his brain. One word stuck. "Shot?"

Tears sprang into her distraught eyes and leaked into the hair at her temples.

"Shot?" He rubbed his chest again. "Through the chest?"

"Through your heart," Winnie said softly as she rested a comforting hand on Spring's shoulder.

Wildly, with no thought for himself, he reached for Spring's hand. "But you're all right? You weren't hurt?"

"No." The sisters shared a glance.

"Who?" Had one of his cousins been injured? Or, Goddess forbid, died?

Spring sat up and scooted to rest her back against the headboard. "Coop was shot in the shoulder and in the leg when he tried to get to me." She swiped at the tears on her cheeks with the back of her hand. "GiGi and Summer treated him. He's going to be okay. I promise."

Although the proof could be felt beneath his fingertips, Knox found it difficult to wrap his mind around what they had told him. He tried to clear away the fuzz clouding his brain and remember the night in question. The last thing he recalled was teasing Spring. "You called me rude, crude, and socially unacceptable." Rubbing the place between his brows, he tried to recall her next words. "I can't remember what else you said."

Color lit Spring's face, and she slid a quick, sidelong glance at her sister before she cleared her throat. "I asked your place or mine."

A bubble of laughter tried to work its way free. Her embarrassment in the face of the fact that he was lying naked in her bed was —*wait!* He glanced down and secured the covers tighter around his hips. Goddess! He was naked in Spring's bed!

Winnie cackled, wicked and knowing. "I was wondering when he'd realize his beautiful backside was showing."

He gave her a pointed glare. "You're engaged to be married. You shouldn't be salivating over another man's *backside*."

Both women giggled.

"When did he become so uptight?"

Spring bit her lip to hold back her laughter and turned over-bright eyes toward him. "I can't be certain, but I suspect always."

"Go ahead and laugh it up, ladies. But I'd better never catch you admiring another man's *backside* in this lifetime, Spring Thorne."

"Only yours, my darling man." She gave a tug of the covers at his hip. "Now give us a little peek."

"You've both had all the peeks you're going to get for the time being," he growled.

"Does that mean we'll get more peeks later?" Winnie asked, the mischief clear in her blue eyes.

"You! Leave the food and get."

"I don't know..." she hedged. "I feel like I need some type of payment for all the hard work I've put into making your breakfast."

"I am not going to flash my ass!"

"How about your front?" Spring suggested.

"I'm not hearing this right now." Knox swirled his hand and closed the door of the ensuite bathroom. "You two are incorrigible." With a simple snap of his fingers, he teleported into the bathroom. Their hysterical laughter could be heard through the wooden panel door. The sound was music to his ears. Knox smiled, even as he leaned heavily against the counter for support.

With a flip of the light switch, he stared at his pale complexion in the mirror. Christ, he looked bad. Dark circles rested heavily under his eyes, and his cheeks had taken on a hollowed out appearance. His gaze dropped to the closed wound on his chest. *Shot through the heart.* How had Spring brought him back? He didn't know a single witch or warlock that powerful.

Other than body aches and a serious need to relieve his bladder, he felt physically fine. No weakness in his arms or legs. No over-powering fatigue. He wouldn't question the blessing bestowed upon him. But if his cousins hadn't already found out who ambushed their group on the alley, he would make it his mission, even if it was the last thing he did. For now, he had to take care of his most pressing need.

Spring picked at the food her sister had left them. It had been a relief when Knox finally moved this morning. When he'd remained in the same position for the entire duration of his sleep, she'd become worried. And when she refused to leave his side, her sisters were kind enough to bring her food at regular intervals.

The bathroom door opened to reveal Knox dressed in a T-shirt and loose pajama bottoms. He padded barefoot to the bed and sprawled next to her.

"You okay?" he asked, resting a warm hand on her knee.

Wasn't it just like the Knox she'd come to know to worry about her? "I'm not sure. It all happened so fast, and I freaked the fuck out." She stroked a finger down his scarred cheek. His glamour spell had fallen away upon his death. Spring didn't feel the need to hide his old wound from the others, although now that he was awake, he might not be too happy she hadn't. "I didn't think to hide your scar."

Knox captured her fingers and kissed the tips. "I don't care. What can you tell me about the shooting?"

She outlined coming out of the club, their saucy teasing, and the second-by-second details of the incident itself. There were times she had to stop and center herself, but she managed to relay the whole night.

"I've heard other witches and warlocks talk about visiting the Otherworld after they'd died. I don't remember any of it." He shook his head and snagged a hunk of bacon from the plate. "What do you think it means?"

"I don't know. I don't remember my time there either."

"True, but Isis said you'd experience a reset and that was to be expected. But I still remember everything leading up to the shooting."

"Did you want to forget?" It had never occurred to her that he might want to start over as she had done. Maybe what had happened to her was a detriment to their relationship? Was it possible Knox viewed her as damaged despite what he'd told her?

He glanced up sharply. "No. I'd never want to forget you or a second of our time before or after your... memory loss."

She was certain he intended to say death. "I think the universe has it in for us."

"It would seem like, huh? I'm glad we have powerful magic on our side."

"Here." She handed him the tray. "Eat up. I need a shower."

"Need someone to scrub your back?"

The hopeful expression on his face made her laugh. "You need to rest. You've only been back in the land of the living for a day and a half."

"Spoilsport."

"You know it." She stroked a trembling hand over his thick hair. "I was so scared."

Knox set the tray aside and tucked her against his chest. "Hear that?" His heart beat a steady rhythm. "I'm fine. Thanks to you, sweetheart, I'm alive and well. Thank you."

"One thing became clear to me; I don't want to go on without you."

"I felt the same way, you know."

She lifted her head to gaze into his serious face but remained quiet, waiting for him to elaborate.

"When you died…" Knox inhaled deeply, and Spring understood the urge. "When you died and Isis told me you didn't want to come back, I begged her to take my life."

"Ohmygod! Knox, you didn't tell me that!"

"I wasn't proud of my weakness." When she tried to sit up, he pulled her back to him and rested his cheek on the crown of her head. "I never want to be without you. I know it's a lot to lay on you so soon, but there you have it."

"No, I get it. It's like the other night. When I couldn't bring you back on my own with the amulet, I was devastated. The future was suddenly so bleak. How was I expected to go on?"

He gave a harsh chuckle. "We're a sad pair."

"We should probably make a pact to not die for at least a good eighty years or so."

"Sounds like a great plan."

They held onto the other in silence. The growling of Knox's stomach drove them apart.

"I'm going to inhale all this food and conjure a whole buffet to fill this empty pit of mine while you grab a shower."

"Coop is across the hall if you want to conjure your table of food in there. I'm sure he'd be happy to see you." She leaned in to kiss him again.

"I adore you and your clever ideas." Knox paused in reaching for the remaining bacon. "I thought you were a vegetarian? Why did Winnie bring meat?"

She paused on her way to the bathroom and spun back to face him. "She's been bringing it with every meal in case you woke up. What can I say? My sister is an optimist."

"Maybe I *should* have rewarded her with a look at my ass."

Spring snorted as she backed toward the bathroom. "Yeah, believe me, she got an eyeful."

"I'm going to die of embarrassment now."

"Nope! No dying remember? Besides, you can trust me when I

say, you have absolutely nothing to be embarrassed about. Your ass is a world class, Grade-A, prime cut."

"You're rude, crude, and socially unacceptable. And when I get back from checking on Coop, we can decide on your bedroom or mine."

Happiness filled her, and Spring laughed all the way to the shower.

27

*K*nox knocked on the door across the hall and entered when Coop's voice boomed out a greeting.

"Hey, man."

"Hey."

He studied Coop and noted his cousin looked as healthy as ever. "You don't look like someone who's been shot."

"I can't say the same about you, cuz. You look a little pale. How are you feeling?"

"I literally just woke up for the first time a half hour ago."

Coop's face went solemn. "Yeah, well, you scared us all."

Because Knox was still a little sore, he sat at the foot of the bed and rested back against one of the four posters. "Any clue as to who was behind this?"

"Not a one. It's terrifying to think we've attracted another enemy."

"Is it possible this was just a random shooting, like the ones sweeping the whole nation?"

A frown and shrug was Coop's answer.

"If we have attracted another enemy, so to speak, the questions remain: who, why, and when?"

"I don't know, but now that you're back with us, we need to call a family meeting. I'm hoping the big cheese himself might know more."

"Alastair?"

"Yeah. He's always had an in with Isis. Maybe he can tap into her wealth of knowledge."

Coop's idea had merit. Knox wanted payback. Whoever had put Spring and her sisters in such terrible jeopardy needed to face a reckoning. Preferably soon. "Do you think I was targeted specifically? Or at least Spring and I were?"

"Yes."

He cast Coop a sharp glance and met his steady regard head on. "Explain."

"I wasn't shot until I went to help her. I think you, and possibly Spring, were the targets, and I got in the way of the bullets meant for her." Coop rubbed his shoulder. "It makes me wonder if someone from Esteban's camp survived."

"I don't see how they could have. I obliterated that whole organization in the days following…" Christ, he still couldn't say the words. Even the image of Spring lying there on the floor cut through him like a damned knife. "This feels different somehow. More personal. If I had to guess, I'd say it was someone attached to Lin."

Coop's head came up from where he'd been probing his healed leg wound. "I hadn't thought of that. I'd just assumed everyone hated him as much as we did and they might be happy that rat bastard is gone."

"I could be off base, but like I said, it feels personal."

"Then we definitely need to talk to Alastair. He's the expert on all things Zhu Lin related."

Knox nodded and slowly rose to his feet. "I'd intended to conjure a buffet of food for us. I'm craving a steak so badly; I feel like I could eat an entire cow."

Coop laughed. "It's close to lunchtime. Let's call Keaton and Zane to join us. Should we meet here or at our place?"

"Here is fine. I can't imagine the Thornes will want to be excluded from the conversation."

"Yeah, Summer would skin me alive."

"You have it so rough."

Coop grinned, and it was clear to see how much he adored his girlfriend.

"When are you going to stop milking your gunshot wounds?"

"Never. Do you know what kind of TLC I've been getting? I—"

Footsteps sounded outside the bedroom door, and, without warning, Coop grabbed his shoulder and moaned just as Summer sailed into the room. Coop, the damned faker, played it up as she fluttered about, fluffing pillows and touching his face.

Knox opened his mouth to reveal his cousin's scam when Summer shot him a wink over Coop's blond head. Seemed like she had everything well in control.

"I'll see you downstairs, if you think you can make it," he told Coop dryly.

"I'll try my damnedest. I may need Summer to lean on."

"Bullshit," Knox coughed into his hand.

Summer's musical laughter filled the room. "More like feel up. It's amazing how he can't seem to find my shoulder for support, but that hand of his zeroes in on my bo—"

Coop clamped a hand over her mouth. "I'm sure Knox doesn't want to hear about our trials and tribulations."

"I tried to warn you a year ago that he was a trial," Knox told her. He shuffled his way to the door. "See you downstairs in fifteen. If you can't cop a decent feel in that time, there's no hope for you, Coop."

Behind him, Knox heard the sound of Coop tackling Summer to the bed. He grinned and closed the door on her giggles. His cousin was well and truly recovered from the shooting.

"NOW THAT THE GANG'S ALL HERE…" PRESTON THORNE STOOD AND tapped his water glass with his fork.

The overhead chandelier caught his dark auburn hair and made it gleam. Spring could almost imagine she saw his fire element flaming to life within those strands. This man was her father. He should've been her rock. Yet, he was still a stranger to her in so many ways. But when Preston cleared his throat, Spring saw a softer, more human side of him and not the stern, autocratic man he appeared to be.

"We've had an eventful year. My brother Alastair returned to the fold, for which I am extremely grateful." He nodded toward the silent blond man by his side. "Summer moved away and developed a thriving practice and a beautiful sanctuary for her exotic collection of misfits." His sunny smile showed he meant no harm. "Autumn and Keaton found their way back to each other after nine long years, and they have a bouncing baby boy on the way." Tears gleamed in his eyes as he looked down at his firstborn child. "You're one helluva fighter and always stand for the underdog. I'm proud of you, darling girl." He shifted his attention to Winnie. "Winnie, what can I say? You are the spitting image of your mother. Lovely both inside and out. Your courage and bravery when facing down Zhu Lin…" His mouth tightened and he nodded, as if he hoped she'd understand his unspoken sentiment.

His penetrating amber eyes turned to Spring, and she gulped. "And my youngest, Spring. You are the family jewel. You sparkle and shine like the brightest of diamonds. Your fierceness and determination are unmatched, except perhaps by the man by your side. I have never seen two people fight to save one another the way you two have fought for each other. Not Lin, not memory loss, and not death itself has kept you apart." He gave her a half-smile and shook his head in wonder. "Maybe we should have all recognized your determination early on. You knew your mind and went after it. Poor Knox didn't stand a chance."

Knox hooked his pinky through hers. "I'm certainly glad she persevered."

"You are a powerful duo and stronger together. I hope you will always remain so. Your love is one for the rest of us to aspire to." He raised his glass. "To Spring, thank you for removing Zhu Lin from the chessboard."

"To Spring!" the family cheered.

Pleasure, and something resembling pride, filled her. From the time she'd reawakened from death, Spring had only wanted to fit in. Wanted to have the awful pressure of expectation taken off of her. It seemed she'd achieved that and more. She'd earned their respect and love.

"I still have one more thing to take care of," she said aloud. "I intend to find whoever shot Knox and Coop, then make them pay."

"There's the brilliant, bloodthirsty niece I know and love." Alastair laughed approvingly and raised his whiskey glass. "Give 'em hell, child."

Uncomfortable in the spotlight and unsure how to handle the sudden praise, she changed the subject. "Did anyone learn anything? The local news reports? Police stations? Carrier pigeon?"

"Whoever it is, the person is protected by magic," Preston informed her.

"How do you know?"

"Because even with the power of three Thornes, we've been unable to bring up the events surrounding that night. It was as if the shooter was cloaked. I have no doubt it was intentional with Knox as the target, I just don't understand why."

"Who has stronger magic than a Thorne witch or warlock?" she asked. She suspected she knew, but she wanted confirmation that only a God or Goddess could set about protecting the shooter from discovery.

Alastair immediately understood her reasoning. Slowly, he nodded. "Only a Goddess."

"Do you think Isis had something to do with this? Did she want to undo my rebirth?"

"It's not her style." Alastair sipped his drink and gazed off into the distance. "Or at least not *hers* anyway. I wonder if another might feel differently."

Without another word, he stood and headed for the stairs. From her vantage point, Spring noted he took the steps two at a time. She shared a meaningful look with her siblings, and they all raced for the attic.

"Whose do you think it is, Uncle?" As Spring approached, Alastair thumbed through their family grimoire. It was funny how they'd all taken that ancient book for granted. The leather still protected the worn parchment pages after hundreds and hundreds of years. Yet, they all used the book almost daily, never sparing a thought to the sturdiness of their spell bible.

"Serqet."

She nodded and stopped his hands. With the edge of her fingernail, she zeroed in on the section concerning the history of the Gods and Goddesses. "Anything you'd find on her would be here." Spring stepped back and left him to his research.

"Why Serqet?" Winnie asked. "Why would she target Knox? And for that matter, how? Isn't she in the Otherworld?"

"Revenge." Knox stated the word in a low, flat tone as he locked gazes with Spring across the distance of the attic. "Spring killed her favorite toy. She wants payback. And she's still a goddess regardless of where she resides." He faced Alastair. "Isn't that where you're going with this?"

Alastair didn't bother glancing up. "It is."

Spring sucked in her breath so sharply she coughed. How the hell was she supposed to get a pissed Goddess off her ass?

In her willingness to assist, Autumn pounded Spring's back extra hard. "Are you trying to dislocate my spine?"

"Pfft. I'm adding you back to the fragile flower category."

"Shut it."

Teasing aside, Spring joined Knox by the window. "I'm sorry. I had no idea she'd try to retaliate against you."

"It's not your fault, child," Alastair cut in. "It's not like Serqet or her descendants have ever been a particularly stable lot."

"But she wasn't all bad. I read about all the good she'd done prior to her emotional breakdown."

All eyes turned to Spring in surprised wonder.

"Uh, I'm assuming I'm the only one who reads the family chronicles?"

Her sisters had the grace to look uncomfortable.

She laughed. "Don't tell me, y'all always counted on me to keep you informed in the past, didn't you?"

Summer spoke up in their defense. "You seemed to like the research more than the rest of us."

Spring hugged her.

"It's fine. I don't mind being the family historian. It's interesting stuff." All the research and studying had paid off. It had also helped to restore her magic at a faster speed than anticipated when she initially recovered. Which brought to mind the entry of that particular spell. "Did any of you create a spell to restore my powers to full force?" All she received from the group was blank looks. If it hadn't been Preston, Alastair, or her sisters, who created the restorative spell? "Never mind. Back to Serqet and her revenge. How do we stop her?"

"I don't know that we can." Winnie shrugged when all the attention turned to her. "When we were in Egypt, Lin told me Isis had foiled Serqet's planned revenge against her lover. He also stated he was a warlock—*one without powers*. His plan was to channel mine."

No one seemed to follow her reasoning. "Where did he learn to do that? What gave him the idea? I'd lay odds it was Serqet." Winnie focused on Alastair. "What if she planted a bug in his brain? It would make sense as why he was always targeting our family in particular and rarely bothered with anyone else's. There are other witches and warlocks he could've channeled for power. I think Serqet is obsessed. She'll continue to find people she can use to come after us."

Silence filled the attic. They were each lost to their own thoughts. If Winnie's hypothesis was correct, it didn't matter who was to blame for the shooting. If taken out, another shooter would take the other's place.

"How are we supposed to have any semblance of a normal life when the next bullet might have one of our names on it?" Coop demanded harshly. "A head shot would have a helluva different outcome than a chest, shoulder, or leg."

A shiver of cold swept Spring's entire body. Would her death have appeased Serqet? By coming back and killing Zhu Lin, had Spring added more weight to the wheel of revenge already in motion?

Knox's arm came around her shoulders in a gesture of comfort. Whether for her or him, she couldn't say. But she knew what she needed to do; she had to right a wrong.

"*W*ill you walk with me?"

Knox studied Spring's earnest face. She had some cockamamie plan in mind. He felt it down to his toes. "What are you planning?" he asked without preamble.

All heads turned in their direction.

Spring's furious glare spoke volumes and told him he was right.

"Sister?"

Spring ignored Autumn and teleported. Had Knox not seen the sliver of movement from the attic window, he wouldn't have known her destination. With a grim smile to the others, he teleported to the clearing.

"What the hell do you think you're doing? In case you forgot, there's a crazy person hellbent on taking us out."

She whirled to face him. "I want to summon Serqet."

"Fuck. No!"

"Hear me out—"

"No, absolutely not. She's dangerous and filled with hate, Spring. You killed her crazy pet human. Do you honestly think she's going to let bygones be bygones? *She had me shot in the fucking heart!*" He knew he was shouting, but his fear was over the top.

"We don't even know it was her."

"I'd say we have a pretty good idea unless we gained a new, unknown enemy in the last week."

Spring's chin rose in the air. "I intend to give her what she wants. A life for Lin's. *My* life in exchange for leaving you all alone."

His mind went blank. Like literally devoid of thought. He'd heard others use the term, but he'd never been able to comprehend how it could happen. Now he knew. It only took one person to say something totally asinine to blow your mind.

When he couldn't form a response, she touched his sleeve. "I want you to be on board with this."

"How can I? You're asking me to agree to have my heart ripped out." He hadn't been aware of gripping his hair in his hands until the pain in his scalp registered. Still, that wouldn't be a fraction of a fraction of what he would feel if his soul was crushed by losing Spring a second time. "Christ, Spring! This is the stupidest thing I've ever heard you say. *Like ever!* What guarantee do we have that she'll keep her word or be satisfied with your d-d..." He couldn't voice the word. Couldn't bear to imagine losing her a second time.

"You have none." The soft modulated voice startled them both. The appearance of Isis always surprised him at every turn.

Knox kneeled when he saw who had entered the clearing. "Exalted one."

He jerked Spring to the ground next to him to honor the goddess before them. Isis was kinder and more forgiving than most, but protocol needed to be kept.

"Rise, children. There is no need for formality among family." She moved closer and laid her hand atop his bowed head. "Such a darling young man." To Spring, she said, "Your beloved is correct. Your plan will fail. My sister doesn't care if you make it easy and sacrifice yourself. She cannot be trusted to honor any promises she makes."

"But she was good once. She helped people," Spring protested as she rose.

Isis's full lips flattened into a straight line, and her amber eyes flashed. Knox experienced a moment of panic.

"You are impetuous, Spring Thorne." Isis lifted her arm and let out a low hum. Within a minute, Mr. Black swooped down from the sky and landed on her forearm. "Show her."

The raven fixed his intelligent eyes on Spring and cawed. He switched to perch on her shoulder and pressed his head into her neck. As her eyes rolled back, Knox lunged to catch her. The three of them —Spring, Knox, and Mr. Black—wound up on the ground in a heap with Knox taking the brunt of the impact. Spring's body repeatedly jerked with whatever magic the bird continued to impart. Tears fell from closed eyes as they rolled around behind her lids.

"What the hell did you do to her?" Knox yelled. It wasn't that he wanted to be smitten, but his main concern was for Spring. Her seizure was magical in nature, but he reasoned it couldn't be good for her overall health.

"I once told you I needed to wipe her brain, that when she was resurrected, she would have no memories. Now, I am restoring the memories without the traumatic emotions attached. She will be able to see what her impetuousness caused."

He stared in dismay. The only solace he'd found in this whole damned situation was that Spring never had to fully know what she'd gone through. Other than the video Lin produced of her death, the truth of her torture had been hearsay. Something from which she could remain detached. A thing that, while horrific, had happened to someone else because she had no true memories or feelings to deal with. But that would change.

"She'll feel shame and degradation for what she's been through. Why would you put that on her?" His voice was hoarse from the raw emotion churning within him.

The gaze Isis turned on him was not unkind. "No one can go through this life unscarred or unchanged in some way, Knox Carlyle. Knowledge is power, whether you choose to believe it or not."

He hadn't realized he was crying until she brushed a thumb over his cheek.

"She will sleep now. When she wakes, show her what it means to be truly loved." She glided toward the widening ripple in the fabric of the space around them. Before stepping through, she cast him one last long glance. "The one you seek was once employed by Victor Salinger, but that is not who commissioned him to hurt you. Many blessings on you, my dear."

"Thank you, Exalted One," he returned humbly, wishing for more than the cryptic information she'd provided but knowing he wouldn't receive it.

As the late-morning shadows darkened to afternoon, Knox held Spring in the cradle of his arms and stroked her hair. The raven had flown back toward Thorne Manor hours ago. He assumed it was to roost in the old barn and rest from the heavy influx and outpouring of magic the poor thing had been subjected to.

A new sensation triggered the hairs on the back of his neck. He sensed the moment they were no longer alone. A malicious, dark force—one he was deeply familiar with—tried to wrap around him.

Knox gathered old, elemental magic within his hand just as he had when he struck down his mother. "Come out. I know you're there."

A woman stepped from the trees. She was tall and had long, flowing black hair that hung to her waist. The curviness of her body would make a saint's mouth water. However, the malevolent energy clinging to her repulsed him. He had borne the brunt of that ugliness in the past and had felt the repercussions of hatred a thousand times over not to recognize it for what it was now.

"That's far enough. Who are you?"

"I am known as Serqet."

Fuck!

Although he didn't rise because Spring rested in his arms, Knox bowed his head in respect, never taking his eyes from her. "Goddess."

"You're hard to kill," she said conversationally.

"I try."

Her lips twitched, whether in annoyance or humor, he couldn't

211

tell. "For years, my supporters have tried. Robert Knox was one of mine, as was Zhu Lin. I eventually turned your mother into one of my followers." She shook her head. "But you and Spring Thorne have systematically removed them all."

He shook his head, stunned stupid by her confession. What was she saying? She'd been trying to have him murdered from birth? Why? "I don't understand. Why would your followers turn on each other? Lin murdered my father. I was there and saw it happen."

"Did you?" She laughed, and the lovely sound was hardened by an evil edge. "You may want to check with those who were there that day. Alastair Thorne and Phillip Carlyle know the truth. You murdered your father, just as you murdered your mother. Alastair was the first to realize you would be in danger from the Witches' Council if the truth came out."

She shrugged as if she didn't care that a small boy might have been hurt. "He came up with the idea to alter your recollection of the events and to make you believe Zhu Lin killed your father. In fact, a single lightning bolt from you had the honor. Did you never wonder why your mother turned on you after your father's death?"

A cold smile graced her stunning face. "Oh, how Marianne hated you for murdering the man she loved. A word here or there fed that hatred. Helping her escape to seek vengeance on you and Spring was some of my finest work. The Witches' Council spelled those prison cells with ancient magic. Magic my family created."

"I still don't understand why you would target a small child. What did I ever do to you?"

"Do you believe in the rebirth of the soul?"

"Reincarnation?" Knox's arm tightened around Spring as he continued to build the elements in his opposite hand. "I've never thought about it."

"You chose *her* over me." Her dark eyes burned with fire when Serqet looked at Spring. "When I would've given you the entire world, you married *her*," she spat. Her face contorted with the fury boiling inside her.

The unease churning in his gut flared into full-blown fear. He doubted he was a match for a goddess, even one who'd been stripped of most of her magic as Serqet had been. If she had the ability to teleport from the Otherworld, then she wasn't powerless.

"You tried to curse us." Spring's voice rasped in the silence that ensued after Serqet's revelation. "I saw it... just now..." she murmured to Knox.

He didn't dare look down. He sensed if he took his attention from the goddess for even a second, she'd strike.

"Yes. And my beloved sister betrayed me to save you. She *continues* to betray me to save you." Serqet gave a slight shake of her head as if to rid herself of a pesky fly. "No matter what obstacles I set in your path, no matter whom I employ to do you harm, you prevail. Robert Knox, Zhu Lin, Marianne Carlyle, Don Carlos Esteban, Tommy Tomlinson—"

Spring gasped.

"Oh, *yes*. Your sweet friend Tommy was one of mine."

"Was?" Knox didn't care for her use of past tense, but if it took one more of her psychotic players off the field, he wouldn't complain.

"Yes. Poor Mr. Tomlinson suffered a tragic end for failing to complete the task he was assigned."

"What task was that?" Spring sat up with great care, placing her hand on the ground. Knox assumed it was for show, a pretense of her shakiness. In reality, she was preparing herself to use her earth element if need be. He silently applauded her quick thinking.

"Shooting you both in the alley, of course."

Knox was tired of the back and forth. Tired of the drama and explanations. Tired of her attempts on their lives. "So you used a non-witch for your own ends and failed. Not surprising considering who he was up against. What now? You're here to do the deed yourself?"

"No. Nothing so mundane as that. I only want to witness your expression as I tell you that the day *will* come when I end your life. Or your lover's life. One shall die, and the other shall suffer the realization that it was his or her fault."

The ground rumbled beneath them, and the trees swayed in response. It was a clear indication of Spring's simmering anger. "Why would it be our fault? Any blame lies on *your* shoulders, you hateful bitch! Not ours."

"Be careful of your tone, girl. I still wield some power."

"Not much if what I've read is true," Spring taunted.

"Spring." Knox hoped his warning got through. This was what Isis had been trying to tell Spring. Her impulsiveness would be her downfall.

Serqet studied them both for a long moment. Her attention focused on him. "Because I hold a remnant of affection for you, I will give you the choice. Leave with me now, be my consort, and I will spare both your lives."

The ground shook again. Knox's hand tightened on Spring's hip. Really, there was no choice. He'd go with Serqet and spare Spring's life if he had to. But Isis's warning came back to him; Serqet could not be trusted to keep her word.

"We'll take our chances." Both women gasped at his statement. "We're stronger together. And if I only have five minutes with Spring, I'd still prefer to spend them with her than a lifetime with you."

An emotion akin to pain flashed in Serqet's dark eyes before she looked away. "So be it." Without another word, she disappeared through a rift in space.

Knox half expected a surprise attack. He glanced uneasily around them.

"No one else is here," Spring assured him. "The plants would put off a vibration, remember?"

"Let's get out of here. I'm under orders from Isis to show you what it's like to be truly loved."

Spring knelt before him and pressed her lips to his. "I already *am* truly loved. Anything else you show me is icing on a cake."

As they walked, hand-in-hand, toward Thorne Manor, he pulled her to a stop. "I wanted to show you something the other day. Are you interested in seeing it now?"

A wicked smile flashed on her lovely face. "Is this a case of you show me yours and I'll show you mine?"

"That comes later when I can have you to myself for hours without interruption."

Spring snorted, and asked, "What is it that you want to show me?"

"It's something I've created with you in mind. If you hate it, we can change whatever you want."

"I'm intrigued. Lead the way."

They detoured through the woods, using a lesser worn path. The plants parted for them to pass.

"This seems shady as hell. Are you taking me out to murder me? You really want that hot goddess, don't you?"

He laughed at Spring's silliness. With a move that would make Gene Kelly proud, he whirled her toward him and dipped her like the suavest of dancers. "There will never be a day when I won't want you. And one day, when we are old and gray, I'll still be chasing you around the bedroom as fast as my walker will allow me to go."

"You've said that to me before."

He stared down into her flushed face. "Before Cartagena."

"Yes. It was in the playback Isis provided for me."

Straightening, he smoothed back her mussed hair. "I suppose we should talk about the before."

"No. There's no need. I'm not that woman anymore. The me standing before you is different, more adult, I think. Can you separate the two?"

"I don't know. You're so much like her, the before-you-now persona. Sometimes it's hard to differentiate the two."

A troubled light entered her eyes. "Is it me you love or a memory, Knox?"

He'd thought about this a lot in the months they'd been separated as she'd recovered from her ordeal. Since Spring's reawakening, Knox had come to the conclusion that she was no different, regardless of the memory loss. "You can't see you're still one and the same. Just because the memories and feelings have disappeared, doesn't mean they didn't happen. Your actions, your personality, your thought process, your beautiful soul… it's all the same. It's what makes you *you*." He traced a finger along her perfect nose. "Can't you see I'm crazy about both who you were and who you are now?"

"I love you, Knox. It was a bolt out of the blue, but your soul calls to mine in a way I can't describe. This feeling—this *need*—to be near you, to touch you, bask in your warmth, I can't shake it, and I don't know that I want to." She caressed his scarred cheek and sighed. "Maybe the reincarnation excuse makes sense, but either way, I don't want you to feel obligated to love who I am now if the old Spring is who you really want."

The words he wished to say backed up in his throat. How did he tell her she was his everything? She always had been and always would be his reason for existing. He went for honesty.

"Obligated? There is no obligation when it comes to you, sweetheart. All I feel is pure love. Take what you feel and multiply it by a million—*a trillion*—and you might be able to understand the scope of my feelings for you." He leaned in and brushed her lips with his. "I've adored you since we were children. Before that if Serqet is to be believed. There is no room in my heart for another, not in regard to this type of all-consuming love." He pressed his forehead to hers. "You are my everything, Spring Thorne, and you always will be."

hen Knox's lips closed over hers, Spring gave into the kiss and matched his passion with a fire of her own. His palms cradled her face as his tongue explored the deep recesses of her mouth. The spark he ignited when he kissed her could be felt throughout her body. It wasn't much different than the way her cells fired up for teleportation. Heat consumed her, and all she desired was to be with him. She wanted to explore his glorious body with her fingertips, lips, and body.

His jagged, harsh breathing echoed around them as he pulled back. "Come on."

Placing her hand inside his larger one, she allowed him to lead her to the destination he'd had in mind when they started their short journey from the glen. When they stepped from the path onto the sizable, sprawling lawn, she halted to take in the view.

Perched on a hillside was a dazzling house. The charcoal gray exterior was trimmed in white with a coral-colored front door and matching sidelights. The wide, wrap-around porch boasted pale gray planks with large tropical-colored area rugs. Teal light fixtures hung down over the sitting area and lent an intimate setting to the porch furniture. With the sun lowering behind the building, the sight was spectacular.

Already, she was in love with the place. "This is your home?"

"I'm hoping it will be ours."

"I don't understand." With effort, she tore her gaze from the beautiful view before her and faced him. "This isn't yours?"

"This property was willed to me from my grandfather. All the grandchildren have land set aside for them. Marianne was never allowed to touch it. Just as any children of mine will have land for their home should they wish it. The Carlyle trust is extensive."

"I'd say so, but I still don't understand. Did you create this?"

"The night of our first meeting in the garden, when you said you were feeling stifled, I intended to show you the land. To give it to you if that's what you desired." He brushed a hand down the length of her back and wrapped an arm around her waist. He turned her back toward the house. "Then when I returned home that night, I had the idea to create this. I kept your shop decor in mind when I decorated. There are skylights in all the rooms and a four-story conservatory off the back for any plants or trees you choose to grow." He cleared his throat. "It's not my intent to pressure you. It's here if you want it. But if you choose to stay at Thorne Manor, that's okay too."

She stared at the landscape with its beautiful house in slack-jawed wonder. He'd made this for her? Because she'd said she didn't feel like she fit in? "Oh, Knox!" Tears burned behind her lids and her nose filled. She was about to cry the big ugly, but she couldn't help it. To feel so loved, so treasured...

The first sob hit and mingled with a snorting laugh at the horror crowding his face.

"You don't have to live here. If you hate it, I can create something else. Or not."

Knox babbled as he held her; each assurance designed to stop her emotional breakdown. If Spring could've told him it was perfect, she would've. As it was, all she could do was cry. It was the first time she'd allowed herself to completely break down since her life had turned topsy-turvy.

"Please don't cry." His whisper was ragged and tortured. "I can't bear it."

"I-I can't seem t-to help myself," she hiccupped.

"I'll take you home."

"I am h-home."

"What?" His expression was something between hope and disbelief.

"I am home," she repeated, her voice firmer. "I'm sure I'm going to love the interior if it is anything like the outside."

Relief flooded his features, and his wide grin flashed. "You had me freaked the fuck out for a minute there."

"Show me our place."

He scooped her up and teleported the distance to the porch. "Open." When the door flew back on its hinges, he stepped over the threshold, and Spring got her first glimpse of the interior. It was, to put it simply, incredible. She couldn't have conjured a more perfect home for herself if she had a lifetime to think about it. Knox had provided her exactly what she needed.

"It's incredible."

"It's also protected with the strongest wards in existence. I wanted you to feel safe."

She placed her palm over his heart and was surprised to feel the rapid rate of the hard thudding. "Are you nervous?"

"Maybe a little."

Spring kissed his chin. "Let me down. I want to explore."

Taking her time, she strolled through each of the downstairs rooms. The kitchen, dining room, and living room all ran the length of the right side of the house. The open floor plan was her favorite. "Did you make it this large for family gatherings?"

"I did. I figured when you were ready, you'd host girls' nights or dinners."

The large red island was topped with a white and silver quartz. She smiled as she poked through the pale gray floor-to-ceiling cabinets of the pantry. "It's pretty sparse."

"I figured you could conjure what you wanted. I'm not much of a cook, and I wasn't sure about you. Winnie might have some suggestions as to the best pots and pans or bakeware."

Spring whirled in his direction. "You've thought of everything."

"Come see the upstairs. I want to see if you like your bedroom."

"My bedroom? Not ours?"

"I'd love it to be ours. I just didn't want to presume."

"If that's what you want, I do, too."

"Sweetheart, it's most definitely what I want," he said feelingly.

She laughed and grabbed his hand. "Show me."

They raced up the steps and into the master suite. The space was easily twice the size of her current bedroom. Knox had created a reading nook and replicated her French design. The blacks, grays, and pinks were bold and yet subtly done so as not to overpower the room. The pale rose chaise took up one corner of the sitting area, while a charcoal-gray leather club chair and ottoman took up the other. The space was feminine yet the distinct masculine touches set it off perfectly. They could each read or recline without giving up their personal comfort. "I love that the wood has the same matching pattern on both pieces. And the dark rose pillow ties in with the chair. It seems you've thought of everything."

"I can change the design if you'd rather have—"

She cut him off with her fingers over his lips and a light laugh. "Stop! I love it. Really."

The twinkle in his eyes warned her of his intent. When he sucked her fingers into his mouth, she watched in fascination. "That's so unsanitary."

His eyes flared wide. "I just realized something. Your OCD tendencies are gone."

"I had OCD?"

"Big time."

She frowned her confusion. "That seems an odd thing to have disappear."

"It was kind of cute. For someone who loved gardening, you wiped or washed your hands constantly, even between plantings."

"You're weird for thinking it was cute, you know that?"

"Maybe, but you love me anyway."

"I do," she laughed.

"I like the way that sounds."

Again, she laughed as he drew her close. "Wait a minute! How do you know how often I washed my hands?"

He froze.

"You're so busted! You spied on me didn't you?"

"I already told you, I did—for your protection." His uncomfortableness with the conversation was apparent in the stiffening of his body.

A little devil perched on her shoulder and encouraged her to tease him. "So, you watched me wash my hands. Did you watch me wash anything else? My legs?" She tip-toed her fingers up his chest, stopping to lightly pinch his nipple. "My breasts?"

"It was for your protection," he repeated, color high and lips compressed in a straight line. "I didn't invade your privacy."

His indignation was adorable.

Spring leaned in and lightly pressed her lips to the column of his throat. She stretched to whisper in his ear. "I like the idea of you watching me. Imagining your hands where mine traveled."

Knox pulled away slightly to check her level of honesty. He offered up a half-grin. "I never did, but I can from here on out."

"I'm cool with that," she laughed.

"Let's get froggy," he murmured against her lips.

She sprung off the floor and wrapped her legs around his hips. "I feel as if I've waited a lifetime for you to ask. Don't pull back this time."

"Never."

"Do we take our clothes off the old-fashioned way or—"

Knox didn't wait for her to finish. With a snap of his fingers, they were both naked.

"Okay, then," she laughed.

"It gives me more time to concentrate on what's important." His breath against her throat sent a delighted shiver up her spine.

Spring dropped her head to the side to allow him greater access to her throat. The softness of his lips as they skimmed the column of her neck caused her legs to tighten around him in response. She rubbed her breasts against the bared expanse of his muscled chest. "I've wanted to do this from the moment I saw you."

He groaned. "Why the hell didn't you say so? I'd have been happy to oblige that night and any time thereafter."

A happy laugh bubbled up.

Knox created a small distance between them and met her gaze.

"What's the matter?" His seriousness triggered her concern.

"I'm afraid I'm dreaming. That grief sent me over the edge in Colombia, and none of this is real."

"Oh, Knox." The sheer amount of love she experienced, combined with the overwhelming desire to soothe him, made it difficult to swallow. She stared at him, helpless to speak. Wordlessly, she leaned forward and kissed him. Not the soul-searing kiss of passion, but the tender love-filled type of kiss that promised everything. When she could manage it, she said, "I love you, and I'm not going anywhere. I think we've proved that we would move heaven and hell to be together, don't you?"

"My early life was hell. That hell revisited me from time to time in the form of my mother and the problems she created. But you have always been the light in the darkness, leading me on. I would lay down my life for you, Spring."

His words required no response, or at least none that wasn't physical in nature. Her arms tightened, and she pulled his head down to hers. This kiss spoke not only of her love, but of her desire. "Take me to bed, Studly."

Her use of Autumn's nickname did what she'd hoped and shifted the mood. He chuckled and crashed on the bed, careful to bring her down on top so he didn't crush her. "How's that?"

"It's a start." She gave his shoulder a sharp love-bite. "Now, let's get froggy."

With an alligator roll, Knox pinned her beneath him with her hands over her head. "Ribbit."

She snorted her amusement, and rocked her pelvis against his. "I thought you were my prince. You know, if the crown fits and all that."

"Didn't I just provide you with an awesome castle all your own?"

"Oh, right. Remind me to discuss the moat after we're finished. I want to keep everyone out so we can stay in bed for at least a month."

"Hell, in that case, I'll snap my fingers right now and create one." He bent his head and planted a kiss on the upper curve of her breast and followed in with his fingertips. "Now shut up so I can get busy."

"You can't do two things at once?"

"Kissing that sassy mouth is a full-time job."

A giggle escaped as she made the motion of zipping her lip. She waved a hand down her body as if to say, "all yours."

Knox buried his smirk against her throat and gently sucked at the skin there. As his teeth grazed the lobe of her ear, she moaned. These were all new sensations to her, but she intended to appreciate each one as they happened. To commit them to memory for future.

As Knox explored her breasts, testing the weight and feel in his hands even as he drew an erect nipple into his mouth, Spring allowed her hands to wander down the length of his back. The tips of her fingers explored the sinewy planes and followed the V down to his ass. Recalling the beauty of that ass wasn't difficult; she'd caught the splendid glimpse of it when she'd stripped him after he was shot, and then again this morning when he sat up to address Winnie. Knox's ass was pure perfection. Rounded, yet tapered down his flanks to show off muscle and fill out his jeans in such a way as to make a woman's mouth water.

Suddenly, her need to see the front of him overwhelmed her. "Lie on your back," she ordered huskily.

His head came up in surprise, but he complied. His erection rose tall and proud, pointing toward the headboard. For a brief second, she had misgivings about the mechanics of lovemaking. He looked larger than she anticipated.

"Spring?"

"Shhh. I'm thinking." His hearty laughter brought her eyes to his face. "What's so funny about that?"

"Because you tend to overthink. Now is not the time for thinking, sweetheart. It's the time for feeling." He took her hand and set it at the base of his shaft, then ran his fingers lightly down her lower abdomen until he reached the apex of her thighs. "Just feel."

As he swept his fingers along her folds, she meeped. He bit back a smile, but she could see the tell-tale crinkle of amusement at the corner of his eyes.

Two could play that game. She wrapped her hand around his shaft and inched her palm upward. When she got to the tip, she ran her thumb lightly through the bead of cum and swirled it around the top. His sharp inhale brought forth her satisfied smile. Curiosity got the better of her. What would he do if she took him into her mouth? Would he be as smug?

Spring lowered her head and licked the length of him.

His throaty moan urged her on, and she swirled her tongue up and down, testing his response. His chest expanded and contracted at a faster rate as his hot, greedy eyes locked with her gaze. With another smile, she took him into her mouth.

"My God!"

With the fingers of her free hand, she explored the fullness of his balls and trailed her fingertips across his well-muscled thighs. The years of riding had made his upper legs pure muscle.

His hand wove into her hair, even as he surged upward to slowly thrust into her mouth. "That's it, sweetheart. Just like that."

Spring peered at his face. A light dusting of color highlighted his cheeks, as his mouth hung slightly open to allow his accelerated breathing. But it was his eyes that mesmerized her. They practically glowed with want and need as he watched her in action. If she lived to be a hundred, she doubted she would see a more erotic sight in her life. Knox in a heightened passionate state turned her on like nothing else to date.

As if he sensed this, his fingers zeroed in on her core and delved into her folds again. With his thumb, he circled her clit. "Your turn," he growled. "Lie back."

Without hesitation, she did as he'd ordered.

"I've wanted to taste you for eons."

Tangling her hands in his thick blond locks, she guided his face toward her. The first swipe of his tongue nearly caused her to explode off the bed. The second swipe ripped a throaty moan from somewhere inside. And when he inserted his fingers, she was done for. Ever so slowly, he explored inside her, now and again changing the speed of his pumping fingers.

Her breath came out in short pants as the sensations inside her built toward some final destination that she was clueless about. Of their own volition, her legs parted wider and gave Knox an all-access pass to her most private area.

Knox being Knox, took advantage and latched onto her with his mouth. The hard suck of her clit and thrust of his fingers took her over the brink. She screamed her release as the waves of pleasure crashed over her. Unable to help herself, she held his head in place as her hips bucked wildly against his face. His tongue resumed, and her orgasm was quickly followed by a second when a pulse of magic flowed from his fingertips into her womb.

The need to feel him inside of her took hold, and she tugged on his hair to pull him up the length of her body. Despite the sting he must've felt on his scalp, he refused to be rushed and slowly kissed her inner thighs. He worked his way across the expanse of bare skin, chuckling when he felt her stomach contract in reaction.

As he got to her breasts, he closed his teeth over her pebbled nipple. Again, she bucked against him. "I want you... inside me... I need..."

"So demanding," he mocked. "Just feel."

"I'd feel a whole lot better if you—ah!" She caught her breath as he eased inside her. "Yes," she breathed on a contented sigh.

She opened her eyes to see him staring down at her with a fervor that stole her breath. Love, possessiveness, and desire all battled for dominance in his look. Spring rocked her hips against him. "I'm yours."

His eyes closed, and a small smile played upon his lips. With a smooth stroke and a hiss of breath, his head dropped back. Four more long, smooth strokes, and then his hips started to piston in and out at a rapid rate.

Faster. Faster.

Spring wasn't aware of voicing her encouragement, but Knox took it upon himself to fulfill her request. His thrusts increased in speed with each of her pleasure-filled moans.

Her third orgasm hit with such force and beauty, tears flooded her eyes and she was sure she stopped breathing. Knox continued pumping his hips, going deeper with each forward motion. Their eyes connected, and a worried light appeared in his until she smiled from her heart. She opened up for him to see all the love and beauty inside her. Immediately, he understood that she was crying with the joy of their joining, and while Spring couldn't be positive, she suspected his eyes became a little misty, too.

With one last drive forward, Knox's body shuddered with his release. And when he called her name, she kissed it from his lips.

For the longest time, they lay there, not speaking but not needing to. Spring idly touched or traced the lines of his body. When she got to the flat plane of his stomach, she smiled. "I didn't realize a guy could recover that quickly."

"This guy can," he murmured as he rolled her on top of him.

THE REMAINDER OF THE NIGHT AND WELL INTO THE NEXT MORNING was spent loving one another—emotionally, spiritually, and most definitely physically. Knox couldn't remember being this happy, and it worried him. But at the same time, he refused to borrow trouble. For now, they were where they were safe.

"I wonder if it's okay to give this to my uncle." Spring cradled the amulet in her palm as she glanced down toward her bare chest.

"You told me Nephthys said to keep it on you. Maybe you should, just in case. It isn't like you can't loan it to him to bring back your mother when the time comes."

"True." She studied it and let it drop back against her skin. "It's odd, but it always seems warm against my skin."

"I'd like to think it's protecting you." Perching his weight on his elbow, Knox trailed a finger over the amulet then detoured and traced her breast and stomach. "That maybe Nephthys and Isis are in league to keep Serqet off your ass."

"We can only hope. But it's time to tell the others what's going on, don't you think? As much as I love our new place, we can't hide forever."

He rolled on top of her and rubbed his budding erection against her. "I'm cool with hiding. My dick wants to hide in your—"

Spring slapped a hand over his mouth. "Rude, crude, and socially unacceptable."

He grinned against her hand and licked her palm. "We can't choose between your place or mine anymore. It's all one and the same."

"I know." She smiled her delight, spread her legs wider, and cradled him within her thighs. "Ain't it great?"

"Yes, yes it is!"

30

*K*nox sent a text to both families with GPS coordinates to the new house and a cryptic message to be there at precisely six p.m. that evening and to arrive hungry.

"Do you think it looks okay?" Spring asked for the fourth time in as many minutes.

"Yes." He leaned in and kissed her in a firm, no-nonsense manner. "Everything looks perfect. Stop worrying."

"What about the meal?"

"Spring, sweetheart, you're having a meltdown for no reason. I promise you, your family is going to understand your need to have your own place." He hugged her against him and rested a cheek on the top of her shiny head. "Autumn moved to Maine before she married Keaton. Summer's main residence is in North Carolina. And your dad travels the world. I think Winnie and Zane will love having the manor to themselves." He rubbed a hand up and down her back. "I think once their triplets arrive, you'll be glad you relocated."

"Thanks for being the voice of reason."

"That's what I'm here for."

She pulled back and lifted a brow. "Really? I thought maybe you—"

The doorbell rang, cutting off what Knox suspected was going to be a naughty comment based on her wicked expression. Damn. He should've told everyone seven. "I want you to hold onto that thought for after everyone leaves tonight."

Her giggle followed him to the door. Knox glanced back to see her wringing her hands and counting plates. "Relax."

The Thornes were the first to arrive with Coop, Keaton, and Chloe arriving directly after. As Knox expected, they ooh-ed and ahh-ed over the house, and Autumn demanded a grand tour.

Coop hung back to speak to Knox as Spring led the others through the house. "We were all worried when you and Spring took off yesterday. Had we not received your message last night, you'd be in deep shit with the Thornes. As it was, I had to convince Summer we didn't need to put out a magical all-points bulletin. They are all still triggered when one of their own goes missing."

"Aww, hell! I didn't even think about that."

"It surprises me to hear it. I know you'd lose your shit if the situation was reversed."

Knox grimaced. "That goes without saying, doesn't it?" And he would. He'd tear someone a new asshole if he couldn't find Spring. He should have been more attuned to the feelings of the others, and he told Coop as much.

"No worries, man."

The doorbell rang.

"Who are we still missing?" Knox asked over his shoulder as he headed toward the front of the house.

"Preston? Who else did you invite?"

Alastair Thorne stood on the other side of the door, facing toward the woods. The large black, wool overcoat gave him a mysterious air.

"Mr. Thorne. Come in."

"Thank you for the dinner invitation."

"Of course. It's not a family gathering without you, sir."

Spring's uncle stared at him through narrowed eyes as if to judge his truthfulness. "I almost believe you're serious."

"I am." So there wasn't any doubt, Knox held out his hand. "You did your damnedest to protect me and Spring throughout the years from behind the scenes. We both owe you a debt of gratitude."

"I'm not looking for gratitude, son. The only payment I expect is for you to live a happy life."

"I don't think that will be a problem."

"Good."

Knox cleared his throat. "May I ask you something?"

Alastair's brows rose in inquiry.

"Yesterday, Serqet paid a visit to me and Spring in the clearing."

Those arrogant brows clashed together, and Alastair's gaze sharpened. "Yesterday?"

"Yes. She indicated I was the one who killed my father. Not Lin."

Knox locked gazes with Alastair and saw confirmation in the other man's blue-steel stare.

"So it's true?"

"It is."

"Why did I never remember? For that matter, why didn't you eventually tell me the truth? You had your chance that day in the clearing."

"What was the point? For you to feel even more self-hatred? You had already piled more than your share of guilt on yourself. You painted yourself with the same brush of evil that colored Robert and Marianne. You are nothing like them and telling you the truth would only have made you doubt your worth."

Spring's arms came around Knox from behind. "I, for one, appreciate your restraint in revealing the truth, Uncle. Can you imagine how much harder it would've been to convince him he was worthy of love?"

The warmth of her adoration wrapped around Knox and chased away the last of his demons. He placed his arms over hers and entwined their fingers. With a quick kiss on her knuckles, he placed her arm back around his waist and addressed Alastair. "I appreciate it, too, as well as all the times you've been there for both of us. This family was ugly to you in the early days of your return. I'm sorry."

Alastair unbent enough to grace them with a genuine smile.

"Apology accepted. It wasn't needed, but the gesture is nice. Now, what's for dinner? I'm starved."

"Come see my beautiful new home, Uncle." Spring, impulsive as always, grabbed Alastair's hand and tugged him toward the foyer.

Knox was about to close the front door when the last of their guests arrived. Preston teleported in mere seconds before Holly Thorne-Hill and her ever-present shadow, Quentin Buchanan. Preston and Holly shared an awkward greeting, mostly on her part while her uncle looked sad and a little lost.

"Welcome!" Knox smiled and strove to ease the tension. "Spring is giving group tours of the house. She just started the second one."

Holly nodded and hurried down the hall, leaving Knox alone with Preston and Quentin.

"Beer in the fridge?" Trust Quentin to cut through any tenseness with a blunt statement or question of any kind.

"Right through there."

"Thanks. Anyone else want one?"

"Sure. Mr. Thorne?"

"I'd prefer an aged whisky if you have it," Preston said.

"Brand preference?"

"Glenfiddich."

Knox pointed to the liquor cabinet in the room on the right, designated for his study. "The good stuff is in there."

"I'm on it." With a lazy, ambling walk, Quentin was off to play the role of bartender, effectively leaving Preston and Knox alone on the front porch.

Without further ado, Knox shut the door and gestured Preston to the comfortable outside seating to their left. "I'm sorry I didn't notify everyone right away yesterday that Spring was with me and safe. We were caught up in dealing with a few visiting goddesses."

A look of concern passed over Preston's countenance. "What happened?"

"Isis showed up first and gave Spring the gift of her old memories—*without* the emotional attachment, according to her. I suppose, for Spring, it was like watching a movie of her own life. Just as she was recovering from that little blast from the past, Serqet arrived to claim responsibility for the shooting and to threaten us."

"Dear God!"

"Yeah, we needed some downtime from drama."

"Understandable. I'd have reacted the same way, I imagine." Preston shook his head and ran a hand through his hair, mussing the coppery locks. "Does Serqet blame you both for Lin's demise?"

"Among other things. Apparently, there's such a thing as reincarnation." Knox still couldn't wrap his mind around the fact he'd been lover to a goddess once upon a time. Or that the same goddess preferred him dead rather than to see him happy with another woman. "Did you know that? Because I'm wondering why I didn't."

"I did."

Knox grunted. He always seemed to be the last to learn things lately. "You should know, Serqet hates Spring. Like with a passion. She's obsessed with making us pay for what she sees as Spring stealing me from her."

"I see." Preston closed his eyes and leaned his head against the cushions. "It's never-ending. All I want is for my daughters to be safe and happy, yet at every turn, old enemies are emerging out of the woodwork, ready to throw our lives into upheaval."

"I'm sorry, sir."

Preston cracked an eyelid. "You have no reason to be, son. I imagine you'd die rather than upset my youngest. I'm happy you've found each other."

Quentin walked out, handed them their drinks, and just as quietly left the men to their conversation. Knox almost laughed at Quentin's ability to assess a situation in mere seconds and get the hell out of Dodge before shit got real.

Dismissing Quentin, Knox focused his attention back on Preston. Would he be so happy if he knew Knox was a murderer? That he killed both his own parents in addition to the men who had been guarding Spring in Colombia?

As if Preston read Knox's mind, he said, "I know the truth surrounding Robert's death."

From where he rested back against the cushions, Knox straightened and leaned forward. "You know I struck down my father with the equivalent of a lightning bolt?"

"Yes. And he damned-well deserved it."

"Absolutely!" Alastair stepped from the gathering shadows. "That's always been my personal opinion. I'm glad we're all in agreement."

Agreement? Knox wasn't convinced he agreed, but he didn't wholly believe he disagreed either. For sure his life had been better off without his abusive father in the picture, but now the weight of murder hung about Knox's neck, and it was heavier than he could ever have imagined. Why had he killed him? For some reason, it bothered him more than the killing of his mother and Don Carlos, both of whom deserved to rot in hell for their attacks on Spring.

Knox's head shot up. He stared between the two brothers. They both wore a look of kind patience, as if they were waiting for him to figure out a puzzle they had already solved. "Why did I kill my father? It was to protect Spring, wasn't it?"

The satisfied curl of Alastair's smile told Knox he'd guessed correctly.

"Why was she there in the first place?"

"Spring had been kidnapped once before. By your mother and father." Preston's faced went grim with the retelling. "She'd been in the clearing. I assumed I'd cloaked it well enough for the girls to play, but it seemed my wards weren't strong enough. You broke through them."

Shock slammed into Knox. "Me? How the hell does an eight-year-old boy break a ward created by a Thorne warlock?"

"How does an eight-year-old boy stop time or conjure lightning bolts from air?" Alastair rolled his eyes and glanced at his brother in exasperation. "I thought he was the smart one?"

Preston's lips twitched, but otherwise he ignored his brother's snark. "I'll tell you a secret only the two of us know." He waved to himself and Alastair. "You are the most powerful warlock in existence, son. More powerful than the two of us."

"But if you say as much, I will call you a damned liar," Alastair cut in.

Once again, Preston's lips twisted into a hint of a smile. "You were gifted your magic from Isis many lifetimes ago. It isn't just built into your DNA; it's built into your soul, like no other witch or warlock alive. If I died tomorrow and was reincarnated, there is a chance I might not come back with powers if I were born to a normal family. But even should you be born to a non-magical family, you would retain your powers. It was Isis's way of protecting you from Serqet."

"The short version of what my brother is trying to say is that Isis wanted to insure you always had the power to take down a god or goddess should you need to. It's why she showed up when Spring died. She needed to temper your rage and prevent you from destroying the entire South American continent."

"No way I have that much power! No fucking way!"

"You do. And luckily, you also have the calmest temperament of anyone I've ever met. But my beloved niece is your trigger. When she is threatened, you become a ticking time bomb. Just as you did as a child." Alastair sighed. "I made up the story of Lin killing your father because I didn't believe you should carry the weight of Robert's death on your shoulders. But Lin *was* there that night for the handoff of Spring for whatever nefarious reasons he'd planned with your parents."

Alastair reached over and touched Knox's temple. "Remember."

All the real memories came crashing back, and he relived the scene.

He'd been in the corner reading when his parents brought an unconscious Spring through the door. She had been filthy, and her dried tears had left a distinct trail through the dirt on her face. Knox jumped up and ran to where they'd dumped her on the sofa. When he moved to touch her, Robert slapped him hard across the face. The ring on his father's finger slashed his cheek open. Oddly, for the first time in his life, Knox hadn't cowered. He stood his ground and glared at his father as the blood poured from the wound.

"She's mine, and I'm hers," Knox cried out.

Robert laughed and grabbed Knox by the hair. "She belongs to Zhu Lin now, boy. You won't want her after what he has planned for her. Take your last look. She'll be gone soon. Maybe then you can concentrate on what we are trying to teach you."

Zhu Lin had shown up within minutes of Robert's ugly words. Knox hadn't known what his father meant at the time, other than Spring was to be taken from him. It was the first incident of frozen time. He'd halted the molecules around him and gathered Spring to his chest. He'd made it to the corner with her when time snapped back.

All the occupants of the room stared at him in wide-eyed wonder. However, his father's rage overrode his wariness of a powerful little boy. As Robert charged toward him, intent on taking Spring, Knox screamed and sent the full force of his magic toward his father. The bolt not only electrocuted Robert Knox, it burnt him to a cinder.

Zhu Lin wasted no time beating a hasty retreat. Only Knox's distraught mother remained in the room, sizing him up and trying to determine the best way to proceed with an angry, terrified child on her hands. That was the moment when the Thornes had shown up to retrieve the family jewel.

"Jesus! I remember it all now." Knox rose to his feet and moved to the rail. As he stared out over his property, he tried to come to grips with the fact that he possessed the power to end Serqet should he choose. "Does Serqet know how strong my magic is?"

Alastair moved to his side and propped a hip against the white railing. "She does."

"So her proposition today was in order to gain that power for herself." Spring stated.

The men all jerked around to face her.

"Sorry. I didn't mean to sneak up on you." Her mischievous smirk said otherwise. "But back to Serqet. Are we to assume she was the one who created those shackles in order to steal abilities? If so, do you think her intent would have been to use them to harness Knox's magic had he agreed to her terms today?"

"Quite probably," Preston agreed.

Spring sauntered to the loveseat and sat beside Preston. She gave him a long, curious look and snuggled into his warmth. Her father's arm encircled her and held her close. They were a lovely picture: father and daughter. How many times had they sat thus, curled up and sharing a quiet, peaceful moment together?

In watching the two of them together, Knox envisioned his and Spring's child down the road. He hoped to be able to sit in that exact spot and hear about his or her adventures. Listen with an open heart and mind about all the magical wonders their little tyke discovered that particular day. The vision was so real as to be a peek into the future. Knox prayed to the goddess that it would be true.

"Knox told us Isis showed you the movie reel of your life."

Spring's gaze sought Knox before she answered. "She did."

Preston nodded slowly and tightened his arm. "Then you will see what a poor excuse for a father I've been." The gruffness in his voice couldn't be mistaken for anything but high emotion.

"I don't think you were a bad father. I understand you have your reasons for your travels." Spring lifted her head to study Preston's face. "But what I *do* know is that you came for me. More than once. You always tried to protect me and show me love. I can only imagine that before Colombia, I knew that and loved you deeply in return. And if you give me time, I'm sure I'll adore you as much as I once did."

Tears escaped down his cheeks as he gazed down upon his daughter's earnest face. "I'm so glad you were returned to us. I will always be in the goddess's debt for what she did for this family. I love you, daughter. And if by some freak accident, your memory of this moment is erased, I will tell you again. But more importantly, I will show you."

"Thanks, Dad." The smile she showed Preston was impish and lovely. "Since I missed Christmas, I've decided to make you a list of things I want."

"Don't let her hit you up for an all-expenses-paid trip to Paris for a shopping expedition." Alastair pushed off the railing and squatted in front of her. With a sleight of hand, he produced a credit card. "She's already secured that gift from me."

"Thank you, Uncle." In one fluid motion, she rose, plucked the card from his grasp, and kissed his cheek, then flipped her hand to reveal a second credit card. "Thanks to Isis's mental download, I remembered what you taught me. Which one should I charge for my trip?"

Alastair's astonishment was priceless, and had Knox had his phone, he would take a picture for posterity. Surprising Spring's uncle had to be a rarity.

With a wink to Knox, Spring handed Alastair the card she'd swiped. "Now, let's see about our guests. I can't imagine it is too comfortable for them with their noses pressed against the front windows."

Sure enough, Knox spied her sisters and their significant others staring unabashedly through the blinds. "Never a dull moment in this family."

"Truer words were never spoken, son," Alastair said with a laugh and a hard pound on Knox's back. "What's for dinner?"

EPILOGUE

*T*hroughout dinner, Alastair silently watched his family interact. Spring was more open and laughed easier than she had in months. Periodically, her eyes sought out Knox as his gaze sought out hers. They would share a soft, secretive smile across the length of the table.

Thrilled with the way things had evolved for them, Alastair turned his attention to Holly and Quentin. They were the next pair on his list to match. Holly wouldn't make it easy. If Alastair claimed the sky was blue, she'd claim it was actually white with intermittent shades of color. He had to be careful with his plan to move forward. If Holly thought he liked Quentin, she'd reject the poor lad out of spite.

Alastair held back a snort. Who would have thought a seventy-five-year-old badass warlock would become a matchmaker?

He shook his head slightly and lifted his drink to take a long sip. Across the table, his gaze locked with Preston's. There was a wealth of understanding in his brother's amber eyes. There was also a promise of help. Preston would do what he could to make sure Aurora Gillespie-Thorne woke soon, not only for Alastair's sake, but for Rorie's and her children's. They both agreed a mother should be present for the future weddings of her daughters.

Before Alastair, Preston, Spring, and Knox joined the others, Knox had mentioned a new threat in the form of Victor Salinger. Fingers tightening on his glass, Alastair fought to shake off the old hatred. Now wasn't the time, nor the place for it. But he hoped to take his revenge on that bastard one day soon. Victor was as bad, if not worse than Lin had been, because his vision was not to obliterate witches and warlocks, but to steal powers and artifacts to boost his place in the world. Salinger dreamed of world domination and would do what was necessary to achieve it.

Spring had stolen Alastair's revenge on Lin by burying their old enemy alive. It had been a fitting end, but he preferred to have been the one wielding Karma's wand. He'd wanted to end Lin in the worst way possible, but he'd settle for taking Victor Salinger down when the time was right. He owed that sick asshole for the endless days of torture while Alastair had been a prisoner in Lin's dungeon.

"You look upset."

He whipped his head around. Holly sat next to him, quiet and watchful. She hadn't always been so. Once, she'd been a spitfire, ready to defy him and the world at large. But her deceased husband, Beau Hill, had changed that when he plunged a knife into Holly's chest. Alastair swallowed hard. If he'd have lost his beloved daughter…

He nodded. "I guess I am a little."

"Are you not happy that Spring and Knox got together?"

"Why would you think that?"

She shrugged and dropped her gaze to her plate. With her fork, she toyed with the crust of the perfectly baked cherry pie. Holly had always hated cherry anything. With a quick check of the table, he swiped his hand over the pie, changing it to rhubarb.

Her blue-green eyes brightened to aqua as she laughed up at him. "Thanks. I didn't want to be rude."

"For the record, I am happy Spring and Knox have finally connected. They've been through a lot." In a sentimental move that shocked the socks off her, he leaned in to kiss Holly's temple. "Just as I wish you to be happy, child."

The rapid blinking of Holly's eyes gave away her tearful response to his affection.

He heaved an internal sigh and took a long sip of his drink. Mending their rift would take more time than he possessed, but perhaps he could provide her heart's desire in the meantime.

"I suppose we should discuss the retrieval of the Cheirotonia Scroll," Alastair said to the table as a whole.

Quentin shot him a knowing half-smile, but turned his attention to Holly. "Looks like we're up next, my prickly pear."

Holly looked like she'd eaten a package of the Sour-Patch Kids candy she loved so much as a child. Her face puckered, and her lips tightened to a crinkled little O.

Alastair buried his face in his brandy snifter in order to hide his grin. Yep, she was definitely a prickly pear and would be the most stubborn of the lot. Matching her with Quentin would require all the tricks in Alastair's arsenal.

FROM THE AUTHOR...

Thank you for taking the time to read *SPRING MAGIC*. If you love what you've read, please leave a brief review. To find out about what's happening next in the world of The Thorne Witches, be sure to subscribe my newsletter.

Subscribe here: www.tmcromer.com/newsletter

Books in The Thorne Witches Series:

SUMMER MAGIC
AUTUMN MAGIC
WINTER MAGIC
SPRING MAGIC
REKINDLED MAGIC
LONG LOST MAGIC

Never fear. All the characters you've come to love—Nash, Preston, and GiGi—will have a story of their own in the coming months.

You can find my online media sites here:

Website: www.tmcromer.com
Facebook: www.facebook.com/tmcromer
TM Cromer's Reader Group: www.facebook.com/groups/tmcromer-fanpage
Twitter: www.twitter.com/tmcromer
Instagram: www.instagram.com/tmcromer

How to stay up-to-date on releases, news and other events...

✓ *Join my mailing list. My newsletter is filled with news on current releases, potential sales, new-to-you author introductions, and contests each month. But if it gets to be too much, you can unsubscribe at any time. Your information will always be kept private. No spam here!*
www. tmcromer.com/newsletter

✓ *Sign up for text alerts. This is a great way to get a quick, no-nonsense message for when my books are released or go on sale. These texts are no more frequently than every few months. Text TMCBOOKS to 24587.*

✓ *Follow me on BookBub. If you are into the quick notification method, this one is perfect. They notify you when a new book is released. No long email to read, just a simple "Hey, T.M.'s book is out today!" www.bookbub.com/authors/t-m-cromer*

✓ *Follow me on retailer sites. If you buy most of your books in digital format, this is a perfect way to stay current on my new releases. Again, like BookBub, it is a simple release-day notification.*

✓ *Join my Facebook Reader Group. While the standard pages and profiles on Facebook are not always the most reliable, I have created a group for fans who like to interact. This group entitles readers to "reader group only" contests, as well as an exclusive first look at covers, excerpts and more. The Reader Group is the most fun way to follow yet! I hope to see you there!*
www.facebook.com/groups/tmcromerfanpage

Lightning Source UK Ltd.
Milton Keynes UK
UKHW011844181218
334231UK00013B/257/P